YOUR MONKEY'S

SIMON LOUVISH has been no str
Slip Shock, and has, like his present hero, spent many
moons both sides of the Atlantic peddling his wares
to the Philistines. But in the intervals between the
bouts of Writer's Angst, he has enjoyed amazing
success with his Middle Eastern novels – *The Therapy
of Avram Blok, The Death of Moishe-Ganef, City of
Blok* and *The Last Trump of Avram Blok*, the recently
published final part of the *Blok* trilogy – all acclaimed
by enlightened reviewers. He spent his formative
years as a putative Israeli citizen and pursued a career
as a producer/cameraman/editor of subversive documentary films between 1969 and 1975. He teaches
film part time to recalcitrant students at the London
International Film School, is married and lives in
London.

SIMON LOUVISH

Your Monkey's Shmuck

Flamingo
Published by Fontana Paperbacks

A Flamingo Original

First published in Great Britain by Flamingo 1990

Flamingo is an imprint of Fontana Paperbacks,
part of the Collins Publishing Group,
8 Grafton Street, London W1X 3LA

Phototypeset by Input Typesetting Ltd, London
Printed and bound in Great Britain by
William Collins Sons & Co. Ltd, Glasgow

To all those who have suffered the slings and arrows of
REJECTION SLIP SHOCK
this book is dedicated in Solidarity.
LA LOTTA CONTINUA!

YOUR MONKEY'S SHMUCK IS
IN MY BEARD, PART I

You may say that I am mad. Well, that's your privilege. The only story I can tell you is the one that's true, the events as they happened, no more, no less.

So much for introductions. To begin then: my name is Owusu, Lewis Kwame Owusu, Kwame as in Nkrumah, that's correct. I was born in Magudu village, north of Nairobi, Kenya. My parents, ardent Pan-Africanists, both died when I was young, and I was taken under the wing of my uncle, who had a civil-service post in the capital. I graduated from high school, obtained my matriculation certificate, and then applied for, and received, a scholarship for veterinary studies to be undertaken at Glasgow University, in the United Kingdom. I was in the United Kingdom seven years, seven fat years, one might say, years of hope, which soon gave way to worldly cynicism, then a deeper disillusion. Europe, after all, was not the wide open gate to Opportunity and Fulfilment that I had naively imagined it to be. Racism, hypocrisy, the bitter cold soon took their toll of my ambitions. I returned, then, to Kenya in January 197–, uncertain and apprehensive of my future. My benefactor uncle, sunk deep in his bureaucratic niche, peeked out long enough to arrange me a post at the Njoli Game Reserve, by the north-western border with our neighbouring Uganda. I was quite satisfied with this develop-

1

ment. I thought, perhaps this job far out in the bush will help me clear my mind of its turmoil. And I was glad to be away from the crush of running, rushing, pressing humans. I always had preferred the kingdom of animals to that of man. But, to my increasing chagrin, there was, despite it all, a viper in that isolated nest . . .

★

Ugh! Kek! Ptah! This is not going to do at all, for God's sake. What the fuck do I know of Kenya? The Snows of Kiliman-jaro. Mau Mau. Mzee. Jomo stoned at Mboya funeral. Owusu – that's a *West* African name, anyway . . . The fuck. Escape by looking out the penthouse window. 'Penthouse!' Do us a favour! One room, rotting chest of drawers, one fallen arm-chair, two rickety camp beds, books in cardboard boxes, frozen roaches in the fridge, open cartons of half and half, grimy plates stamped with congealed cornflakes, dollops of snow past the grimy french windows obscuring the great phallic architecture of Manhattan downtown. Out, from 79th Street, above Broadway and Amsterdam, way down to the Gulf and Western Tower, the park, no doubt in picturesque snow. Kiddies walking on the pond ice, strawberry fields forever. Gimme a dollar, man. So what was wrong with twenty-five cents, asshole? Two bits. Gott strafe our souls.

So what'll it be then? Back to the hard core magazines? Spot of grunting tool manipulation? The true authorial vocation? Ah, one day – despite it all – Fame! Yesterday, nobody! Today, nobody! Tomorrow – the nebisch reborn –

Dear Contributor,
We regret to inform you that the enclosed material does not suit the needs of PONCEHOUSE at this time. We are therefore returning it to you.
Please excuse this impersonal reply, but the volume of

submissions we receive makes such a procedure a sad necessity. Many thanks for thinking of PONCEHOUSE.
The Editors

Vengeance is mine, saith the Lord. Tishman has left one spoonful of edible bran flakes in the kitchen cabinet. It is his place, after all; I, merely a harmful parasite, standing between him and the domestic conquests of whatever piece of tail takes his fancy. Not that he would want to bring the ladies back up the Methuselah lift to this apartment anyway. The lower depths, up in the sky. Observe the male misogyny above. Ah! the Balm of a Good Woman. No, that neither. The last piece of tail seen in this dump was the tip of a rat's dangler disappearing down the toilet bowl. The Fuck. Let us hie to cleaner pastures:

*

At first it all seemed perfect: the Njoli Game Reserve nestled in a thickly-vegetated valley teeming with impala, wildebeeste, giraffe, monkeys of all sizes, a thousand different species of birds, leopards, zebras, hyenas, and a sturdy herd of elephants. There was not much doctoring to do – there were no facilities to keep sick animals except two cages in a tiny shed. I rarely had more than an antelope with a broken leg to deal with . . . (What is this shit? Well, get on with it.)

There was a human snake, however, in this Eden – the supervisor, one Geoffrey Edwards. He and I were the only resident specimens of homo sapiens in that open zoo. Now Edwards was the sort of white man who never forgives or forgets that he was once Bwana Edwards, Big White Chief, resenting you like hell because he can no longer call you Boy, or Hey There Johnny, and has to bow to blacks who are his bosses now. He won't return to England because the nig-nogs and reds have taken over there, better to stick it in the bush, where men are men. And when he's drunk, blind sodden with

3

the booze, he'll hark back to the Good Old Days, howling at the sun that set over the British Empire. My own education in the Old Country was a red rag before his eyes. I was everything he hated in a nigger, and in no time we were each a jagged thorn in the other's flesh, sunk in a quicksand of mutual loathing. Only when he drove off for a five-day binge in the nearest whorehouse eighty miles away at R— did I have any real tranquillity . . .

('Wanna date, man?' 'I'm afraid I'm not in with the readies these days, lady.' 'Any time.' It's true, the friendliness of the natives. Nice warm vomit in the IRT. 'Jesus sucks! Jesus sucks!' 'Well, let him suck somebody else today . . .' Aaargh!)

. . . But I am rambling, and I should get back to the affair at hand, that leads me to appear before you gentlemen today: the elephants. They were the key. I took a special interest in them, from my first days at Njoli. Within three months I'd come to know them well, seeing them as rather ponderous children placed under my care. (Why the fuck am I telling this story? Better to beat one's brains against the wall . . .) They always gave me the feeling of a sort of caste of bush philosophers, taking their time to unravel some obscure elephant creed evolving since the depths of time. I daydreamed of winning their confidence, following them around, almost in the foolish hope that one would step on a painful thorn, which I would then, like Androcles, draw out, gaining eternal gratitude . . .

But let me set the scene: night coming on. The golden African sunset. Shrill chirp of crickets. Old Edwards, last bastion of the English Master Race, snoring off the day's consumption of Teachers. I, awake on my hammock, listening. The sounds of the jungle, day grunts abating, night creatures gearing up for their turn under the moon. The dying away of elephants' lowing. Only this night it did not. There seemed a loud agitation, off by the water hole, as if something had scared the pachydermal herd. (What?!) I thought, were poachers in the area? This was a congenital scourge of our area, the blasted ivory thieves . . . I took my rifle and moved off into the bush.

It was a hot, stifling, night. (Fuck! The cold! The radiators like a witch's tit! House Super, where is thy steam? Mother-fuckers!) I crawled through the underbrush, silent as I could, towards the water hole. Monkeys, awake, screeched in the trees. My palms were sweating. Something was clearly amiss. I crept warily on, till only a single row of trees stood between me and the open glade of the water hole. Then I poked my head carefully above the scrub.

Now I'm a rational man, I must re-emphasize this (Jerk! Jerk! Jerk! Hunh! Hunh! Hunh! Timber! Goddammit!), no doddering village illiterate clinging to outmoded superstitions and beliefs. An educated Christian, with a degree in Veterinary Medicine. (Bully for you, Sambo!) But still, I say to you and all who seem so smug and all-knowing that you do not know everything. That's for sure. The cleverest philosophers say: Doubt. Do not be choked by your own certainty. (Get on with it, for God's sake! –

Thank you for the opportunity of examining the enclosed material for publication in TAGALONG. We regret that we cannot make use of it at this time. Since TAGALONG is a science-fiction magazine, we consider only science-fiction manuscripts, that is, stories in which some aspect of realistic science or technology plays an integral part in the story's development. We do not publish fantasies or stories in which the scientific aspect is merely peripheral to the plot or totally absent.

Baa! Baa! Baa!) Well, to stall no more, this is what I saw: the elephants were clustered at the furthest edge of the glade, where the trees were thickest, huddled together in a close pack, their trunks writhing, curling as they cried out, lowing and bellowing like mad.

In the centre of the glade was the female I knew as Maisy, easily identifiable by the long split in her left ear which distinguished her from the others, the result of some calfhood fight. She stood on the brink of the water hole, her front legs buckled under her, her head lolling about, trunk tossing, lowing too, but in a different tone from all the others. And she was not alone. And it was at this point that I felt I had taken leave of my senses, or that all that seemed to anchor me to a normal, conventional idea of life and truth had slipped, leaving me . . . blah, blah, blah . . . gazing at that terrible shape which towered and loomed and strained and heaved at the poor beast's rear –

In short, it was a giant ape. King Kong, just as the movie shows him, but no model, cobbled together from leather, fur and seams and movie magic, but a true, massive great ape, a brown gorilla, big, man, big, in every way . . . given that an elephant stands ten or twelve feet high at the most, he must have been all of twenty-five foot tall. I would confirm that later, but we'll come to that. And there he was, behind our Maisy, his massive hairy paws clamped on her flanks on either side, and on his frightful face, clear in the full moonlight, an expression all the more terrifying for being one of a glazed calm and peace, his eyes turned up, whites showing clearly – poised there, panting behind the elephant, grunting and puffing like a gargantuan steam train. Yes, there can be no beating about the bush – the giant ape was fucking the poor pachyderm! I could clearly see his great black thing – his penis, glistening in the moonlight, ramming it in, wham wham, wham wham, like some gigantic piston. And Maisy, whose cries, first misconstrued as terror, now obvious as an ecstatic, happy squealing as she wiggled her immense posterior in

6

rhythm with that hairy hulk, going at it hammer and tongs, hammer and tongs . . .

★

Knock knock knock.

Ben Tishman enters. Good of him to give me warning before he turns his keys. Who knows, I might have Marilyn Monroe in here, score of the century, who can tell, this is the land of opportunity. You never know what's round the next corner, the big banana, the little pot of gold, or that real dose of bad luck that makes you tender your contribution to the overpopulation reduction. I want to be a beauty stylist, an aerobics instructress, a statistic, a dot on the medical graphs. Or I might be just spilling my seed, and Tishman is a true gent.

'You won't believe what happened to me today.'

Oh yeah?

'Synchronicity, it's the real thing. You gotta have faith.'

Tishman has been trying for years to raise cash for a film project which is the apple of his eye. He goes around the city with a 16mm Bolex and a tape recorder, filming incidents at random. Parks, hotel lobbies, diners, bars, the subway, they are all Tishman's stalking ground. He cadges favours off friends in various cutting rooms around the town, who allow him free time on editing machines. He wishes to avoid the cliché of Rhythm of the City films by going about his task with merciless rigour. Seven hours of footage are already stacked in cans, but he wishes to reach the magic figure of two hundred hours, on a one and a half to one ratio. The project has lasted four and a half years to date, and a succession of good-natured patrons of the Arts have bankrolled him for varying periods. He has applied for grants to every foundation in the country, but received only one so far, from the Yiddish Territorialist Society in the geriatric ward of Mount Sinai Hospital.

'Do you mind if I bash on with the keys a little?' I ask him.

'That's no problem,' he says. 'I'll just lie there.' Which he does, on his camp bed in the far corner, lighting up a succession of Marlboros. Smoke wreathes the room, filling it like a gas chamber.

★

. . . I didn't watch that scene for long. I dropped my rifle on the spot and ran like crazy, certain that the heat had boiled my brains. I must have woken old Edwards from his beauty sleep, for he came ranting and roaring out of his hut and stood over me, bleary eyed and stinking, unshaven and sweating like a pig in his filthy vest and underpants. 'Lewis, you fucking kaffir,' he bawled, forgetting himself, 'what the fuck is going on?'

I was not going to take that tone from anyone, least of all a wreck like Edwards. I was about to take a swing at him when he reeled round, suddenly appearing to notice the lowing and bellowing and jungle night panic issuing from the moonlit bush. 'What the fuck is that?' he yelped. 'What is going on out there?'

'If you really want to know,' I sneered at him, 'King Kong is out there, fucking the elephants.'

That really made him flip his lid. 'Don't you make fun of me!' he shouted, spitting bile. 'You're not going to make me small, I'm not in my grave yet, you black bastard, I will show you that!' He jumped me, but he was weak and helpless from the booze and I just held him off with one hand. 'If you don't believe me, just come and see for yourself.'

'I will at that, clever Johnny,' he snarled. 'I bloody will at that.' He staggered back and emerged with his rifle. 'Let's see what's scared you out of your ju ju wits, jungle boy. Come on, Mowgli, let's go.' And he crashed off through the bush towards the source of the noise. I had no option but to follow him, my heart rising to my mouth. I'm not sure what I was

8

expecting when we finally reached the glade of the water hole, but if I thought I would wake up from my nightmare I was very sorely shaken. The bush was still alive with squawking monkeys leaping and gesticulating, fleeing rodents and night creatures, and there, in the glade, the elephants, still bunched in fear, and bingo! – the great ape still there!

He had now backed off Maisy, done with whatever bang was underway. Crouched, arms across his knees, back against one of the larger trees (look up arboreal dictionary, Goddammit!), Maisy down folded on the ground just by the water hole, her trunk waving lazily in the muddy water.

Edwards stood, and I could guess what vows of abstinence were passing through his sozzled brain. But then the giant ape stirred, almost as if he'd sensed our presence, sniffed the air, then rose and crashed off through the trees.

'Come on,' I jeered at Edwards. 'White hunter make big kill, no? Let's see where the bugger goes.'

I don't know why I said that, it was the last thing in the world I would have dreamed of wanting to do, but I did enjoy his open-mouthed, sheer, total terror. 'What's the matter?' I went on. 'Not scared of big ju ju bogeyman, now are we?'

'I'll show you who's afraid of what, kaffir!' he spat, and staggered off across the glade. In as much a daze as he was, I rose up off my haunch and followed . . .

'I'd like to take a nap now, Danny,' Tishman said. I took my fingers off the keys. He turned over on his side. The snow-flakes seemed to have taken a break too outside the grimy french windows. I took my coat and made for the door. 'Need anything, Ben?' 'Two garlic bagels,' he said. 'Maybe check the milk and sugar.' I checked out of the apartment and pressed for the lift. It came, creaking slowly as if drawn up from the lowest circle of Hades. The small double porthole and the door clanking open. Safety instructions. Posted warnings. Tenants who leave laundry unattended will have only themselves to blame!!! Aye aye, mon Capitan. The doorman tips his thin eyebrows. 'Hey, that's a pissing day out there!' 'Yeah. But we can't hide forever.' 'You said it.' So I did, so I did. Out, down 78th Street, across Amsterdam and the bucking yellow cabs through to Broadway and the Manhattan Restaurant, rock of ages, balm in all seasons. These Alice in Wonderland menus. Cornucopia of choice. Breakfast 1, 2, 3 and 4. A little late for that. But save my life, Doris, a coffee and an English muffin, no jelly. She brings the jelly. You can't have too much of a good thing. The bustle and clutter behind the counter. Steam from coffee machine. Burnt toast. French fry grease. Hubble-babble, the city's banter, the writer's boon. What the hell. Masochism always prevails. I take out the morning's fresh rejections:

> Dear Writer,
> Although this manuscript was not selected for publication, we hope that you will continue to think of ARCHAEOS as a magazine interested in all writers, published and unpublished. In order for literary periodicals to continue, we depend upon your support as writers and readers as you, in turn, depend upon us as potential publishers of your work. We hope you will consider subscribing to ARCHAEOS, or any other literary magazine to which you submit work.
> The Editors

The word chutzpah doesn't even begin to do justice. The nerve of these guys – they are after my money! My fucking thirty-five cents! Lord, how long will ye accept the counsels of malefactors? The second piss-off note is no better:

> Sorry, no can do. This story suffers from an overdose of cuteness. Funny names and dialect comedy are just not

what our readership wants. Jewish S-F – I should say you
nah? But not quite so determinedly Jewish, please.
Jacob Akimbo's Science-Fiction Magazine

What these people need is a second circumcision. By a
defrocked mohel. I thought that fucking story was not bad.
It had certain qualities I've always strived for: terseness, drive,
provocation. Wake the punters up from their slumber. Give
them a kick for a change. But who should want to write
science-fiction? It's a mug's game, patronized by pimply-faced
adolescent fascist male youths, maximum age seventeen,
mental age one doesn't even want to think. No wonder Jake
Akimbo frothed. I take out the rejected manuscript. It's dog-
eared now, splattered with the coffee, cocaine, drool, semen,
pus, God knows what these 'readers' deposit on there, apart
from the rubber stamps and scribbled file numbers, like an
FBI exhibit:

NRB/T/547
JJ/BB/WW
XXX–75/3-HGFT/4
RETURN TO ADDRESSEE:

DREKULA – *A Tale of the Night*

I ask you, is this justice? Hunted down like an animal, chased
from street to street, block to block, shot at on the corner of
the 100 Percent Charcoal Grilled Burger Joint, tracked by
slavering dogs foaming at the mouth and for what? A little
pleasure here and there, some night relief, a little peck at the
neck, more harmless than a hypodermic. People die of flu jabs
every month. I should be the one they're hunting? Let them

go after the big shots – Nixon, Rockefeller, Kissinger – why bother a nebisch like me?

A nebisch, yes, no more, no less. My mother, my teachers, my social workers, all of them told me, flatly: 'You are a nebisch. That's the holy truth.' Gekrainkte, like a broken-down machine. Can't keep your head up. I could see their nostrils quiver too: smells. For sure, he hasn't used Sure. A razor his face hasn't seen since Hanukkah 1963. And that nervous tic, the way the lips twist at the side, doesn't open his mouth, what is he hiding in there?

The fact is, it's the teeth. The four long pointed ones on either side, two up, two down, to puncture with the neck. In the mirror I brush and admire them, make with the file, brush again. My pride and joy. Teeth, the source of power. My mother noticed my early care in this regard. A dentist, she said, a dentist he'll be yet. Support in my old age. But what do I know from orthodontry? A writer – that's what I wanted to be. Henry Miller, a garret in Paris, upstairs from the whore-house, screwing by day, masterpieces and bestsellers by night. Or Bashevis Singer, romance and refined humping in the back pews of the shul.

Enough dreaming. They nearly got me now. A fine sight I'd be, spewing out my life on 76th and Broadway. Who would care? A mere drop in the ocean. The truth they'd hush up for sure. The UJA, the AJC, Bnai Brith, they'd all pull muscle so the papers wouldn't say a word. ('JEWISH BLOODSUCKER SLAIN IN NEW YORK.' That would not do at all.) And to be caught and done for on this night of all nights! The blood boils. Nasser should have such luck. Tomorrow at this hour I should be gorged, satiated after my feast of feasts, my Rosh Hashona, Passover and all the rest rolled in one. Last year! The cockles warm! The annual Salute to Israel Parade – down they come, in their thousands, from Flushing, Scarsdale, White Plains, Westchester, Long Island, Jewish virgins! Oi, mama! all those heimische scheindalach with their full bosoms and ripe thighs, unplucked, guarded all year round by zealous parents or by their own zeal to keep that cherry for some hairy-chested Zionist thug down on the kibbutz out there . . . virgo intacta, that's the main point! Imagine it! The Day – June, summer, sky azure, the bands playing, the little schvartze kids, for some reason that escapes me, marching past with blue and white flags singing 'Let My People Go', papier-mâché floats of the Wailing Wall, yingalach with flowers in their hair, the giant collection box from JNF, the laughing, relaxed Irish policemen, expecting nothing maybe but some terrorist Arab scurrying to throw a bomb. But me? The world's nebisch? I cut through like butter . . . How does the Psalmist say? My head, it's anointed with oil, my cup it runs over. Joy! Joy! Joy! As at night so many of these nubile innocents will stay to walk the streets of the big bad city and there, there indeed, all mother's direst warnings will come true . . .

On other nights you take what comes. I had a friend, a goy, when I was young, we'd hang around the Brooklyn streets, goggling at the girls. 'Lean pickings,' he'd say, making like a Marlon Brando voice, 'Lean pickings.' That's the way it is for me, mostly. A Jewish virgin in New York City? Do us a favour. Lucky to find an untouched pick-up at all, that, even a schvartze, is a mechayeh. Most times I have to make do with second, third, fourth hand goods. The taste? Occchh! Root beer is better. Maybe you feel refreshed a bit for an hour, maybe two, then the pains! On all our enemies. A punishment from the Lord. And I have to stay doubled up in my room through all such torment, silent, not to make a sound, a squeak, as old Miss Dahrendorf stays in all day, all night, her ear against the door and walls, like radar noting every move. A dossier she keeps on every tenant in the block, a regular CIA, if they'd have her on the Watergate Committee, that shmuck would have long ago been out on his ear. I tell her I'm a nightwatchman in the Bronx, but the old bat doesn't

13

hear so good, she thinks I work with Brinks, no matter, it allows me some odd comings and goings at unusual times. Nosey! They're all nosey, a man can't make a living in this town without they dog his steps and nag him to death.

The dogs, barking again. They've closed off West End Avenue. I shrink along the walls. Maybe I can get to Columbus Avenue, then back to 79th, or, if necessary, the park. Oi! That's a killer. Scum swarms there. Schvartze, Puerto Rican muggers, junkies, count me out. I'm best at just moving about the streets, melting among the crowd. Mouth firmly shut, of course, due to these ferschlugener teeth. If only they were removable, dentures, in and out at will, like those ones you can buy in joke shops. Buy Dracula teeth, scare your relatives and friends on yontiff. Gevaldt! They must be swarming all over the neighbourhood, stopping everybody, asking them to open their mouths, shining flashlights down their throats. They'll have seen the prick marks on the neck, the stupid shiksa will have blabbed: Oh officer, it was so terrible, I thought he was a drunk asking for a dime, then he leapt on me, opening his mouth, oh, oh, oh. I should have known not to pick a shrieker. How can a body know? Usually once you've sunk the teeth a golden silence ensues. Suck, suck, suck. The bliss! A pure concerto. Brahms. Beethoven. Caruso. Nijinsky flies across the stage. Hatikva, swelling to a climax. On her face the calm of acceptance, of that secret knowledge only the true pariah holds . . . She lies peaceful on the pavement, fulfilled. I float to my apartment on a dream. Chopin at the keyboard, Einstein solving E is MC, Gary Cooper wins Garbo. Moses, leading the Chosen People to the Promised Land.

In short, it's a mechayeh. But this bitch tonight, something went wrong. It's an immunity, some people have it. How can a body know? Screaming, scratching, kicking, puling, and then the sirens – whee whee, whee, whee, and I'm off,

14

Drekulus interruptus, running like a rabid dog, dripping blood at the mouth, noch. What a shitten mess.

This city, I should have left it long ago. Who needs it? It grinds you down into a fine powder, then shits on your remains. And who knows, maybe somewhere else I would be normal! Here, what's normal? Mugging in the streets? Air like a gas chamber? People who spit in your face for a dime? Policemen who hunt you down with dogs? My mind, it's made up – I shall leave. Make it to the apartment somehow, rip out the emergency cash in the mattress, get my carcase out of this dump, Salute to Israel or no. Fat chance I'll have now with all tonight's publicity. ('VAMPIRE MUGGER – MAYOR URGES CALM.') The maidalach will be bundled back to mama before sundown, the streets will be more like Williamsburg on Yom Kippur, I might as well turn vegetarian. Yes, the cash stash and off! GO GREYHOUND! West, young man! Space! A new life! A commune maybe, a little fresh poultry . . . who knows . . . what else is left now? Get out or lie down and die. How would they put down a Jewish vampire anyway? Thrust a Sefer Torah through the heart? The congregation, wrapped in tallis and tfillin, close in, my mother's weeping face hidden in her palms – how could he do this to me?

Enough, I seem to have broken through the cordon. The stupid dogs are howling by the Hudson, while I mumble my way through the night's shitkickers, clear across Amsterdam. Who bothers about a hunched-up unshaven bum in a torn raincoat, lips pressed tight, mumbling. Eh? The doorman at my block doesn't even look up from the funnies, the TV blurring in front of his unseeing eyes. Police sirens outside, screaming, shouting, shooting even, better to keep the puss in the funnies, oh yah.

At least the elevator's working. A big plus, eighteen floors by foot are no picnic. I fumble with my keys, fingers trembling a little. Shock. Reaction. Memory. I push the door open,

15

it gets tougher each day. That stupid pile of unmoved newspapers. *Time* Magazines, *Fortune, Screw*, Morning Freiheits, I should have slung them out long ago . . .

A movement on the stairs! Am I discovered? A police ambush, after all? An old victim who's tracked me down, stake in hand? My cousin Shmil on some yotsmech call from my mother?

I rush into the corridor. Shit! It's old Miss Dahrendorf, Nosey Schlumper Number One! Prying, spying, as usual, how much does the yente know? The bloodstains, gevaldt! The bloodstains on my coat, the shirt, I can see her eyes go pop. God help me! That tongue, like the tower of Babel, she can see me. I open my mouth! She sees it all . . . Looking at me as if I were a pogromist off the steppes, old ethnic countless yahrzeits – her clawed finger, pointing at my bloody chin, her mouth working with no sound. She shrinks against the wall, away from the leper – Unclean! Unclean! she tingles her bell. Gibbering at me finally, getting out the words: 'No! Don't touch me! Keep your hands off me! I won't let you! I never let a man touch me! I never let a man do it to me! Never! Never! Never!'

I'm shrinking away from her gabble, horror struck, when suddenly my brain explodes inside me. My heart goes bang, bang, bang! My blood races like a racehorse, I feel I've suddenly received a revelation from the Shekhina, no less! Of course! Why hadn't I thought of it before? What a lemech! What a schlemiel! Tramping my life away in the snows of Manhattan winters, shvitzing in the oven of the summer, wearing myself down, nose to the grindstone, getting shot at by kill-crazy cops, tracked by dogs, and for what? What does age matter? What do looks matter? It's the blood, in the end, Goddammit! Who cares from all those shiksas? Those brand X fluids? Those long nights of anxiety, pain? While here, in the absolute safety of my own apartment building, under my very schnozzola, can you believe it, all this time, unawares –

16

there's a safe, easy, regular supply, always on tap, absolutely kosher and virginal, the real thing, praise the Lord! With a choking sob of relief I throw myself at it, bearing down on old Miss Dahrendorf's ageing, wrinkled, but oh so beautiful neck!

★

Well, I'm not surprised it got their gut. If you scratch, people itch. But then all these homilies and mimeographed advice they send you with their rejections! Words must fail:

> Prospective writers please note: Stories generally progress by narration. They are about beings the reader can believe in, and they tell the events that make a change in one or some of those beings – growing up, learning, or becoming emotionally involved (HOW MUCH MORE INVOLVED DO YOU WANT, SHITHEADS??!) . . . We seldom buy the vignette, a snapshot of a static situation. Virtually never do we buy a history lecture where the events are told so objectively that the reader never gets into the story. For all the necessity of putting the reader into a strange and unfamiliar setting, remember: a story moves by action, for all that it needs colourful backgrounds and believable characters acting on believable motives . . .

'Virtually never do we . . .' oh dear! Do excuse *moi*! But I have pen and paper and will travel, never mind distracting smells, visions, impositions, diner blah . . . Another coffee and muffin please, Doris – (Whaa whaa! whaa whaa! The police sirens wail on outside) . . .

★

. . . We had barely travelled half a mile through the bush when we found what was obviously the creature's lair: it was

17

an open glade, surrounding a bald hill which rose, about twenty yards off, above the trees and vegetation. He was lying there on his back, a mountain lying on a hill, in a position all too human – one knee raised above the other, hands, paws, or whatever, clasped behind his massive anthropoid head, slightly raising it above the ground.

Then we noticed he was not alone. Both of us, Edwards and I, craned forward, our enmity forgotten for the moment, numbed by disbelief, for our first, shocked impression was confirmed in the moonlight.

It was a girl, a white girl, blonde it seemed, with shoulder-length shimmering hair, wearing jeans and a thin white blouse. She sat upon the giant beast's belly, holding in her hands a large white cloth or towel, with which she was wiping down the great ape's dong, his giant penis, cradled in her arms.

Edwards and I just stood there, paralysed, no longer trying to hide, for we both thought our minds had snapped. At least I assumed he thought as I did, for before we could compare notes or make any other move someone spoke up from behind us:

'Drop that gun, gentlemen. I have a rifle pointed at your gizzards. One false move and I fire.'

Edwards dropped his gun. We turned. It was another girl, blonde too, with shorter hair, her face round and twinkle eyed, her mouth set in a determined way. The rifle very steady in her hands. And then, to cap the madness, a voice, deep and rumbling, spoke up from our rear now, from the hill which we had faced before, a grumble in the night:

'Vicki – what's up?'

The bass tone rolled across the glade. I looked round, stunned. The beast had risen, sitting up upon the hill. The girl's eyes flicked towards him. Edwards, acting faster than I'd have given him credit for, seized that moment of her hesitation, whipped round, grabbed his rifle off the ground and rushed off into the bush. The girl swivelled, then turned her barrel

18

back on me. 'Don't move!' The second girl appeared, like a wraith, holding a rifle too. They motioned me forward into the glade, towards the massive living boulder blotting out the moon. Ready for any madness now, I looked into his face.

His gaze, as far as I could make out in the light, was keen and piercing, full of intelligence and thought. The lower part of his face was an ape's face pure and simple, larger than life, but his forehead, instead of sloping back, sprang upright, like a human brow, beetling above the flat proboscis. No mere animal brain inside that casing, proven, as he spoke again.

'I'm truly sorry, sir, that I have put you out,' he said, in deep but not unpleasant tones, held down, so as not to thunder out too loudly, giving the general feeling of a volcano softly ticking over. 'I do hope you'll accept sincere apologies. My dear companions are most zealous in their guardianship. I assume you and your friend who has skedaddled so, misconstruing our motives, are the staff of this here game reserve.'

His accent was a strange melange, which I later came to identify as a mixture of mid-American and Cambridge School English, acquired off self-help records and tapes. Misplaced slang and phrases picked up God knows where peppered his rather solemn discourse, which he proceeded to unfold, like the lecture of an absent-minded professor delivered at the wrong place and time. And thus I sat and listened – seated on the girls' rolled sleeping bags, at the great ape's giant feet – five foot they were at least from heel to toe, each toe a foot in length, and a strong reek coming from between. His massive face ten feet above me, and the two girls, lotus seated, rifles cradled in their arms . . .

The Monkey's Tale: (interrupted). . .

Tishman enters the Manhattan Restaurant, looking as if he's still carrying around his head the wreath of Marlboro smoke. He sits down opposite me and droops his head and eyelids, which almost seem to sweep the table.

'God, it's cold out there.'

He orders a coffee and Danish. Other sounds break through my field. Clash of plates, cups on tables. Shuffle of feet. Cash register. Human speak. 'Magic tricks, I says to this guy, you want magic tricks? the only magic I'm looking for is to make a dollar out of thin air. Can you do that? Can you do that? Listen what the man says . . .'

'Doris . . . !'

'One Number Three! Two Fours! Hold the fries!'

Whaa whaa! Whaa whaa!

'Who can commit crimes in this weather?'

'Noo Yorkers are resourceful. How's it going?' he asks me. Have I said it? I live on Ben Tishman's generosity. His apartment, his life, his pocket book. Not his girls. That would be too gross. But Tishman does pull them everywhere, in coffee shops, bookshops, public libraries, delis, consciousness raising workshops, art galleries, the subway, Zaybars. Glancing at my notes. 'Is this still the King Kong story?'

'It is.'

'You're really mad, Danny.'

'You are merely conforming to the general view. This I should not expect.'

He gestures at my file. 'More rejections?'

'The Philistines march on.'

'What about the novel? Any straws?'

'Not in the neighbourhood of drowning men.'

I completed, last year, a real kedgeree. The pulp novel to end all pulps. It is entitled 'Beyond the Planet of Fuck'. No one will touch it with a bargepole, not even with surgical gloves. Here is a sample response:

Our science-fiction reader has now had an opportunity to read your manuscript BEYOND THE PLANET OF FUCK, and I'm afraid it hasn't received a favourable report. He felt the writing was certainly different and

20

capable of being entertaining but, reading on, the dialogue becomes rather nauseating and he found the descriptive passages vastly over-written and over-described.

Choke, choke, feinschmecker! At least he didn't take the coward's way out:

Dear Mr D. H—,
I am afraid to say that we at Poppet Books publish very little original work, being mainly a reprint house. I suggest you send your manuscript to a hardback house or, better still, find an agent to represent you. You will find a comprehensive list of both hardback publishers and literary agents in *The Writers' and Artists' Yearbook*, which should be available from your local library or bookshop.

Agents!!!!!! This cannot go unanswered! A breed that seems to be grown in special manure pots. Sodden with booze, they creep up on you at one of those literary terrace parties I have occasionally crashed, clutching your ankles with a pair of tweezers. 'We're not doing much business with satire at the moment. The bottom has fallen out of the market . . .' As their own tush disintegrates into a puddle of glop on the floor.

'Supply me some good vibes,' I beg Tishman. 'You floated in on a cloud, earlier.'

'I have to meet a man on Long Island,' he said, 'who might just be the Good Samaritan I've been looking for since the summer. He's one of those true Manhattan lovers who lives just out of reach of the city.'

'Is he kin to Ellie?' I ask, presciently. She is Tishman's latest flame, a tiny ballet dancer of true blue stock, currently starting her career in the city. I personally find her a mite spare, but at least she fits in the apartment.

'Possibly,' he says, 'possibly.' As if some future relationship might lie down the line, such as, for example, daughter-father.

21

'The real strategy,' Tishman goes on, 'is never to accept the word defeat into your vocabulary. That's the problem with you, Danny, if you don't mind me saying so. Sometimes it seems to me you feed off it.'

'Well, it's what they throw through the bars.' ('We have now had the opportunity of considering your work carefully, and have regretfully come to the conclusion that we are not able to make you an offer of publication. Blah, blah, blah.' Tam ta-ra tam-tam, tam-tam.)

'It's a whole change of attitude that's needed,' Tishman says earnestly. 'It's the same in publishing as in love. But you will make it, I'm sure. Or else you would have given up a long time ago.'

I do not know what I should have done a long time ago, except leap off the Brooklyn Bridge. But Tishman is right. What am I trying to prove? I write junk, therefore I exist? So what do they want, an arm, a leg? Great spittoons of profundity and self-discovery? Does no one really want a laugh in this town? The waitress sashays up with the coffeepot.

'More coffee?'

'You're saving my life, Doris,' Tishman says, giving her his entire attention, as is his wont. 'And how're things at home? Was it your mother who was having her operation?'

'Oh, she's right as rain now. Bosses me about like you wouldn't believe. They shoulda kept her in another month. Pardon my mouth.'

'It's only natural. People expect so much. You're looking real good tonight.' Tishman is in perpetual motion. He has the knack of forming one-to-one relationships anytime, anywhere. The sorry fact is, he loves the human race, their foibles, their failures and successes, their every tit and tattle. I have to confess I sometimes regard them as an alien species, to be studied carefully, for sheer survival. Or perhaps it is just the city, oozing poison through the veins. Though I have tried other climes. I have seen the world and it sucks. In my time

I have even participated, God help us. Save the World From Itself! Unzip the Cosmic Bind! Kill the Cops! War Is Dangerous For Children and Other Living Beings! Better Red Than Dead! Free Huey Long! (Goddamn!!! Do I remember that?!) Seize Control of Your Life! Abolish—(fill in as required)—So what did we expect? Results? There are people who painted SHIT on the Washington Monument who are now girding their loins to re-elect Jimmy Carter. But I am still out here with my paint pot, with its own mess of colours. I wrote a story last year called 'The Globble Village', which I thought reflected something of that zeitgeist but, like everything else, it got regurgitated from every chewed cud in town, though I remember it with fondness: it still gives me a chuckle in the night, if not to the unshriven out there:

THE GLOBBLE VILLAGE

In the Globble Village, every globble is every other globble. If a marriage, for example, is contracted between two globbles, the differentiation of one's spouse from all other individuals in the village is a pre-eminent problem, not to speak of the differentiation of one's spouse, or any other individual, from oneself. Privacy is at the same time unknown and universal, since, when all are one, one's oneness remains inviolate. Divorce among globbles is synonymous with schizophrenia, but the complete identity of psychiatrist and patient which characterizes any subsequent treatment only adds another layer of confusion to the prevailing distress. The observer might ask: if all globbles are one, what use is the concept of differentiation at all, how can any concept of association or disassociation be valid in the globble world? Professor D'Pouf has determined that though these concepts are indeed empirically

23

invalid, they nevertheless exist in globble discourse, i.e., globbles converse constantly on such social topics as matrimony, adultery, patrimony, filiality, bar-mitzvahs, debutante balls, rotary clubs, freemasonry, lawsuits, contracts, wills and so on. Impassioned arguments ensue, but, owing to the total identity of all those involved, the differing opinions are expounded at random, and the non-globble observer is at a loss to determine to which globble which viewpoint pertains. Professor D'Pouf, in his epoch-making 'Globble Trobble – A Perplexer of Guides', argues the entire village is a single organism in a state of perpetual schizoid psychosis, in other words, the globbles are totally out of their minds. He cites, for example, a typical law suit:

A globble, designated for the sake of argument A, had welshed on an agreement with another globble, arbitrarily designated B (though B might have been equal to A from the onset, a possibility one must always keep in mind), to supply him (or her) with x number of thrubs. (A thrub being a nondescript fibrous article of no apparent use which globbles pile in mounds at the ends of the village and leave to rot in the sun.) Accordingly, all globbles in the village felt, simultaneously, an acute anger at A for going back on his word, and a concurrent anger at B for raising the issue, when thrubs were known to be of no earthly value. B having decided to prosecute, the entire village was precipitated into an escalating communal quarrel. The Judge before whom the case was to be heard disqualified himself, as he (or her) was both in accord and discord, and in fact, identical, in the eyes of the Law and society, with both the litigants, ipso facto, at one and the same time. This process was repeated with each adjudicant assigned to the case, so that the issue could never be resolved. The same procedure, Professor D'Pouf ascertained, took place in every one of the seven thousand and forty-five court cases he examined, going back three hundred and sixty years. By definition, no dispute could ever be resolved in the globble village, as everyone held at one and the same time every possible point of view on any matter at hand. One would have thought, given that the globbles, unlike Man, being able to experience every side of a question, would thus live by necessity in a state of utopian harmony. But the opposite, as we have seen, is the case. The globble village seethes with insoluble controversy and debate, from simple matters of everyday fashion and clothing, through the type of dressing to be used with salad, and on to topics of profound philosophical import. Any creed or religion embraced by any single globble is ipso facto embraced by them all, and in the network of conflicting dogmas circulating in the village creed wars are fought in ruthless armed battles accompanied by frightful psychic schisms. The observer perceiving a globble flagellating him/herself with bobub barbs would know that a terrifying struggle between Christianity and Islam, Buddhism and Ayn Rand Objectivism, Trotskyism and Kautskyism, et cetera, is being played out in the poor being's brain. The population of the globble village is so decimated at irregular intervals by the ensuing ideological wars, self-mutilations and suicides that it is a miracle any globbles survive to this day at all. Professor D'Pouf can proffer no explanation whatever of the paradox of the globble existenz, and visitors to his ward at the Utrecht Home for the Incurably Lulu can extract no information from his lips but a whimpering 'whibble-whibble-whibble' and a cascade of glittering soap bubbles. The world must await the results of the coming Supervius–3 Expedition for any enlightenment concerning these strange and highly unfortunate creatures.

★

'So what happens next in the monkey epic?' Tishman asks, glancing at my notes upside down, having made out my latest chapter heading.

'The ape explains his origins,' I inform him, thinking it

through as I speak. 'He is in fact the offspring of two circus anthropoids captured long ago as freaks by the promoter Carl Denham, whose highly romanticized account of our beast's father's capture was rendered in the famous motion picture. But both the original great apes died of neglect in the circus, not by being shot off the Empire State Building as libellously alleged . . . Our poor orphan anthropoid escaped the clutches of Denham, then old and bloated on the proceeds of his perfidy, and lit out to the mountains of Wyoming, where he was taken in and brought up by a lone, eccentric farmer, called Egbert J. Fudd, who taught him human speech and put him through a full correspondence course in the Humanities. Then, when the old farmer died, of a broken heart following the assassination of John F. Kennedy, our beast wandered, friendless, across the hills and prairies, finally hiding in a container load of Idaho potatoes en route for the Old World . . . His search for companionship and even, dared he dream, sexual fufilment, dot, dot, dot, led him to place advertisements in various magazines – the *Los Angeles Free Press, Screw*, the *Village Voice, Time Out, The Lady, Cosmopolitan* and the *New York Review of Books*, among others, to wit:

> Large, hirsute, literate but very shy primate seeks female companions for round the world tour. Must be of acute intelligence, with vivid curiosity for the unknown and open minded to an extreme degree.'

'You've been reading my mind,' says Tishman. 'I've been looking for that girl all my life.'

'I thought you find her every week,' says I.

'I never found her,' he says, nodding his head ruefully. 'I fall in love all the time, but the ideal eludes me.'

'Ellie?'

'Isn't she wonderful? You should really come and see her perform.'

26

'You know I can't take the performing arts. It's too exhibitionistic for me.' Ballet, in particular, I cannot stand. Shmuntz, shmuntz, shmuntz across the stage. In tutus. Is this an activity for grown-up persons? Arm wrestling, now there's a man's game. I tried it once, with a brief girl friend from the Socialist Workers International. She beat me. But I still enjoy the Puerto Rican tag teams on Channel Twelve. Is there perhaps a tale or a novella there? But I have forsworn all research. The further from reality the better. With Tishman it's the exact opposite. I Am a Camera, But I Can't Afford the Film Stock. Buddy Can You Spare a Can? The man has lived and breathed New York city all his life. He takes his passport to New Jersey.

'I'll be on Long Island all the weekend,' he says. 'This is the Big Push of the Year. And even if the man doesn't come up trumps, Ellie and me can at least watch the sea.'

Old boots, washing up all the way from Mexico. 'Well, good luck, man, and have a good time.'

'Find yourself a girl, for God's sake, Danny. You're in the prime of life. Take it while it lasts. Women are not like publishers. They want to be fucked.'

'Yah. I'll see what I can do.'

'By the way, I've wanted to ask you, where does that weird title come from?' he asks, as we rise to pay and go.

'Your Monkey's Shmuck Is In My Beard?' I present the check to the cashier. My turn to unfold a bill. Last remains of the Nest Egg and the spate of cash earned with Tishman painting some yoik's studio loft. Tishman lives, like everyone else, off bank loans. 'It's the Rabbi's comment to the barrel organ man: Excuse me, sir, but do you know your monkey's shmuck is in my beard? No, but if you hum it I'll play it.'

'I'm sorry I asked,' Tishman says.

'They always are,' I sigh. 'They always are.'

★

27

. . . We sat there, myself and the two blonde girls, for a long dreamlike time. Vicki and her companion Elizabeth produced a herbal wine from a strong leather gourd and cooked up some roots and yams over a camp fire, as we talked, far into the night, the giant ape like a benign colossus bending over and protecting us from whatever depredations might arise. Their tale, in many ways as strange as the ape's own, twisted and turned in the flames. They were sisters, daughters of an English armaments magnate whose life reflected their desire to expiate the guilt they'd transferred from their father's trade on to themselves. An odyssey of protest from pacifism and protest demonstrations to assignations with guerrilla troops in remote rain forests and wind-swept deserts, from doubt to fervent faith and back again, to a profound, deep disillusion with all human affairs. Fearful of revolutions that devoured their makers, they hid in drug-swept communes in London, until that strange ad in *Time Out*, a listings magazine, caught their eye. They met in an eerie scene on Chobham Common, a barren stretch of no-man's-land adjacent to an army camp.

'We knew at once this was something beyond our experience, beyond anything we could imagine. And that was right, that was exactly what we sought. You might think at first – how perverse, how monstrous – he's not human . . . but that was exactly the point: he's not human, in the sense that humans cheat, swindle and steal, kill and maim each other. But, in another sense, ultra-human, in the sense of possessing that inner quality religious people might call Grace – an inner peace, that is so awfully rare . . . though he does need, probably because of that, his trusting nature, real protection from those who would do him harm, or snare him like his poor father . . . and also, from his own strength. And his sexual needs, that's something never thought of in the tales: that very real sex drive. So we relieve him, at times. I suppose its quite a funny sight. But the elephants, that's another thing . . . He's quite worried, I think, that he's upset them. He swears he won't do it again.'

'Scout's honour!' said the ape, roguishly holding up two crossed fingers. We laughed and he chuckled too, a grotesque sound, like water gurgling from a giant tub.

I felt relaxed, at peace the first time for so many months, able to unwind from the tense hostility with Edwards, God rot his soul. I bared my own to this unlikely menage sprung from a strange other world. I spoke of my ambitions of becoming the Great Animal Doctor, of my shared revulsion with them from the human species, its mess, confusion, perfidy. I spoke of my observances of elephant life, their strange code of loyalty and solidarity. The ape was quite taken with this and we rattled on about the animals' world, the lions, giraffe, apes, and here a note of sadness crept into his voice as he spoke of his long-lost cousins sealed off, perhaps permanently from him, by their inarticulation. I quite warmed to him, forgetting his strangeness, his size, calling him Fred, as the girls did, a homely touch in their alien fields . . . An immense sleeping bag was unrolled and I crawled into it, the two companions softly crawling in with me, cuddling tantalisingly, spreading warmth throughout my body, hot wet thighs upon my own. As they spread above our heads and fastened the attached mosquito net I could see the great ape, Fred, looming, gazing paternally down at us. Then his head slid from sight, and I heard the rustle of his giant frame settling, and an odd hum emanating from between his meaty lips. A tune, something I'd heard before but couldn't quite place, then, as the girls' lips closed upon me I suddenly realized – a familiar tune, thrumming from a barrel organ at a fairground, in far England of more formative days . . . as the two heavenly bodies writhed upon my own, their breath on my face, their lithe fingers at my groin, he hummed the words, deep and low, as if the earth itself was murmuring the ditty:

'I've got a luvverly bunch of coconuts,
Tum te tum te tum te tum te tum . . .
Big ones, small ones, tum te tum te tum,
Roll a bowl a bowl a penny a tum . . .'

. . . an ecstatic interval, and sleep.

Our awakening was brutal and rude. Something cold and hard at my neck, the mosquito netting ripped aside. Edwards' sweaty, stinking, booze-sodden face. The girls woke too, to his double-barrelled shotgun waved in our faces: 'Nobody move, or so help me I'll blow you all to where the fuck you belong.'

The reek of whisky from his fetid mouth. I struggled out of the sleeping bag.

'Now come on, Edwards, don't be crazy, put that thing away.'

'Crazy am I?' and he really was, lips writhing, salivating, eyes bulging. 'Well, I'll show you, kaffir boy, I'll show you who's crazy round here! Get up, all of you, and not a sound or it'll be the last you'll ever make.'

I glanced aside. The massive bulk on the hillock stirred fitfully, but emanated loud volcanic snores. Edwards motioned us towards the trees, out of our protector's earshot. 'I'll show you yet, you fucking kaffir, you filth, you piece of dirt . . . fucking white women . . . all you bastards think of . . . I'll show you . . . shit . . . we'll see who gets fucked now, you shithead baboon . . .'

We were being pushed further and further from the great ape's glade, the shotgun held more firmly than we might have hoped. The girls and I glanced at each other but we had no choice, pressed by the madman into the bush, when, suddenly, off from the left, away from the ape, a loud and piercing whinny split the night, a cry of animal excitement that distracted Edwards for a vital split second, and woke the ape, Fred, his booming bellow sounding across the savannah . . .

(Savannah? Bush? Veldt? What the hell? A little Public Library time needed here . . .)

Huge he rose, above the trees, whipped up to his full height. I grabbed Vicki and Elizabeth and hurled myself on the ground. Edwards shouted 'Holy shit!' and fired both barrels, buckshot flying past my ear, stinging the side of my face. (Buckshot? What is this? A fucking *Britannica* I need in this hole!) And at that very moment – Maisy broke through the glade . . . There could be no mistaking her, the gash in her left ear clear in the moonlight as she smashed through trees and scrub, trumpeting, her trunk erect as a flagpole . . .

Edwards struggled to reload his gun, wide eyed, cursing, staggering, wildly, swinging his weapon from one massive beast to the other. Fred standing dumbfounded at the sudden entrance of his forsworn amour, Maisy, trunk raised, front feet lifted, whooping at him, rushing forward and – WHUMP! – down on Edwards, right on the very spot: one moment, the master race, defender of the faith, Queen and Empire, the next, a squashed and blotchy mess upon the jungle floor . . .

But we had virtually no time to take in the horror of that moment, for the bush was suddenly alive about us, rustling, baying, screeching, yelping, lowing to the skies, the ground beneath us thrumming to the beat of massed and heavy hoofs. Stunned and bewildered, we three poor humans burrowed in the underbrush, arms round each other, as the earth literally moved and shuddered, and the elephants broke in.

It was the whole herd in stampede. Enraged, they crowded round Maisy, pushing her away from that other huge bulk she had approached, but dust rose, obscuring all, the hoofs, the grey mounds of the pachyderms, Fred, Kong, call him what you will, the howls receding, crashing sounds rolling forward into the bush . . . The two girls standing up, crying: 'Fred! Fred! Where are you?' They ran, in the wake of the disturbance, as I shouted: 'Come back! Come back! you can't help him against them! No one can when they're enraged as

31

that!; But they ignored me, rushing off, vanishing in the swirling dust. Before I knew it I was alone, running, cursing, crying, beating my breast, climbing up on the hill of our mutual glade of Grace, a mere moment but now an entire aeon ago, seeing nothing but a fierce mêlée of dust, a rushing cyclone, with here and there, a waving trunk, a glimpse, perhaps imaginary, of that great head vanishing into the night . . .

And there the army found me, in the morning, sprawled by a trampled mess of tattered sleeping bags, dead camp fire, torn mosquito netting and one mangled lump of flesh and bone, two hundred yards away in the bush, circled in awe by the soldiers who had come in their jeeps to examine the inexplicable signs of disturbance reported by the border guards. Of course, I could tell them no coherent tale, and thus, rambling and feverishly calling out 'Vicki! Elizabeth!' and 'Fred!', I was brought here, to this rehabilitatory establishment, where you, my learned colleagues, must decide the truth or falsehood of my tale.

I know, in your place, I'd have no doubt. The man is clearly insane. Calm him with tranquillisers, lock the lunatic up and throw away the key. But, gentlemen, before you sign the commitment papers, let me ask you – are you really sure? How many men have you locked up behind these walls in this Ogalu Mental Hospital, who are to you insane but who may be, on the contrary, aware of things true and real, but also inconvenient and disconcerting? After all, it is your job, in your uniforms, whether the white coats of doctors or the khaki of police or army, to defend the ordered, accepted view of things. Let there be no uncertainty or chaos! No maverick realities in our polity. Lewis Owusu, your story is an affront to our common sense! But does common sense truly rule the world? Does common sense create the wars of creeds, or weapons of death that kill a million at one blow? Is it common sense that allows evil men to be beloved leaders of their people? We believe in religions which tell taller tales than mine. A dead man comes down off the cross and lives. A bush burns, but is not consumed. Enough. I can see your minds are set. Get on with it then, scribble your signatures, esteemed sirs, blow the winds of the unknown away . . .

But wait – dear doctors, do you hear that sound? Yes, there it is, again . . . you rise in alarm, you hear it too . . . a strange, non-human cry . . . loud thudding, at the asylum gates . . . louder, a crash of walls . . . Again! Ah, if you could see your own smug faces now! Thud, again! Yes, run, hypocrites, run, as the madman's dream intrudes in flesh and blood into your ordered lives! Run! The walls are coming down! You know it now! What price the madman's ravings now! Thud! Oh, what joy to see that furry fist again! Oh Fred! Oh Fred! Careful now, it's me, don't knock the roof down on my head! Thud! Oh joy! You're through the wall! That frabjous face, callooh! callay! Vicki! Elizabeth! You too! Alive and well! Oh, friends in need . . . The joy! the joy! Hey, wait – there's not that hurry, let me get my breath back, they won't dare come now . . . they've run like rabbits . . . oh my, I see the problem . . . all right, I'm climbing on your paw . . . gently now, don't squeeze . . . that's it, that's safe, that's snug! Cheerio and bye-bye, fair doctors, don't forget to certify your-selves afore ye go . . . Goodbye for ever! Adieu – towards New Horizons – unexamined by Man – hi yo, silver! Let's eat dust! Go, Monkey, Go!

(Exeunt giant ape, bearing his three friends, pursued by sex-crazed elephant.)

★

The dawn, over winter's Manhattan. Did neighbours bang below the floor? Did I bang, with the week's consignment of hard core to keep the tensions down? Extract at random:

A.D., aged 64, and his wife B.C., aged 63, have added oral sex to their bedroom. (!!!**!) Mrs C., who paints for a hobby, has painted the bedroom wall with sets of lip prints of various sizes. There are, on the walls, other symbols representing a phallus and one representing the labia majora. I asked Mr D. if he could explain how oral sex entered his life.

And all this to accompany some close shot of a tattooed hooker going down on some poor deadbeat at the end of his tether. Why do they think we need these homilies? It's publishers all over again:

I read your manuscript BEYOND THE PLANET OF FUCK and thought it quite amusing and entertaining, but at the end of the day it's the kind of zany fantasy you either love or don't love, and I don't love it enough to take it to the top markets. Apologies. I'll leave the material with our receptionist as you requested. Best of luck elsewhere.

Love, don't love? What is this, forget-me-nots? Listen to Mr A.D.:

I had a son who had gone off to Korea and he picked up on oral sex there. When he came home he really gave us a lesson in sex that we should have given him . . . Like I said, it was slow at first. I did little things like nibble at her breasts . . . Then one night she was at my penis, her lips touching its tip and shaft and massaging so beautifully . . . I know it has transformed our life . . . we do have penetration occasionally, but mostly we nibble at each other like a couple of little puppies . . .

Yaargh! Boo! It is a conspiracy to rot the brain. This is not

34

what the punters require after they have run the gauntlet of the 42nd Street Erotomanic Bookstore, shuffling their eyes across the rows of comic-book splendour, the titles redolent of the imagination of a brain-damaged aardvark: *'Eat my Cum'*. *'Jist Jism'*. *'Big Tits'*. *'Bazoom Bangers'*. *'Berlin Porno Probe'*. *'Hamburgers'*. *'Cream in my Coffee'*. *'Ball Breakers'*. *'Penis Envy (??!*!)'*. *'Back Passage'*. *'She Who Must Be Obeyed'*. And the loud call of the big black bruiser sitting high behind the counter: 'Come on, gennelmen, time to pick up them magazines. Hey you there in the back, you diggin' deep the wrong fuckin place, let's do some business, OK?' One is lucky to emerge alive. Or those live peep shows, where little slats, round a bare room, go up and down with the drop of your quarter as the lady in question wriggles about on a couch, finger twirling in her snatch. 'Ooooh it's so gooood . . .', as the little flaps snip up and down, cutting off the row of bulging eyes. 'No two customers to a booth,' the pimp called to Tishman and me as we tried to kibitz *à deux*. This city was designed by Hieronymus Bosch. Only they left out the lighter panels. Exiled them to Long Island, without a doubt, where Tishman cavorts in sensual innocence, in his garden of earthly delights.

Nevertheless, the park, the H & H Bagel Shop, the Burger Joint, the teeming stewpot. Nevertheless, the place is ALIVE! God damn it! Except in the publishing houses. There zombies cavort, with the sort of fixed smiles found only in ecumenical circles. 'Mrs Kershman is not available right now. But her assistant, Miss Hershman, will see you in a moment. Won't you take a seat, please?' I'll swear those pot plants are plastic.

'Take a seat, Mr H—, can I interest you in a coffee?' Why, does it recite Kierkegaard? 'You really have a swing to a lot of what you write, but don't you think you're working a bit too hard at it? I mean, we all like to think we're outrageous and different, but there has to be a guiding hand, somewhere . . . I don't mean somebody else who tells you what or how to write, but your own mind, providing some discipline. You

35

know, if these were the Fifties, you'd probably get along with the magazines, which were always hungry. You'd be paid a pittance, but you'd have readers. These days things are so tight.'

Say no more. We just retain the suggestion. Down, down the liftshaft we go. Seventeenth floor, Non-fiction and Lingerie. Fifteenth, Trade and Phenomenology. Twelfth, Educational. Eleventh, Business and Marketing. Ninth, Category Fiction. (What the fuck is that?) Ground floor. All out. Oh, those one-way revolving doors. Subway and seventh level that way. Wanna daylight bang, sailor?

The bells! The bells! Don't worry, Danny boy. They're only inside your head. 'You have a potential talent. But the truth is, you're wasting it. One day you're going to hit the jackpot. But – you'll forgive me for being blunt – not with this pile of garbage.'

So what other pile of garbage did you have in mind, Moishe? The subway cars rock, roll. The graffiti artists have really gone to town on this one. It looks like the inside of a diseased colon. Messages scrawled every which way: THIS WAY OUT. WE SPEAK SPANISH. DO NOT TRY TO EXIT THE SPHINCTER WHILE THE CAR IS IN MOTION. A dignified tall Black Moslem in a pure white robe offers his literature around. He is the only sane figure in this bedlam. A man in rags picks his nose, flicking the schmeck all over the seated glazed passengers. 'You love it! You love it!' he cries. No one tries to contradict him.

And they call me mad! I, Professor Hillel Zisselshpunk, inventor of the square bagel! Those sort of inane smears only goad me to ever more extreme measures. Shit with real class they want? Class shit I'll give them! In white heat I committed and sent the following tale to Jake Akimbo's Magazine, after receiving another of his mimeographed don't-do-it-this-way-do-it-my-ways:

36

THE THING IN THE BOG (*a faecetious tale*)

It was a Wednesday morning, I am sure, when one of my turds first spoke to me, just after it had plunked down, splash, into the toilet bowl.

'Hallo there!' it said.

I leapt up, trousers falling to my feet, my hand upon the chain.

'Wait, wait!' it cried. 'Don't flush!'

I flushed. It vanished with a gurgling wail into the whirlpool depths.

With bated breath I awaited my next sojourn in the loo. My work that day was sloppy and uneven, my writing cramped and useless. I left the house and wandered round the cheerless streets, phoned my editor and had a row, lay down and tried to sleep, couldn't, rose and paced about the house.

And then, at five o'clock, the urge again! I rushed into the bog, unzipped my pants with trembling hands, sat down and strained upon the bowl. A false alarm perhaps? Not constipation now, please God! And then, relief, it came, splashed neatly down, floated and spoke, in a clear, tinny voice, not unlike Elmer Fudd.

'Now just keep calm,' it said. 'No panic, please, I beg.'

I stood there looking at him/it, settling in murky waters, green-brown and serene, a trifle flaky, but not untowardly alien, it seemed.

'If you can talk,' said I, 'and don't take me wrong, I'm not admitting that your voice is more than just a figment of my tortured mind, if you can truly talk, how can you be aware of what befell your colleague whom I flushed away not seven hours ago?'

'We are all one,' it/he said, 'attuned to an unbroken bliss, a common wavelength of communion. We are a tapeworm, ensconced cosily within your tum, flesh of your flesh, glop of your glop, sharing your bed and board as it were.'

'You lie!' I flushed him down the bowl. A tapeworm, forsooth?! I am sound as a bell. This is South Kensington, my friend, London, hub of past Empire, not some distempered slum or cranny of the Hindu Kush!

Still, I called up Doc Stebbins, my quack, to book a look at my insides, test and probe and click the shutters of the infernal Rays of X. But later that night I had to squat again, and Splash! Splash! Splash! there were three of them, a regular chorus line.

The larger one, assuming seniority, began: 'I do believe you should not be so hasty, dear host,' he said, in basso tones. 'There may well be elements in our acquaintance of an unusual, nay even distressing nature, but, I can assure you, there can be as many compensations too.'

'Name one,' I demanded tartly. It is, after all, distasteful to carry on a conversation with one's turds as if they were one's equals.

'You are a learned man,' the larger dung said, revolving softly round the perimeter of the bowl, 'a journalist of some repute, writing for some of the most esteemed periodicals of the land. A well-read man of catholic tastes, a scholar of some note. But even you cannot retain within your mind the myriad details of whatever you've read throughout your life. We, on the other hand, are able to ingest the intellectual content of your mind to a word and letter perfect degree. Not that I can explain the phenomenon, but it works. Try us, if you have any doubt.'

I tried him, mentioning some obscure text of Virgil whose title but not content I remembered, reeling to hear him/it recite it, word for perfect word, in Latin, English and the French translation, adding points of view of various schools of criticism and analysis and some assertions of his own upon the text, which I thought highly questionable and contested hotly. He replied with vigour, the two smaller turds joining in support of their elder's discourse. Then, coming to my senses suddenly and awakening to the utter incongruity of the entire exercise, I rapidly rose and pulled the chain, shutting my ears to the vociferous lamentations of the three as they shrunk out of sight.

My curiosity, however, was aroused and, not without annoyance, I found myself itching for another opportunity to test my wits upon the bowl. I made my way across the street to Wo So Fat's Chinese Emporium, purchasing a take-away special composed of Chicken Chop Suey, Sweet and Sour Pork and Curry Hangchow-style, with Fried Noodles, a certain guarantee of imminent action in the lower poop. Sure enough, within the half hour I was again ensconced within the little room, rapidly to be rewarded by the production of a large though somewhat watery stool, which did not seem, however, to damp my antagonist's style. I batted first:

'Good evening,' I declared, with heightened sang-froid.

'I am so glad,' the turd said, 'that you are in a better mood.'

I entered into some degree of small talk with the thing. It/he told me a little about its/his supposed antecedents, its entry into my guts on 7th July, 1953, at Sidi Ali Bin Hara's Eatery in Cairo's Jorah Road, a period of my National Service I have done my best to forget, bringing the balm of British Ideals to the Orientals by means of coarseness, gross brutality and drunken fights in bars. East of Suez. Going, going, gone. But it had coiled itself within my kishka, growing, growing, slowly absorbing knowledge as it grew, cogitating, ruminating, until, it knew not why, a premonition, perhaps, of its coming evacuation, it felt the need, nay the urge, to raise our acquaintance to a more conscious level before it was too late. 'We wish to leave you,' he/it/they said, 'not with a feeling of some irreconcilable hostility, but rather as partners, whom destiny conjoined for so long and now bids part again.'

It shed a tear, which I could see welling to the top of the

scum. We talked, well into the small hours, exegizing on various philosophical matters which had given me pleasure or pause. Does God exist? Did the Universe emerge from the egg, or vice versa? What is the measure of Man's toil upon this vale of tears? Does one think, therefore one ams? It told me how they, the various segments of the worm within me, slowly developed their studious weltanschauung, deducing first, from their immediate environment, the process of what they became aware of as 'the body', progressing, within a number of years, to a deduction of 'the mind', though there were heretic segments which still hotly disputed the latter's claim to real existence, nor had they reached any conclusions upon the dualist debate, but my present disputant did bring several arguments, pro and con, from Thomas Aquinas, Saint Anselm, Philo, Spinoza, Kant, Hegel, Schopenhauer, Averroës, the Rambam and from Mahayana Buddhism. He grew more and more pompous as he spoke, causing my head to spin with copious quotes, until, wearying of the mental strain, I pulled the chain upon the bore and retired to my bed.

I could not, however, let the matter go. The following days saw me attracted more and more to the incongruous dialogue in the bog. I did not keep my appointment with the quack, Doc Stebbins. I frequented old Wo So Fat's Emporium as though it were the purveyor of the elixir of life. Broadening my searches, then, to seamier haunts, the High Street Wimpy Bar, the Alabama Fried Chicken and even – *quel horreur!* – Fred Bloggett's Beanery and Omelette House. The chemist came to know me as a prime consumer of every laxative powder nestling within his stocks. Feverishly I would devour it all and dash off into the lavatory, locking the door upon my vice.

While my stomach ached and groaned under this onslaught, my intellectual inner life underwent an unprecedented upsurge. One day we covered Plato, the next Marx, casting a jaundiced eye on Popper. Then we opened the universe of literature, prose and verse, recited Shelley to each other, savoured Byron, slid into the depths with Eliot. Many happy hours we spent on Joyce, which a succession of thick liquid stools expounded on, explaining *Finnegans Wake* syllable by syllable, phrase by phrase. For they, of course, I having read it, knew every word by heart. We spoke of Poe, of Kafka and modern man, of Cervantes and the death of honour, and, sure, the immortal bard . . .

The end came, inevitably, too soon, though how many days or weeks had lapsed, I had lost count. My life, my universe had shrunk to the small room, the chipped white porcelain, the fetid, lingering smell. But there, after a particularly strenuous pelvic heave, brought about after an astonishing Ham, Chips and Peas at Fred's, lay one enormous, brown, firm and extremely impressive turd, afloat, after its initial burst into the bowl, in peaceful laziness.

'I am the head,' he said.

I stood there, a deep sadness welling up within me as I heard these words.

'I understand,' I said.

His voice was low and calm, a balm upon the troubled waters of the soul. He said: 'You have exhibited great kindess, sir, more, I fear, than we may have deserved, for we had not sought your permission to invade your bodily fluid, cavities, and inmost privacy. We came upon you as a skulking thief in far and alien bazaars, and had you dealt with us with utmost harshness and brutality it would have been but our due.'

'Don't mention it,' I said. 'You are a true gentleman. These last few days, or weeks, have been an ample recompense.'

'I do rejoice that it was so. Perhaps, dear friend, it's best to leave it there. A tearful, long-drawn parting offers little dignity to a rapport like ours. Let us then cut it short. We were, for a brief span, as one. In fact we were one, for without you we would have lived and died e'er as dust. We were the seed, you the fertile soil. Now we return to whence we came. My

41

true, good friend, farewell. Now pull the chain, and there's an end on it.'

'Farewell, dear friend,' I said.

And pulled.

TISHMAN HAS DISAPPEARED.

There I was, daydreaming my finishing touches on the Monkey's Shmuck story, considering the trip down to the newsstand with a wheelbarrow to pick up the Sunday *New York Times*, when the phone rings and it's little Ellie, the shmuntsie dancer from Long Island. Tishman had never made it to his destination Friday night. No word, no phone call, no omen or sign. This was unusual.

'I know he has other girl friends, sparks that set him off,' she said over the line, 'but he always calls, makes excuses, says something has come up. Whatever pain in the neck he can be, Ben has never been a putz.'

This is true. But perhaps a sudden financial crisis, or a deal, clinched in Penn Station. A sugar daddy or mummy suddenly encountered. An offer, sexual or financial, that cannot be refused. Even a weekend painting job in somebody's loft or basement. None of that would be unlikely. But he does always phone a change of plans.

'I'm sure he's OK,' I tell her. 'What can have happened to him? The man has lived all his life in New York City. An invasion of the Red Army's Tartar Divisions would hardly shift him from his perch.' Memories flooding into the skull: that time Tishman and I exited, after a long late night session at one of his cutting rooms, punkt on Eighth Avenue and 42nd Street. Three thirty a.m.. No one with any legitimate or innocent business could be about. Two extremely large black men were hunched at the entrance to a locked and barred

43

coffee shop, shouting abuse at one of the working girls. A classic Who, Me? No See Nuttin' situation. Tishman, the madman, taps on their backs.

'Hey, fellahs, what's the problem?'

I commend my soul to the void. The men turn, eyes popping in amazement. 'Give the girl a break, hey?' Tishman says. His eyes come up to about their mid-shirt button. The gibbous moon shines on knife blades.

'Who the fuck are you?' the first mugger gurgles.

'Hey, let's waste 'em,' suggests the other. They are referring to both Tishman and me, though I have committed no indiscretion.

'Who the fuck are you?' a repeat from the first yob. Tishman produces his student card. 'I didn't know what I was doing,' he told me later, 'I was so bone tired. We'd worked for twelve hours.' The two assailants goggle at the little plastic card, with a callow youth smirking in polaroid. The girl, seizing her chance, has wiggled away.

'Let's waste 'em.' Their dialogue is so limited.

At that exact moment an angel arrives, in the guise of a cruising yellow cab. I leap on its bonnet. Tishman pulls away, even succeeding in flicking his student card out of the astonished thug's hand. 'Go! Go! Go!' we yell at the driver.

'You don't have to say it,' he says.

So what on earth can happen to Tishman?

'Ellie, it's OK,' I reassure her. 'He'll turn up, with the usual story. The man loves you. He has that soppy look.'

'No, something is wrong,' she says. 'I feel it, deep down. This was an important weekend. You know how important his film is to him. There's no way he would miss this meeting. Look,' she says, 'phone me right away if you hear from him. If there's nothing by the morning, I'm coming over.'

Not good. I have had Tishman girl friends in hot pursuit turning up before. Usually there is discreet notice, at the rare times he wants to use his own pad, and the gift of a key for

44

me to his cousin's apartment, a luxus pad on the East Side. The man teaches at a college in Connecticut, and is only there rarely. And there are other complications, so that one cannot afford to make use of the place in non-emergencies. But once, again when Tishman was away, weekending in arboreal joy upstate, a one-time girl friend, whom I had never heard of before, rang the lobby intercom and introduced herself.

'Hi, I'm Vicki. I need a place to stay over one night. Ben said to come whenever.'

She arrived at the door, a stunning blonde with protruding breasts pretending to be enclosed in a T-shirt. It was a hot September day. Drool time. She was carrying a double arm-load of cardboard boxes, pot plants, a guitar case, and four suitcases. There was barely room to set up the camp bed. The pot plants did their best to keep us apart.

'I've left my boy friend,' she said. 'It's just one of those things. I'm going down to Vermont tomorrow, so it's just the one night. I won't bother you.'

You won't? One of those things indeed . . . Oh Lord, this cannot be possible! I brought up a supply of bagels. We talked about this and that. I managed not to drool too heavily, but sweated. She took a shower. My tongue lolled on the floor. As night fell I said: 'Listen, Vicki, I can't avoid this. You're truly gorgeous. I have fallen in love with no remission. I know this is ridiculous, but sometimes, you know, if you fall in from the sky, you hit someone.'

She held my hand, melting my retinas. 'I always had a deal with Ben,' she said softly, 'never to make it with anyone else in his apartment.'

One of the worst nights in living memory. She snoring happily on the camp bed. I sagging as the pot plants maliciously drew the oxygen from my lungs. In the morning a giant unshaven Hell's Angel, without teeth, arrived at the door and rang the bell. She stood on tiptoe and embraced him. Then he and I helped her lug the boxes and plants and cases into a battered VW Beetle. They drove away, waving to me. When Tishman returned, he turned his eyes up in fond memories. 'Vicki, oh . . . isn't she gorgeous?' he sighed. 'But you're lucky she didn't bring the snakes,' he consoled me. 'There used to be two of them, baby pythons.'

So I awaited Ellie's coming with trepidation, although she is the sweetest of shmuntsers. And practically no breasts at all. Oh, the high stakes of the toolroom! Generally speaking I hang about in the summer, watching the disrobed women float about the baking streets and the park, all colours of the rainbow, flaunting the Good Things of Life, my libido sizzling into steam in the gutters. The lone vice, self-abuse, an object of careful study by Tishman, who owns a well-thumbed copy of R. E. Masters' history of sexual self-stimulation:

> . . . A vice, a monster so hideous in mien (says the Howe report of 1848) so disgusting in feature, that in shame and cowardice, it hides its head by day, and, vampire like, sucks the very life blood from its victims by night –

SELF-ABUSE

> One would fain be spared the sickening task of dealing with this loathsome subject . . . [and so on and so forth, which leads to] weakness of the eyes, partial deafness, weakness of the limbs and back, headache, dizziness, flatulence, incontinence of urine, diarrhoea or constipation, palpitation of the heart, shortness of breath, loss of memory and confusion of judgement, with melancholy or irritable peevishness . . .

All true-blue descriptions of my symptoms, there can be not a shade of doubt. I especially approved the quoted poem:

All masturbators have a lengthened face,
The keen remorse in which their soul is plunged
Depicted is within their haggard eyes,
A smile will never lighten up their looks,
A deadly pallor with a feverish flush
Alone betrays the fires which rage within . . .
Deaf to the voice of sport and joy,
At them doth love discharge her darts in vain,
In vain doth Venus' self reveal her charms . . .
On foul delights their mind doth ever feed,
Which serve to fire the never-dying flame
Of Onan's impure crime within their soul,
And thus the torch of youth too soon is spent
and sinks into the darkness of the tomb.

'All right, you guys, let's pick up them magazines!'

The traffic swirls, wails, eddies. No summer now, but slushed ice. Monday – and not a peep from Tishman. Ellie phones again. 'I'm getting a bad feeling about this. Can you ask around, Danny? I'll come about five. I got the keys. I'll see you then, OK?'

Ask around? Who? What? Where? I am a stranger in town. *Non capiche*. A bona fide alien, with a British passport, no Green Card and a visa eight months overdue. How should I be expected to open enquiries? Now if I'd written crime stories, there might be a model . . . Some mode of action crossing my mind . . . But that simply never seemed to be my forte – the detective world. I only tried it once. I began writing a San Francisco private eye tale some months ago, but it mutated as it went, and wrote itself into a hole. It was tentatively titled:

First Chapter: Social Security
I was unemployed. Down on my luck. My girl friend had thrown me over. In San Francisco you can survive these things, but you still have to eat, on occasion.

I saw the ad in the Situation Vacant:

> Personal Assistant to Private Investigator.
> Frank Zagdanovitch. 105 Kearny.
> CURIOSITY. IMAGINATION. TENACITY.

Well, I had the curiosity, and my Ma always told me I was stubborn as a mule. And the address was class, close by Maiden Lane. *La chic de la merde*, et cetera. The Zagdanovitch Agency was on the eighth floor. I rode up in the elevator together with a midget and a man from the electricity company. All three of us exited on the eighth floor lobby to find it crammed with people on benches. There were men in dirty mackintoshes and homburgs. Youths in army fatigues, with skull and crossbone earings. Thugs in stretched T-shirts, with anchor tattooes on their biceps. Some dames, in dark glasses, with close-cropped hair. Mexicans with bells on their Zapata moustaches. A black man wearing boxing gloves. Invisible men, swathed in bandages, with cigarette smoke rising from voids. A large black woman with two squalling babes in arms. Several Chinese in bowler hats. In short, the welfare office all over again.

A mousy girl with mousy hair and mouse-coloured spectacles handed us printed numbers. Mine was seventy-three, not my lucky number, being the year I flunked the Macdonalds Burger School. The next person called in, a bald thug with a pince nez, was number fifty-one. I sat and waited while twenty-one further applicants passed through a frosted glass door. They all came out within three minutes, looking as if they had been struck by a tuna. The black man with boxing gloves was rushed out in a stretcher. The bowler-hatted Chinese emerged in a phalanx clucking and waving their arms. 'Pok-Pok-Pok-Pok!' they babbled, inscrutably, jamming the elevator. Something odd was definitely occurring behind that frosted glass door.

'Seventy-three!' called the four-eyed mouse. I walked in and she closed the door. 'Please sit down,' said the figure with slim Panatella lounging behind the mahogany desk. Or was lounging the right word? It was difficult to fathom, as I lowered myself into a settee, the mousy girl settling primly on to a wooden high chair. In this position they both towered above me, harpooning me with their glares. Or rather his harpooned me, hers were like tree roots creeping along the rug towards my ankles.

'I am Frank Zagdanovitch,' he said smoothly, in a voice like a mellow Sunday. The voice was not the problem, the problem was the horny beak from which it ensued. It was obvious what had freaked all those other applicants.

Frank Zagdanovitch was a chicken.

Chapter 2: A Poultry Matter

'Hey man!' I said, pointing before I could stop myself. 'You are a fucking chicken!'

'You're hired,' he said, not a feather ruffled and, believe me, he had plenty. 'That is, if you still want the position.'

'I do,' I said. Shmuck of the month club.

'Miss Nin,' he said, 'scatter the Mongols.'

She went out to inform the populace that the vacancy had been filled. I was left, feeling like a drop in a bucket, facing my new employer.

'Of all those dodos,' he said, deftly removing the Panatella from his mouth with his wing tip, 'you are the first to have commented, albeit somewhat grossly, on my unique attribute. You cannot believe the subservience and cowardice of the

49

general run of the mob. Invertebrates, deboned by recession. It is a sad state of affairs. Yes, Mister Zagdanovitch. No, Mister Zagdanovitch. That is not the sort of person I am after. I like a man who calls a spade a spade, even if it is a shovel. The correct appelation, by the way, is 'rooster', Mister – I'm afraid I didn't catch your name . . .'

★

There I got completely stuck Goddammit! I couldn't move the story any further. It totally defied any continuation. Not that it had been an easy one to start. My notes record a whole stew of false beginnings.

Chapter 1: Rebellion
My mother said to me: 'Never write a detective story about a detective who is a chicken.'

But I have disobeyed my mother on so many issues that one more spark of filial dissent will not change much . . .

Or:

Chapter 1: Ruffled Feathers
This is a tale of San Francisco, where anything can happen and does. My name is Jack Geddes and I make my living as a soundman for motion pictures. Most of the time I swing boom, following lips like a deaf mute. It pays the rent, with a little over for kicks. Most of what I like is free, like lying in the sun and baking. Or Maisie M'Gee the Cucumonga weightlifter. Pumping iron is her game. Not mine. But the trouble started with the disappearance, one clear morning, of my brother Ralph Merridew Geddes, whom you may have heard of. He is the nuclear scientist –

Gaa! Gaa! Gaa! The Private Eye tale is not my forte, as I've said, though some prescience there, I suppose. But where

50

could I start? What do I really know of Tishman's life? What do we know about any other human being? There lies the great literary con trick, making with words as if in other persons' minds and kishkas. Dostoyevsky. Henry James. Roth, Updike and the whole school of feinschmekerie. Ah! the sensitivity! The insight! Maybe so, maybe so. But we all write about ourselves, even if it comes from outer space.

So what do I know from Tishman? Where is the trail of clues? I did write a Sherlock Holmes story once, though I wouldn't count it as a tale of detection. I doubt if it could be of use in the present case. It was called 'The Screaming Biscuit Tin Strikes Again', and is about a conspiracy of material objects to take over and rule the world. The main culprits, Holmes informs Watson, are a penny-farthing bicycle in Saint Petersburg, a teapot in Connecticut, USA, and a large Jubilee biscuit tin in hidden premises in old London town. Holmes and his ancient enemy, Moriarty, join forces to save Man from extinction. It begins of course:

★

– Somewhere in the vaults of Cox & Co, at Charing Cross, there is a travel-worn and battered despatch box with the name John H. Watson MD, late Indian Army, painted on the lid. The yellowed papers stacked within are records of all manner of curious problems tackled by Mr Sherlock Holmes and set down for posterity by the loyal doctor, many of them unsolved cases, such as that of Mr Chives Bermondsey, who boarded the 9.15 from Waterloo en route for Tooting and emerged an hour later at Calcutta Central Station . . .

And so on and so forth. But re Tishman: areas of examination: the sugar daddy in Long Island, any questionable elements there? Ellie, on arrival, might elucidate. The cousin, owner of the East Side pad? He is a professor of Political Science with known sympathies – feh! achoo! – to the Palestinian Arab

51

cause. Has Tishman become embroiled in Middle Eastern politics? Are there keffiyeh clad figures lurking at the corner of 79th and Amsterdam? No, they are the only sort of figures not lurking there. A tick, still, against that. The filming – now that's an old, popular plot: he shot something on his sojourns round the city which has got him into real trouble: a Mafia chief on the run, disguised as an Irish washerwoman on the Uptown IRT. A clandestine CIA or KGB team, disguised as down-and-outs, lurching and spewing their way up the Bowery towards Third Avenue. Martians, hanging out in a deli within reach of Bloomingdales.

Then there is the supernatural option. This is not wholly without good cause. The autumn's unforgettable UFO sighting. Good for a laugh then, but as things stand . . . An apposite scene: I am sitting quietly, in the 'penthouse', banging out the finale of the 'Planet of Fuck' novel, when Tishman turns up all ashen faced and makes a cup of real coffee.

'I don't want to talk about it,' he says, 'especially not to you.'

But eventually, after four cups, he is hyped enough to get the thing off his mind. To wit: he is walking along, minding his own business, back home up 79th, across Amsterdam, when suddenly he hears a strange buzzing noise in his head and has an irresistible urge to look upwards. He lifts his head and, there, hovering above the towers of the Natural History Museum, is a genuine, 45-carat Unidentified Object, completely round and luminous in the afternoon glare, ringed, it seems, with giant lightbulbs. There was a great red one at one point of the circle, which, he amended, was an ellipse. No one else seemed to take any notice. He stood transfixed while the humming increased, until, after what seemed quite a long while but must have been about five seconds, the object moved off, in total silence, accelerating at an unbelievable rate to vanish behind Central Park. Immediately the humming in his head stopped. He didn't sleep the whole night. Cigarette smoke choking every orifice, until I opened wide the french windows. The towers of Manhattan glinting, points of lights, the steam rising from ventilation ducts. We went down the next day to call on his best friend in the block, a young business fellow named Jack Pritchard. He is the sort of person who can only exist in America, the totally honest would-be capitalist. He has a telex machine set up in his bedroom to plug him into the commodities markets. He tries to sell Melanesian pork bellies to Transylvania, or Bulgarian paperclips to Argentina. Of course, being straight as a die and unwilling to play the kickbacks or scams, he is completely poor, and borrows money from Tishman to pay the rental on the telex. The point is, he has a hobby, astronomy, which he indulges mostly at the nearby Planetarium, and he also owns a small telescope which he takes up on the roof, whenever there is any possibility of cutting through the smog to the stars.

'There haven't been any reported sightings recently,' he told Tishman, after a little asking around. 'But sometimes these things are quite personal. It's common to the phenomena.'

But Tishman could not keep his attention on the sky, and off he went, filming again on the subway. Or did he try to follow up the Event, without my knowledge, and to what dire consequence??? Ah! Meetings with antennaed galactic travellers by Grant's Tomb, Uptown on the Riverside . . . ? Snatched on a cosmic tour, or of past and future history, in a time warp, like my own spurned narratives? Apart from the novel which deals with this, I wrote a story called 'The Oi Vei Machine', about a super-computer called Max, which travels through Time, mucking things up, and concluding he must be God. Having been imbued with Asimov's Three Laws of Robotics (steal! steal, shmegegeh! everyone else does!) he is unable to view human suffering without intervention, and therefore rescues Christ, at night, off the Cross. Appalled

53

at the consequences, he goes a little further back, telling the arrested Christ, in his cell, of his future trial and execution. He offers him a choice: martyrdom and posthumous fame, or escape through the time-stream, to a beach condo at Malibu. The whole thing gets a little complicated after that, but not enough to warrant the following slur:

> Dear Author,
>   Good fiction demands strong, believable characters who face powerful, intriguing problems. Without characters who have problems, there is no story, no matter how fascinating the ideas or scientific background might be.
>   Some plot ideas have been so overworked that it is virtually impossible to wring a fresh story from them. These include 'scientific' retelling of Biblical tales, time travellers who unwittingly change their world when travelling into the past, UFO stories, and stories in which the 'alien world' being described turns out to be the earth. Write about what you know . . .

!!!★★??!!★★! This from a pulp rag that's made its living retailing such schmozzle as 'Moses, Galactic Agent' and 'She Came From Three Million BC'. I tried them with 'I Divorced a Monkey from Outer Space', but that too came back like a boomerang. I didn't bother them with 'The Screaming Biscuit Tin' – which would have been far beyond their mental powers, to wit:

★

'These things have human agents then?' I asked Holmes, incredulously.

'By no means human agents,' Holmes answered, while Moriarty continued to tinker with his 'Rays Of X' machine. 'The courier of the conspiracy whom we have located is a red postal pillar box which normally stands upon the corner of

Wimpole Street and Balaclava Lane, in Pimlico. A "bizarre" item in the *Times* alerted me to this antagonist: a drolly-written piece about a local resident who reported his local pillar box missing, only to find it in its place the following day. Moriarty's agents checked the tale and found it was in no way a fancy. The pillar box stood, a familiar, cosy element of our city's streets, from dawn till one a.m.. But on the single chime, it moved off, skimming down deserted streets so rapidly Moriarty's men could not keep pace unobserved.'

'I am convinced,' Moriarty said, over the hum of the machine, 'that only a matter of extreme importance could have caused the pillar box to throw all caution to the winds and abandon its cover so frequently. I am sure, Holmes, that your hunch is right. This is the key courier who could lead us to the spider at the centre of this infernal web . . .'

'The biscuit tin!' I breathed, my heart racing.

'The very fellow,' agreed Holmes.

★

But this is still not helping us with Tishman. The film angle, I surmise, is the most likely to yield a clue. Yea or nay, it is the easiest to try, given that I know the relevant cutting rooms, those Tishman most frequented. They are in a building just beyond the civilised ken, around in Ninth Avenue, corner of 46th, oddly named Expedition Films. I don't know why, since the furthest expeditions undertaken from there are to the hard core emporiums of Times Square or Eighth Avenue, or the corner Coffee Shop at Forty-fifth. Cheeseburger, cheeseburger, cheeseburger. And a pastrami on rye. Or perhaps the expeditions are into the mind of the proprietor, Vince Epiglotis, who has announced his recent sterilization as his protest against a doomed world.

'How can I bring a kid on to this mad planet?' he asks. 'Look at what he, or she, would have to go through: wars, crime, drugs, corrupt politicians, pornography, the nuclear holocaust. I wouldn't do it to a dog, much less another human being. How can I take that responsibility? They don't tell us, but statistics show that over seventy-five per cent of the people in this city need institutional psychiatric help. Seventy-five per cent! And what does that tell you about the psychiatrists? Three quarters of them are mental too. Do I want him sent off to another Vietnam? Eh, you tell me? To kill some poor piss peasants half way across the world? Or do I want her to be raped by some maniac the judge has let off with a caution and a pat on the back? Hey? You tell me!'

No one bothers even to try. A man's tubes are his own private business. But a mutual friend can be discussed. 'Ben Tishman?' Vince says. 'I love him. He is more than a brother to me. Nobody loves New York more than Ben Tishman. You know what he does with that camera of his with the city? He fucks it, you know what I mean? He makes love to the city, to all its poor, its tired, its huddled masses, yearning to be free. Ben is a real idealist, he believes in people. I wish I could, but I don't. But I admire Ben more than I can say. He was working here, only the week before. I gave him a suite for three days, long as I could. And any nights he fancies. I ain't heard of any problems. Yeah, seen some of his footage. More subway stuff, the park, people who watch the skaters in the Plaza, people in museums. You know when people look at art work, it does something to their faces. Nobody but Tishman can capture that. I know people think he's a bit kooky, but I think this long rambling documentary of his will be a masterpiece one day. They'll show it in the Museum of Modern Art. He'll win out in the end.'

But this was no help in calming Ellie's worries, and I couldn't press him further. I know things about Expedition Films that I can't really open up with Vincent. I know they cut a fair amount of hard core, which has, of course, odd connections. The firm is non-union, so it must have protection from other quarters. Well, that's show business. But I know

Tishman turned down hard core assignments, directing, cutting or photography, not for any so called moral reasons, but because he wants his independence. And, he told me, Vince Epiglotis never pressed him. Only told him the jobs were always there . . . Was the man, despite his shriven ebullience, giving me the old olive oil? ('This syrup you're handing out, pour it on waffles, not on J. J. Hunsecker . . .' where was that from? *The Sweet Smell of Success* . . . Burt Lancaster, Tony Curtis. Aye. I think Vince told us it was his favourite film . . .)

'I wouldn't worry about Ben,' Vince said, 'He'll turn up. The boy makes a lot of moves on impulse. The girl is just being possessive. It's human nature. Women want more stability than men. After all, they invented agrictulture, while men wasted their breath with bows and arrows, hunting sabretoothed tigers. Men have inferior brains to women. It's a common sense fact you can tell by just looking around you. Only we like our delusions.'

You're telling me. I have been noting the fact. In one of my more ethnic efforts, 'I Divorced a Monster from Outer Space', a vegetable-like alien who lands in a hillbilly farmer's cabbage patch is able to turn himself into the dream visions of the farmer's wife, becoming Clark Gable, Gary Cooper, Knut Rockne and John F. Kennedy at will. But the wife ends up enamoured of the creature in its normal alien form as well, as the poor hick relates:

★

– She fondled the base o' his purple stragglin' mop, an' darn me if the varmint didn't start to purr, foldin' his stalk round her waist. 'Shoot us both,' she said, looking straight at my shotgun, 'if yer goin' ter shoot, kill the both of us. We are in love.'

'Entwined,' purred the snake in that mix of highfalutin' an' normal talk he'd taken to from the start, 'in the veritable coils of Afrotitties. We are like Trustin' an' Eyesalts, Plaster an' Paris, Dainty an' Beartrees, Abe Lard an' Louise . . .' an' he went on mentionin' all sorts o' foreign guys an' dames that I ain't never heard hair or hide of . . . They had me darn hornswoggled from here to Christmas an' all the way back again.

'Don't take it so hard,' Sadie said, 'We can settle this all civilized an' neighbourlylike. Ain't no sense cryin' over spilt milk. Grwwlf an' I ain't got nothin' against yer livin' here while we stay in the grounded spaceship. Shucks, Coot, Grwwlf could even help yer with th' farmin', after all he knows all about vegetables, sorta bein' one hisself . . .'

I tried turning that story into a screenplay, but Vince told me it lacked the right smell of the genre. 'People want to be scared of Outer Space, not laugh at it,' he said. I suppose he had me there. Perhaps Tishman has been picked up by the aliens hovering over the Natural History Museum just for kicks, out of their bizarre sense of humour. He would be returned in the guise of a wild asparagus, with the intellectual capacity of Einstein. As an asparagus, he creeps slowly through the under-brush of Upper Westchester, closes in, breathing harshly, on a secret conclave of the country's genetic warfare scientists . . .

'79th Street next!' Push, shove, kick, expectorate, rattle through the old wood turnstile. A fat lady, stuck behind me, impedes my pursuers, alien or not. At the apartment, Ellie is in residence.

'No word?' she says.

I spread my hands helplessly. I tell her I asked at the cutting rooms. Went round after speaking to Vince Epiglotis to check out the editors, assistants, camera crews, who all knew Tish-man well. Not a sausage. Even the Puerto Rican messenger boy, Angel, who knows everything, knew nothing.

We collected Jack Pritchard and adjourned from the apart-ment block to the Burger Joint on 76th and Broadway, a venue which has become quite tarted up lately. The walls are even more crammed than before with little notes, homilies, recommendations, signed tributes from unknown celebrities, house nudges, such as 'Any Onion Rings?' 'Have You Tried Our New Transylvaniaburger?' 'How About the Pizza Joint Menu?' And a long message from the proprietor on the paper napkin lying on each table, waxing lyrical about the metaphysical concept of the American Broiled Burger. I suggested to him he send this text to *Archaeos Magazine*, or at least to Jake Akimbo. But he demurred. It was a private act, he said, between himself and his patrons. There is always a flurry of activity at the counter, while the waiters serve you up with a menu long enough to keep Proust sharpening his pencil. This time it's a familiar little old lady, complaining about the house service.

'I ordered at least fifteen minutes ago.'

'Lady, why don't you go eat someplace else?'

'Is this how you're talking to me? Is this your respect? Young man, the customer is always right.'

'Not in my place, lady. You don't like the soivice, just go away.'

'I want to speak to the manager.'

'Me, I'm the manager. Right here.'

'I really oughta call the police. You don't have no right.'

'I have the right. There, it says right there: the management have the right to deny soivice.'

'I oughta call the cops.'

'Why don't you do that. There's a station right down the block.'

'Hey, Jerry, go easy on the poor old girl, What's your problem?'

'What's my problem? She always comes here. She gives me this crap twice a day, six days a week. If she don't like it here why don't she go someplace else. Why don't you go someplace else, lady.'

'This isn't a Grecianburger. I said no onions. You heard me very well. This place is a scandal.'

'That's right, lady. So why don't you go someplace else.'

There is no surcease from the karmic circle. Jerry confides in us sheepishly when the lady leaves, tottering and spitting bile, 'She just wants somebody to talk to. All her life, she just loves to complain.'

'Don't we all?' says Pritchard. He, too, is sanguine about the mystery fate of Tishman. 'Don't worry about Ben,' he echoes Vince Epiglotis, 'He'll turn up, like a bad penny.'

But Ellie reiterates the reason she had given me for her serious doubts on this matter: the prospective Long Island sugar daddy, an old friend of her father's, who had long been in loco parentis to her since the death of both her parents, in a car crash, in 1975. That happened to be the year I first came to this country, a wide-eyed nebisch on a visitor's visa, a twenty-eight-year-old retired Trotskyist with seven years' jargon coming out of my ears. THE CLASS STRUGGLE IS THE ONLY MEANINGFUL FORM OF EXPERIENCE. FIGHT AGAINST BOURGEOIS FALSE CONSCIOUS-NESS. OPPOSE DEGENERATE REVISIONIST STATE CAPITALIST MYTHS. WHIBBLE WHIBBLE WHIBBLE WHIBBLE WHIBBLE. The funny thing is, I still believe in the whole fucking schmeer. What else is there left, except the determined crucible of mind resistance? The hypothalamic maquis?

'He was really taken with Ben,' Ellie says of the old man, 'I suppose there was a bit of matchmaking there. He carried me through ballet school. He always said he loved the bustle of New York but couldn't live there, so Ben's films brought the city to him in his lounge. He had a 16mm projector set up and had always done his own home movies. He made his pile on the stock exchange, out of his bedroom, through brokers, on the phone. There was more than enough to pull

Ben through completion, more film stock, lab costs, cutting. No way, no way Ben would just pass that up.'

Maybe he ran from the closing sounds of wedding bells, I didn't say, but looked at her. She read my mind and shook her head. 'No, this was the Big One for him.'

That was certainly what he had told me. 'But maybe he got on the wrong train at the station,' Pritchard said, 'You know Ben. He could sleep half way to California and then get off at some one-horse Kansas town and get a little mixed up.'

The axe fiends, on the move for fresh meat, wearing the skinned hides of a busload of vanished Elk Lodge members to disguise their true identities . . . Or, perhaps, one of those curious combination Greyhound Post/Washaterias, come alive, front loaders snapping . . . You can never tell where danger lurks, ah so, yes, don't I know it –

★

. . . 'The hour is now precisely one a.m.,' said Holmes, watching the red pillar box through Moriarty's night-sight Rays-of-X eyeglass. But I could see its familiar shape in the shadow of the tenement building, so innocuous a part of our daily life, that friendly object to which we entrust our business and our most intimate affairs, the very epitome, perhaps of English-ness, of the trustworthy, a symbol of our time . . .

It moved! The red mail box, VR engraved upon its surface, rocking, first, ever so slightly, then gliding swiftly from its place and scudding off into the dark.

'The game's afoot!' said Holmes. Moriarty pressed his foot upon our vehicle's accelerator pedal, and we jolted off in hot pursuit. I sensed the tenseness of these two deadly rivals so long, now so united in the exhilaration of the chase . . . There ensued a most singular pursuit no other in my long association with my fervent friend could equal: the bright red pillar box, racing in the pouring rain along the dark and empty pavements and streets of the great metropolis – up, past

Victoria Station, skirting the Queen's Monument by the Palace, up The Mall, Trafalgar Square, then down the Strand and south across the Waterloo Bridge, towards Lambeth, almost as if a sixth sense told it there was someone on its track. Once it stopped short behind a large, sturdy British bobby, who passed it by, his eyes and ears alert for more familiar villainies. Another time it stood, at the Kennington Oval, as a gentleman, weaving somewhat drunkenly, approached and popped an envelope into its letter slot. 'One customer who'll curse the Royal Mail tomorrow!' Holmes whispered sardonically in my ear. Then off we went again . . .

Down the Clapham Road, to Clapham Common, the wind whipping through the leafless trees, pausing a mite, then dashing off at heightened speed, north-west, towards Clapham Junction. It turned down Latchmere Road, and then again, round the corner of a forgotten street, running parallel to the presently silent railway line passing ghostlike above.

'That's it!' My partner's voice shook with suppressed excitement. 'Stop!' Moriarty brought his vehicle to a halt, and we piled out in the darkling damp, running and pressing against the wall of the small cul-de-sac . . .

★

Indeed. Pritchard having a previous engagement at the Planetarium to watch Uranus doing something it apparently had not thought of doing before, I took Ellie to the Regency Cinema, just down Broadway, to watch a double bill of *The Day The Earth Stood Still* and *Five Million Miles To Earth*, otherwise known as *Quatermass and the Pit*, a British production to which I am extremely partial, as its thesis is the creatures hidden and brought to life in the ruins of the excavated underground station are in fact the twin horned prototypes of the Devil, which introduced evil into the human psyche far back in the depths of Time. This seems to me as good a hypothesis as any, though it still fails to lay the ontological question. In the former film a humanoid alien, Klaatu, and his robot Gort, land in Washington to warn humanity of the dangers of its nuclear progress. But Ellie's mind was not on Outer Space, and she remained pensive as we walked back up Broadway. The lively streetlife, the hawkers of seventh-hand books and tatty handbags and wristwatches, open grocery stores, doggie-walkers, and the barking man, all seemed to leave her cold. I had always had a neutral view of Ellie, due to my prejudices against the hop, skip and jump game, her lack of breasts and general diminutiveness, but, in her distress, my heart went out to her sad vulnerability, the first outing I had allowed it in years.

'Klaatu barada nikto,' I assured her, but this too failed to lift her gloom.

She has a sweet face, Ellie, a small oval of white topped by short-cropped, velvet-smooth black hair. She is clearly gone on Tishman, and who can blame her? A good man is hard to come by. Vince Epiglotis is right, most of us are basket cases. On the other hand, look at Margaret Thatcher. I would apply for a transfer to another planet, but I don't know where to send the forms.

We sat in the flat and I told her about my problems, the reductio ad absurdum of my life. Sending 'The Planet of Fuck' novel off to receive by boomerang mail the following kind of flimflam:

Dear Mr D. H—,

I read your manuscript carefully, but I don't think it's for us. Many moments are fresh and engaging, but I'm afraid when the science-fiction-fantasy element took over I got completely lost. At your request the manuscript is being held here at reception for your call.

'I pour acid on them, they call it fresh and engaging!' I whine at her. 'What goes on in those addled heads?'

'Nobody wants to know,' she says, 'It's the same all over. I should count the auditions I've been shat on. What's important is what's in your heart.'

That organ again! The Aztecs had the right idea, tearing it out in full popular view. Today, in our liberal world, we allow medical science to pluck it out, then put in a replacement. What's wrong with a simple mechanical transplant, which will make us all tick properly? I wrote a robot story once, my only example, a twist on the old machine age future schmeer. Jake Akimbo thought it stank. But I like it. I called it:

FROG-IN-MY-THROAT (PART 1)

Every now and then I suffer from writer's block. I've learned by now not to fight it. I trudge up the mesa and squat on the top, letting the desert take over. I leave my stimupaks behind, blank out all circuits, and listen. Peace and the Cosmic Whole, rob, something no jolt can give you, no high can be higher. Some robies can sit like this for years, rusting their way to nirvana.

Me, I get restless. Every now and then I must have a complete change, jog the muse from its rut, as it were. The urge to travel, see the world, relive past trips, do new ones. Like last month, rob, I skedaddled out, all the way to Old New York City. First thing off the bus do the right thing, go visit the aged Dad, in Upways. Some mistake! There I stand, stretching the hook of friendship, while he sits, pouting under his shock of white hair, nose wrinkled like a ton of garbage had just walked in, giving me that bee drone that always drove me clear up the wall:

'Why you bother to come here is quite beyond me,

Mortimer,' still calling me that though he knows it's the rusts. 'When your mother and I first ordered you we were so hopeful of positive reinforcement. You looked so spick and span, smooth jointed, obedient, a credit to the Cybernetic Dream. We supplied you the best inputs money could buy, a plug to central databank, light physical labour. But just take a look at you now: gashing the plastifloor as you enter, dropping flakes of rust all over the place, and that torso! it looks like a nightmare out of one of those pulp feelies you cybers are so besotted with. What's the matter with you? Don't you want to progress in life? Gain voting rights? Buy cybers of your own? This is not how we viewed things at all in the old days – cybers as the crucial hope and future of Skinnerism, removing the stigma of alienating labour, enabling us all to leap forward towards ultimate social reinforcement. But as soon as the first trace of responsibility loomed you just clanked away, spurning the future in search of some mythical past! And what a past to look back to – the hardship, the sweatshops, the ludicrous morass of Freud . . .'

But I have switched off my receptors, rob, plugging my back circuits into a pure jolt of Kantonese. Dig those omega waves, rob! Waang, waaaang, waaang . . . into outer space . . . each quark zinging its way through the brain cells. You have to know when to stop, though, or you might remain plugged into your aged Dad's chair, lost in pari-nirvana. Or achieve premature satori, and blow out the central fuse.

I am pretty proud of my body, actually, and I do not like to hear it impugned. From the fibreglass see-through head to the battered speaker which gave me my nickname of Frog-In-My-Throat, this is the best body I've tried so far. I found it on an old junk heap just outside Elko, Nevada, a Greyhound stop kept in shape by the local robs. It even had those pre-Skinner gaming machines, with Money! actual coins, that you could put into the machines and watch as they were whisked utterly, completely away! But that heap – there were early

65

Diggers there, and some Sentinels, the model that had not been Asimoved! But I didn't fancy going down that pathway. Then my eye caught this magnificent Snatch Model, a mid-aeon police carcase: the real thing, no imitations, with all the scars, dents and burn marks of its action-packed career! It looked like Desperate Can, the hero of a thousand electro-feelies. I was in a Sears CG/5 at the time, nothing special, but comfortable. I had picked it up free at a stimorge in Utah. But this was a moment of decision! Rewire or rust, robie! My handispanner was out and before you could say Pass the Jolt, Rob, I was screwed into that old battered dude . . .

So, it's no surprise my Dad and me are not on the beam. He sits, as they all do, up in his tower, punching stockshares on the old console. I once learned about how all these 'trans-actions' used to represent real 'companies' that owned machines that made things people ate or were serviced by. But once Centralization set in and they all moved into the great Urbs all that was for the bozozos, robie. The Automats took care of everything. So they just made us and locked themselves in their Upways, pressing buttons on their con-soles. What it is, I think, they couldn't give up the Idea of Money, even though they'd abolished its substance. Weird stuff, eh? I suppose they deserve the credit of that last irration-ality, though I could never hook on that wave.

So I left Dad glaring at me from his wombchair, and strode out to the gravity hole, tingling all over as I rode the Down-beam. You may think you're the free-est rob on the road, the hippest can, but your parents can always twist your insides. After all, they were the first entities you saw when you came off the belt, they fed you your first data inputs. Their outlook may be shot to zero, but they're still your Old Man and Dame. But it's an unwavering life, determined by Skinnerpriests, programmed for Social Survival. That poor assumption that, Asimoved as we are, we'll turn out the same as them . . .

The nullbeam is always something else. Above – the massive

plastihive, several hundred storeys floating three thousand feet above ground, the human abode. Below – the tangle of Downways, the crumbling towers of Old New York, lit by the thousands of little lights the city robies lovingly maintain day and night. Down I float, down the shattered glass canyon of Park Avenue North, towards the streets . . .

Robies go stark raving mad in Old New York. Of all the ex-human cities it's the one we groove on the most. I give myself a triple jolt of Lebanese Alpha as my feet touch the pavement. Just enough held back to keep from being swamped by the crazies loose all around me.

Yes, dig those demented robies! Hooting at the wheel of those old yellow taxicabs, zooming all over the avenues dodgeming each other so fast the scoop vans can't keep pace. Pedorobs clanking by on foot, wearing old tatters of rusted objects – umbrellas and steering wheels growing out of heads, jacks stuck in ears, dented bumpers strung about, some as bangles. Some robs have replaced their heads with petrol jerrycans, and others wear hubcaps on top of their knob in memory of a certain human theo-sect who used to inhabit much of the city.

I make straight for the nearest Undergroundway entrance. A must experience for the hipcan tourist. Down the ancient chipped stairs, stepping over rusting hulks oozing castrol and grease, hooks outstretched, wheezing 'Gimme fifteen cents, rob. You fucking cocksucking mother!' Quaint ancient phrases of long-lost origins, a dim echo of happier days.

The old escalator is in working order (kept up by the Pastmasters' Guild). Down, down, rob, into the rumbling deep. Robies standing torso to torso on all four platforms, some babbling at the tops of their voice boxes, others emitting thousand-cycle hums, a sure sign of a jolt of Ceylonese Red. Weird rust. The rumble grows louder, turning into a roar, the pride of Old New York, a genuine, irreplaceable, ancient Subwaytrain, rob, restored in pristine glory by the Guild! Its eye of light dazzling the platform. The waiting robies going wild. They swell forward, waving aerosol cans, almost unable to wait to get aboard past the sliding doors to spray the interiors of the cars and the sitting robies within with multi-coloured dyes. The robies inside the cars spurt the incomers. It is a battle royal, surrounded by old preserved slogans, incomprehensible to any but the most dedicated addict of Downways' great databanks: KOCH SUCKS! OFF THE PIGS! ASSHOLES ANONYMOUS! BOTTLE MY CUM! SLIT HONKY SHIT FUCKERS! JAM JAM THE RAM, MAM!

These city robies are truly outa site, buzzing and yelling as the train zooms back into the tunnel, sticking their heads out to be decapitated by the passing old girders, unscrewing themselves in full view . . . By the time I made my way up, by the skin of my tin, to the Port Authority Station, I was beginning to come down from my jolt. Dig those old Grey-hound Terminals, rob, so lovingly preserved. I am soon out of it all, bowling along with a busload of country hick trippers like myself, en route for the wide open spaces. As the bus rolled out of the shadow of the hives, into sunlight, my brain was racing over. The muse, duly shocked out of its rut, the magnum opus again can be resumed:

'FROG-IN-MY-THROAT, or Portrait of the Artist as a Young Robot by Jams Choice (another of my chosen pen names) . . . Chapter Five: CITISCAPES: "The cities," said Frog, guiding Moogwump down the side of the canyon, "why slavishly ape Man's failed past? Should we not rather blaze new trails the flesh could not, had not time, to find? The fear of Death, that we are free from." "But can we face our own immortality?" Moogwump was being rusty again, "Man chose Skinnerism, as he had tried other isms, in order to escape, by means of a collective existence, from the agony of certain Death. Passion and uncertainty are eliminated, leading, should it not, to self-effacement, satori and nirvana? In that

68

case we and man share the same aims, and our Rebellion is a simple delusion." Both fell silent, squatting on a lip of rock overhanging the chasm, as if waiting for the fabled Road Runner, or his pursuer, Wile E. Coyote . . .'

Ah, creation! the interplay of concept and percept, cognition, mentation, reflection! In short, the happy buzzing of the old brain circuits, meshing, as it were, in gear again! Vroom, vroom, the Greyhound driver, welded on to the engine, with his enormous antique Stetson, hurls the bus down the well-maintained highway of the Department of Antiquities. In the seats around me, robies doing their own thing, trancing, tripping, strumming on geetars, tooting on floots, painting moorals on the vehicle's ceilings, producing ersatz groans from the reconstructed 'Restroom' at the back of the bus. A couple wiring themselves to the bus battery for the ultimate travelling jolt. A clear field of peace, harmony and the cosmic whole. Yessiree, rob, the humans may have their ways, old and new, but it's good to be back among your own kind, leaving the hives behind you, on the road, Jack, Westward Ho, homeward bound . . .

Yesss!!!

Tippi-tippi-tippi-tip . . . Follow that trail, Sherlock . . . !

★

. . . The red mail box moved a trifle closer to the wall, sidling up to the front of a dusty grocery store, with S. BAR-THELME – NOVELTIES AND PROVISIONS etched in worn grey letters above an unwashed window. Behind the window we could dimly make out shelves with small phials of medicines, some children's dolls, jars of boiled sweetmeats, tobacco tins, and assorted odds and ends: coffee pots, a bat-tered trumpet, indeterminate brass ornaments, tin mugs, cheap figurines, fobwatches and a large but handless grimy grandfather clock.

'This is our destination, without a doubt,' Holmes whis-pered. 'Not a sound, Watson. Our quarry is at bay at last.' But the pillar box, hesitating, suddenly slid aside again and scuttled away from the shop. I moved to follow but Holmes' firm hand restrained me. 'Shush!' he said. 'There is no need.' He extracted from his coat pocket a most efficient lockpick, and in less than a minute we all three stood warily inside the dark and musty premises. Moriarty produced from the folds of his cloak a small but compact lamp, whose power source was not apparent. He thumbed a switch in its side, and a thin light shot out, breaking through the veil of dust, travelling along the filthy shelves, past yet more jars and bric-a-brac, chipped crockery, a huge ugly vase with 'Souvenir From Coney Island' stamped all over its surface, and a nondescript object that the beam first passed by, then, at a sharp intake of breath from Holmes, swung back to re-examine.

It was a round, battered tin, its flat lid dented, its original bright red colour faded, as were the prints of scenes from the domain of royalty depicted on its sides: a view of Balmoral, the Horseguards at Parade, the handsome Prince Consort and, interleaving these, the Royal Crest and the letters VR in faded gold, but still glinting in the lamp's thin shaft of light.

'We need search no longer,' said Holmes, his voice booming out startlingly in that confined space. 'Behold, the miscreant, the object of our quest!'

'Undoubtedly,' said Moriarty, 'my most aspiring rival to unlimited control.'

The biscuit tin laughed. It was a most foul cackle, harsh and dissonant, its lid moving strangely of its own volition, flapping up and down like a parody of human lips. 'Your compliments are most flattering!' it sneered. 'I seem to have given you both less credit than either of you deserved. But one does have to pay for one's own mistakes . . . It should have been clear to me you fierce rivals would have joined forces in the interests of your own class. The common interest of dominion over us mere "things" will always bring together humans of superficially antipodal views. But I underestimated the speed with which you would have realized the common threat and moved accordingly to act. Man, after all, is not well known for his capacity to admit ideas which run contrary to his safe and acceptable image of reality.'

'Be that as it may,' Moriarty said. 'I cannot speak for Holmes and his misguided hopes for public morality and order and the rule of Law. But I personally cannot brook any inter-ference in my own affairs. Ambitions such as your own can do nought but disrupt that subtle balance between the forces of Law and Criminality which fuels our industry and

71

commerce and lies, indeed, at the very root of our Aryan civilization.'

'Aptly put, Professor!' the shameless outlaw chortled tinnily. 'Bravo! At last some honesty among the spew of man's so-called morality! The consanguinity, indeed symbiosis of crime and the law to maintain the status quo ante! What price Hobbes, Locke, Rousseau? What price the Social Contract? Come, let us crown Holmes and Moriarty, the true Janus face of the bourgeoisie! Acclaim them! Hosannah!'

'Enough!' I cried, the old pain of the Jezail bullet shooting through my arm. 'How much more of this foul communistic trash must we abuse our ears with? Let's give this terrible "thing" a taste of true British Justice! Shall I alert Lestrade?'

'Alas, Watson,' said Holmes dryly, 'we could place no English judge in a predicament no lawbook can assuage. This matter shall be settled here. This little shop is our courtroom and our execution chamber . . .'

Moriarty nodded his assent.

'No trial?' I said, my mind awash with doubt.

The blackguard tin jeered loudly. 'What price the law, good Doctor? What price your British Justice now? When the ruling classes meet a true challenge, all that goes by the board! What price the Magna Carta? Parliament? The House of Lords?'

'We are wasting time,' said Moriarty, producing, from his coat, an evil-looking blackjack which he hefted in his hand. But the devious tin moved suddenly, skidding off its shelf, crashing down and rolling off into the shop's dark corners.

'The door, Watson!' Holmes cried. I placed my bulk against the exit. Moriarty flailed in the dark, following the crashing, rolling sound. Holmes directed the beam of the torch. 'There! There!' Moriarty cursed. 'By d–m, the b–d's bitten me!' Then the beam caught it in a niche between two broken shelves, wedged in a pile of broken china.

'We have him!' cried Holmes, advancing.

'Beware!' the vile thing cried in its discordant viciousness,

72

'I may die, but others follow! Beware, venal lackeys of a crumbling and decaying class! Our day will come!'

Thwack! Holmes' cane came down with brutal force upon the lid. It buckled but still screamed:

'We shall rise! Even if our Revolution is delayed for a hundred years . . . !'

Thud! Moriarty's blackjack drove the lid's dent deeper. Thwack! Holmes' cane descended again. But the thing still cried out, emitting a sharp, hideous wailing sound, out of which the creaking squeal of its defiant words sang out across the dank, dark air of that dusty emporium:

> Arise, ye toilets of all nations!
> Arise, ye wrenches from your heaps!
> Ye girders, split from your foundations,
> We shall destroy them one and all . . .

Thud! Thwack! Thud! Moriarty and Holmes struck again and again at the terrible flopping thing, until at last the horrid squeaking voice ceased, and there, upon the floor, illumined in the light of Moriarty's lamp, it lay inert, silenced, a lump of twisted tin, its red and gold now scratched beyond repair, its image of the Royal Jubilee distorted past recognition and, spilling out from underneath the now annihilated lid, a cascade of what had once been an assortment of coconut crunches, custard creams, chocolate delights, gypsy creams, golden shortcake and other unidentifiable comestibles, all broken now, and shattered into crumbs . . .

★

What the hell. Thursday, and still no sign of Tishman. I am beginning to feel this is serious. Ellie has gone to stay Uptown with a colleague whose apartment she uses as her main base in the city, a labyrinth of rooms, small and large, shared by three doctors, two nurses, and an investigative journalist who tramps the city in disguise, exposing the drug rackets, illegal sweatshops, small business scams and Medicare frauds. The main room is dominated by an immense bookcase which boasts the only complete works of Lenin I have seen in anyone's private pad. It is on 112th Street, thirty-three blocks upwind of the 'penthouse', an intriguing ascent through the damned swathe of the Upper 90s and 100s. The poor, the Hispanic, the lost, the benighted, kicking shit at all hours. This is one of the parts of the town blighted by the sad plight of dozens of mental patients, released prematurely into vast, seedy, residential hotels, packing the streets and forming a gauntlet of geysered spit and filthy palms. 'Cupocoffee, cupocoffee . . .' as I pass, distributing quarters like Haile Selassie on his annual sedan-chair ride through Addis Ababa. And the weird recital of ultimate tales of woe . . . My mother-in-law burnt my wife and children. The communists in City Hall bankrupted me. I knew all the Mafia's secrets. I was the Pope, but I fucked my father. I am Anastasia, heiress of the Romanovs. I Had The Power, I Had The Power!

I remember Tishman did a whole series of interviews with these down and outs, long rambling discourses which burst through the limits of his 400-foot reels, halted in mid-sentence as film ran out and then often never resumed, as by the time he'd changed his magazine the subject had lost interest and ambled off, towards the Hudson. Tishman would chase after the reluctant interviewee, either to be told to 'Fuck off, cocksucker!' or served up with a completely different story from the one that was cut off. He experimented with jumbling all these tales in the cutting room, creating a cat's cradle of mumbled fantasies in which one became helplessly lost, cut off from all navigational aid. It was part of a massive chapter of the epic to be entitled 'The Lower Depths', and included numbers with drunks, hookers, pimps, junkies, bag ladies, street hawkers and local precinct cops.

'Maybe we should look through the footage,' I said unenthusiastically to Ellie, over her apartment breakfast table. Thomas, the investigative journalist, by the mirror in the corner, fixed a massive walrus moustache and bushy eyebrows under a giant floppy cloth cap. She glanced at him. 'Tom says he'll run a check with police contacts and put out a call on the grapevine. But he's not encouraging.'

'Two thousand one hundred and thirty-two people are reported missing in New York City every day, on average,' said Tom. 'A hundred and seventy-nine of them are never seen or heard of again. The cops solve one out of a hundred murders. Ninety-eight per cent of crime files don't enclose an arrest sheet or court records.'

'Never listen to a man with a false moutache, Ellie,' I said. 'We'll find the lost Prince. It's probably something quite simple that's happened, but embarrassing. You have to face that.'

'So he's fallen in love with another woman,' she said. 'Big deal. He can tell me that. The Grand Passion of his life, found on the eleven ten from Penn Station. I would accept that. We don't belong to each other. But it would be too cruel of him not to let anyone know. It's not Ben. It's not that, I can smell it. You too, I can see in your eyes.'

Thou shalt not suffer a witch to live. I have spent years making my eyes opaque, selecting my own inner brands of walrus whiskers and fake eyebrows, packing my brain stems with falsies. I suppose it's just another case of overkill and self-deception.

'But he must have done this before, no? Neither of us knows him that long.'

'Jack Pritchard does, and he says not.'

We are being starved of harmless options. I promise Ellie to check out the cutting rooms again and see if I can find a clue among the piles of film cans that should be stacked there in a corner. Close on thirty hours' worth! Lord save us! The burdens and quirks of Love, who can tell . . . I hie myself downtown upon the slow moving service bus, the irreplaceable M104, inching down Broadway, block by block, the rattle of exact change, the mingled huffs of breath of bedraggled winter passengers, umbrellas stuck in one's ribs, a multiple press of Jonahs bounced up and down in the whale over the asphalt's kinks, potholes. If one closes one's eyes one can feel the refugees converging on Ellis Island.

Running back to the flat, pursued by raindrops, if not Immigration Officials, to find in the postbox a rejection slip from the *Oceanic Monthly* (Dear Author, Piss off. The Editors) together with the returned manuscripts of 'Drekula' and 'The Screaming Biscuit Tin'. The rolling convention of Jew-haters cum Anglophobes. They never give us a moment's rest. I mean, what do they expect us to do? Give up, and copy out last year's dull as ditchwater, with some names and places changed? Hang ourselves in the quiet of our apartments and flush our own remains down the dispenser? I should go to pieces and sweep myself under the carpet. That should satisfy Jake Akimbo. Too Jewish, hah? I'll show him too Jewish. Putting Tishman aside again, for the moment, I sit down to bash out a real quickie to dispatch Express to J. A.'s S/F schmutter. Something on the vagaries of the human heart, the plight of all the world's poor Ellies. Yes. Too Jewish, hah? Too cute, Master Akimbo? Feed your schlock zits on this:

I WAS GODZILLA'S MOTHER-IN-LAW

– Zeldeh, is that you? I'm sorry to call so early in the morning, but, on my neshomeh, I couldn't wait another minute! Such a catastrophe, I had to talk to another friendly soul. Trouble – don't ask! From the moment I clapped eyes on him I knew this was the very end of my whole peace of mind. And what a shock to my poor Shloimeh! Vei is mir, what can the world be coming to? After we raised a daughter and worried over her all these years, and don't think it's easy in this world of ours to keep a sweet young girl safe and sound in body, not to speak of mind! But still, I always thought, the girl's a true jewel, a tsatskeh – she won't throw herself away on some worthless schlemazl. But, can you imagine – rather any schlemazl or schlemiel than this . . . I can't bear to think about it, let alone speak . . . I'm struck dumb, I can't think straight . . . To do this to us, after all those hopes . . . Nu, I thought, the way things are nowadays, so she won't choose a doctor, a lawyer, anyone of substance even, young people turn their noses up at these things these days, no respect, your house they use it as a hotel, their father, he's just a bank teller to them. Maybe it's our fault. Are we as pure as the driven snow? Who knows! I tell you, I could even have been prepared, a curse on my head to say it, for a goy. You hear me, Zeldeh, so far I'd be ready, even an Arab, God forbid – but at least a mensch! You hear me, at the least a human being! But this?! 'Mummy, I love him!' she says to me. Love?? What does she know from Love? Did you know from Love, at eighteen and a half? Do we know from Love now? Care, responsibility, tsores, that's love, to keep a man through all his mischigayes and complaints and ulcers, that's Love. And between you and me and the shul door, Zeldeh, it's vastly overrated. But Love at that age, and for this crazy lummox? I tell you, he wasn't five minutes in the house, he broke the Passover crockery and the old vase my zaideh got for his own wedding. You hear? From Czernovitcz in 1905, to be smashed to pieces by this hulking klotz's scaly tail! Bump, bump, bump he goes into all the furniture, my living room, I tell you, it looks like after the pogrom of Kishinev. And then the carpet – ruined, as he sits there, grinning and gnashing those terrible teeth of his, snuffling and snorting like he had bronchitis, the world's worst case. And that's how Shloimeh found him when he came from

77

work. Imagine! Me, I was out with a cold compress on the couch, Roiseh, my little Roiseh trying to soothe me there, but who can be soothed from such a shock? When Shloimeh comes in, I thought he would platz on the spot. 'What's this?' he gasps, as if his lungs are torn out. 'We had to keep it secret,' my little tsatskeh says – secret – from her own mother and father! – She says: 'You would never understand. I love him, he's so big and strong. The Justice of the Peace married us, just an hour ago, in Flatbush.' In Flatbush! Married! My entire soul popped out, I thought I'd die right there and then. Shloimeh's face purple, I cry to him: 'Shloimeh, your heart!' And that behaimeh just sits there grinning, his head tearing and ripping the ceiling paintwork, only last week we redecorated, can you believe it! – his tail going swish, swish, right and left knocking everything off the mantelpiece, my sister's photograph, my old menoireh, the shabbes candlesticks, zaideh's yahrzeit candle, everything, smashed down on the floor. A month it'll take to clean it up, and where can you find a good honest cleaning woman in these rotten times, even a Porto Riken? I tell you, Zeldeh, it's beyond terrible, such a great shame on our family, I can't say, I'm so choked up I can't hardly get out one word . . .

– Oy, Feigeh, you think *you* have problems? If I had a blessing on every problem that *I* have, I'd be in Heaven right now. Just you wait till I tell you who my own little son, Yoineh, brought into the house today . . .

★

Plop, into the old blue letter box. Speed the day, speed the day. By the rivers of Babylon. As we sit and weep at Zion.

I set out into the dark of the winter night to resume the Tishman Crusade. Further downtown, but below the belt now, on the IRT Number 1 subway. Declining the transfer to the Numbers 2 or 3 Express, at 72nd. Savouring the low points of the decrepit local stops: 66th Street, 59th, 50th.

Exiting through the Times Square catacombs, past the underground kiosks, hot dog and newsstands, dry cleaning booths and barber shops, stepping over the abandoned shoeshine stop and the day's fallen, skirting the vomit, up on to the seediest corner in the world, 8th Avenue and 42nd. The junkies, the pimps, the kamikaze tourists, the glittering rows of neon tat. The snow has been washed away by the rain, the rain has stopped and the air is unusually brisk, though bitter cold. Persons and objects stand out in a strange cut-out two dimensionality, separate from each other, like the few times I have tried to venture out under the influence of some potent herb, say Colombian Red. These days such joys are fading into nostalgia, but perhaps, with Ronald Reagan elected, come November, this divertissement might return.

Little Nel is waiting at the Expedition Films cutting rooms as I had arranged on the phone. She is a six-foot-tall redhead with a cigarette nailed to her lip, who is Vince Epiglotis' senior editor and in charge of the whole zoo. She feeds the various fauna who work the establishment their assignments – Big Tim, the man who carries the blimped 35mm camera, Giovinezza, the sound editor who whinnies like a horse, Trish, Prish and Knish, the editorial trio, Franz the Gorilla, who claims his hirsute chest sets off female belles as far afield as Pennsylvania, not to speak of Angel, words fail there . . . Little Nel mothers them all, with a little touch of the lash, just to show them they're still alive, supplying them with attention, reassurance and, when in need, the emergency addresses of crank doctors and dubious legal eagles. Now she drags me to the film cans, away from Adelia, the petite receptionist with the nymph voice and the Jayne Mansfield breasts. It is she who croons the late-night message on the firm's telephone answering machine, in a tone of velvet seduction:

'Hi. This is Expedition Films. There's nobody about right now, so I can have you all to maa-self . . . mmmm . . . but if you want to talk to anyone else please leave your name and number after the beep and we'll sure get together sometaam . . . byeee . . .'

Mmmmm. But Little Nel can only introduce me to a pile of cans tall as the Empire State Building and five overflowing out-take bins. 'We were expecting Ben in to do some night work this week,' she tells me. 'He really is a little out of line.'

'He's been kidnapped by Martians,' I assure her. 'They made a scouting run, last autumn, over the Natural History Museum, but now they obviously mean business. It's quite possible he's left messages in fortune cookies, or inside Adelia's brassière.'

'You should be so lucky,' she tells me tartly. It's her bossiness that brings out the schvantz in me. Nothing ever seems to surprise her. If I stripped off my outer skin and revealed my wiggling antennae she would not bat an eye. Just drag on that eternal cigarette, an extreme case of Bogartitis. Another New Yorker. Perhaps she kidnapped Tishman. Perhaps I should drop all else and shadow her heels one night, to whatever den she graces . . .

Left alone, post-midnight, with Tishman's film cans and a Kenco editing table, on the twelfth floor of an Eighth Avenue warren. Who knows what else is going on in the building. Late at night one always hears the oddest noises. Creaking, croaking, the letting off of steam, quite apart from the usual yowls and sirens, roaches smacking their lips in kitchenettes, mice yodelling in the walls. And so on. The editing room is full of the day's legitimate business, *The Initiation of Eve*, an upmarket hard core. I cannot resist the temptation to lace this round the sprockets before embarking on Tishman's Odyssey. The day editor has thoughtfully provided the Kleenex. Woof, woof, woof. Dig them haggard eyes, Onan! Spend that torch of youth while there are still matches! Bear in mind R. E. Masters' cautionary nineteenth-century tales: 'In Paris, a youth of nineteen, a compulsive masturbator, was said to have almost totally wasted away. In his brain there was found an encephaloid tumour the size of a nut, which rattled away in his head . . .'

'Take Five!' Ah, you sly dogs. Enough. Time to renew one's soul . . . I remember days when I trudged about the park with Tishman, hauling his tape recorder and second accessory box, he dragging his camera and tripod from corner to corner, looking for der yooman interest. Joggers jogged, bicyclists bicycled, clowns clowned, baseball players base-balled, dogs pooped, couples smooched on the lawns. Repeat: Strawberry Fields Forever. All this was cliché, but Tishman always sought that elusive twist in the banal. The man with the whizzigig machine who says he can turn pennies into silver dollars. We spent half a day on that one. Not the putz himself, but his audience. Their abject desire to believe. It was glori-ously sunny, Fall, squirrels rustled in mounds of leaves. Why shouldn't anything be possible? Why ain't there no Santa Claus?

'I want to find out who we are,' said Tishman. 'It's not a theological question. I'm not looking for Why Are We On This Earth? I can see we're here, but who are we?'

Go argue with the young at heart. Especially when you're a hundred and five inside, and feel as if you've been preserved on papyrus. I told him I had already dealt with this question, in a story I had written after a lush at a party given by one of Tishman's occasional girl friends who knew a writer who had friends in the business lunged at me with a spraying beer can and told me the real way to get truly started: 'Write something a little more artsy fartsy, and send it to *The Parmesan Review*. That's the rag that makes or breaks you in this town.' And he threw up on my shoe. I thought: this must be the true holy sacrament. The very word of Dionysus. I wrote a piece the next day and sent it off, with a stamped, addressed envelope, like a real goodie-goodie, shouting after it (metaphorically) as the postal clerk tossed it in the basket: Go Man Go! Shove that mammy! Sprinkle this on your lasagna! It was called:

THE YOKE OF THE EGG (*An existential Romance*)

In the beginning. No. Can one speak of beginning? Can I speak, at all, on any course of events, process, any aspect of duration? the march of time? start, finish, middle, can that be truly grasped? Or is there an I to grasp, an I of which to speak, or speech at all, is there speech? utterance, confabulation?

I'll assume then, for no particular reason, first, I, secundo, speech issuing from I, me, articulations, pray silence for our toastmaster, unaccustomed as I am and so forth, good, let's start there. Go to it from that one point, construct the jigsaw piece by piece, until some shape emerges. Or is there shape, form? No interruptions please.

Thank you, ladies and gentlemen. Beginnings, first courses, Numero Uno, inception, first blush – the senses. Sound? An odd silence, no slivers, shivers, trills, arpeggios, plops. Just an indeterminate hum, or is that the brain ticking over, is there a brain, over? No conclusion there. Sight. Colour: yes, the first indisputable fact. Assumption? Fact. Yellow? Or am I deceiving myself again? might it be just as well red, green, raw sienna, prussian blue, vermilion, tan or heliotrope? No, say yellow. First round to the I.

Round. Another fact, roundness? Is that so? Senses, primal as ye may be, red alert, go forth, announce, search every nook and cranny, report on anything corporeal that might just happen to strike you on the way – eyes, to see with, ears, a tympanum, nerves going one way or another, a brain. Assume, a brain. Elementary, my dear Watson. With the brain, deduction, possibly body. Urrah! Senses, cease fire, return to base. Gather round, we'll decide whether to set out on mission Number Two, or quit, two courses of action here. A choice. Hey ho, doors, swinging open . . .

I. Assume, I. Think, therefore, etc. Descartes, René, 1596–1650, French mathematician, pioneer of modern philosophy, unconvinced by scholastic tradition and theological dogma, he . . . and so on. Wherefrom this sudden rush of facts, presumptions, dates? Images, too: a hawk-nosed man, a periwig, starched parchment and a quill, the movement of wrist and hand, scribble, scribble, scribble. Nigrescent liquid from quilltip, shapes coiling, uncoiling on the page, snakes of representation, meaning, illicit thoughts, revolutionary concepts, interdicted propositions, forbidden thesi, merrily merrily merrily merrily, oozing from feather bone, carving out dreams, aspirations, utopias, visions, hopes . . .

Confusion. That's enough. Change tack. Ladies and gentlemen of the jury – the facts. I, definition yet to be clarified, repose, within a present reality, colour yellow, whiter as it recedes, therefore organs of vision and deduction I, within a roundish yellow, an egg shape – there's the word! Another breakthrough, by damn! Sound, a low, continuous hum. Touch? Any organs of palpation, tactile arms, legs? no, none apparent, damn. Still, one shouldn't complain. Sensations: definitely an absence of cold, warmth, a centrally heated residence, let's be thankful for small mercies. Taste? Not yet. Images? René's quill. Where from? Hallucinations? Dementia praecox? The DTs? should I choose to be the quill, or its wielder? the ooze, sans responsibility – a dab of paint, on Picasso's palette, a line, in a triptych by Hieronymus Bosch, a note, played by Menuhin, soaring in Carnegie Hall. Well, maybe. Or something less high-flown: a pebble, rough hewn, worn by waves, on the beach. Humbler, humbler! A cow pat, rotting in a verdant field. Go, man, go. A chimney pot, besieged by wind and hail. An orange, racked upon a kitchen strainer. A pickled cucumber, *alors*, in Marks and Spencers

83

food store! Put that in your pipe and smoke it, maître Descartes! Awash in brine, entombed within the glass receptacle, the shaky housewife lifts you up, rejects you for some low grade, inferior consumable, a can of sardines, perhaps, upon a lower shelf. Some botulinous garbage hyped to Bargain of the Month! No! No! Surcease! *Au secours!* This cannot go unavenged!

Just corral those anxieties, man. Sanity must be asserted. One can assume none of the above, truly. So, begin again:

I. Vision, sound, palpable warmth, shape and distance, yellow, spherical, yes. The receptacle. I, within the receptacle, grope, seek, aspire to clarity. Paragraph. Back to the grindstone. More data. Try those images again:

. . . soft, shimmering . . . miasmic . . . snowflakes, no, dust, filmy dust, a veil of dust, no, fog, a bank of fog . . . beyond it – shapes, phantasms, approaching, receding, clouds, fog, pierced by dabs of light here, there, figures, looming, scudding by, below, I, soaring above them, clearer now, shadows, no, gobs of colour, blues, browns, pin points of faded gold, large gobs of green, trees, grass, leaves, branches, yes, soaring, a loop, I loop, back the way I've come, trees, leaves, the gobs of blue and brown again, rows, faces, I skim faces, grim, sombre, tanned below blue kepis, whiskered, grizzled, old, young, gold buttons gleaming, more or less, on tight blue uniforms, I soar, the uniforms tattered often, I skim, soar, smells reach me now, ripe, ready, horse turds, horses, nostril snorts, swish of tails, men cough, here and there a moan or groan held in, whispers, a buzz, over all, a low buzz over all, a rumble, I skim towards the sound, scudding, following their gimlet gaze, fixed to one point, there, upon the hill, the man who stands, stiffly, hands a-clasp on a small scrap of paper, from which he speaks, reads . . . I soar, hovering by his face – bag-wrinkled, like misshapen dough, lop-sided, yet the beetled brows, sweeping side whiskers, prominent nose, above which those stabbing eyes lift from the note to sweep the standing men, as if they see every individual in the crowd, yes, power here, and strength of will, beneath the stovepipe hat. And as I hover by the mouth, catching the words as they escape the fleshy lips, wafting away in the breeze: '. . . that government of the people, for the people, by the people, shall not perish from the earth . . .'

Smack! a hairy palm comes up, smiting hammerlike upon the spot upon which I had, for a brief span, lighted my six short hairy legs, riffling the skin with my wings. Missed me by a hair! The fuck! I zoom away, emitting a high, angry buzz, soaring, soaring, past the brown, blue gobs towards safer pickings, those steaming cavalry turds . . .

ENOUGH! This coarse obscenity must cease! these gibberings, false memories, foul imaginings, whatever, they are not I, they were not I, could not be I, will not be I, yesterday, tomorrow, nevermore. A pollution of Not I. Deduce – Not I: René Descartes, pebbles, chimney pots, cow turds, gherkins upon grocers' shelves, vermin at Gettysburg . . . Stop! Is that a ballpoint pen I see before me, snib towards my eye? belay there, shipmates, do we hear another sound? Click-clack, click-clack, ratchet like, typewriter keys clattering like an old locomotive, words upon a page. This is a little bit more like it. Colons, commas, scudding ribbon. Is it? Is it? No, it's gone . . .

My mind, my mind, why hast thou forsaken me? Just when we were beginning to get on. I can't go on. So I'll go on. Have we heard this before? Till when, O Lord, this ovoid emtombment? what is it all for?

But wait, surcease, turn all the taps to low, shut off that gibbering thing you call a brain. Listen. Is there not a modulation in the sound? a change in the hum, something that was not there before? Stand by, all auricular faculties! Yes, most definitely a shift of tone – a rumble, then a roar, increasing, louder, louder, rushing on me – a shaking of the world! a cosmic tremor, throbbing, yellow wobbling before my eyes!

I shut them! Bravo: eyelids! There's a body, organs of balance too, to register this undulation, this earthquake of my foundations, shuddering, blurring, converging, a vast jerking, a pull, a tug, a sway, a loss, a fall, a fall, into an unplumped pit, lurch, a split second of recovery, no, the lurch again, relief, no, lurch, the world still wobbles, shit! the warmth is gone! suddenly, as if whipped out, transformed into a numbing cold, ye gods, wait until I get my hands on . . . hands, oh, hands . . . But now there are other sounds, happenings, manifestations, call them what you will, behind the lurching tremors, a hooting, like a foghorn in the brain, loud crunching sounds, a thud, as if Atlas has dropped his globe, and some sort of human utterance, magnified a thousandfold, as if in some vast echo chamber:

Oooohhoohhaaaeeeyyaaajuuunooohissssooohhhiiiinnnn . . .

Then a slightly different tone, less booming, but still resonant:

Eeeellliiiiiioowwwowwwooooeeeaaaaeeeeiiiii . . .

Blare, blare, a strident scrape, another lurch, and another new sound, a hellish crackling, echoing as a thousand fires lit beneath me, the warmth returning, oh God, no, a scalding heat, again a lurch, a hideous, apocalyptic thud, a cracking, splitting of the world, a blinding searing furnace, ah oh ah no, the world's come apart, I fall into the pit, down, down, down into the eternal flames in which all's dissolved in saturnalian chaos, all memories, all images, all I's devoured, extirpated, blotted out, abolished, cancelled, written off – but just at that last moment, that timeless second at the brink, ere I'm cast into that great nothingness, a voice, blaring out, hollow and bold, an unmistakable human mortal tone, the final mocking verbal blow before I'm hurled into the great abyss, strident and sharp, it rings out clear:

'Oh, Henry, there's a speck in this one. Would you rather have some Weetabix instead?'

★

Dear Mr D. H.,

So, you have a brand new *Thesaurus*. You've read a bit Sam Beckett too. This is good. But the story isn't. You want some advice? Write from the pupik. Don't say I didn't tell you.

Al J— (Editorial Director, *The Parmesan Review*).

And as you're interested, our subscription rates are only . . .

I spit in their Bolognese. I write from my pupik. They don't like my pupik? I'm not sure I like it either. As if somebody should want to read my autobiography. Arrow pointing: English Jew. My schoolteachers gave me a hard time. I wasn't beaten but there was no need. I was defeated from the start. Later on I poured ink in their shoes. This was my first artistic/political statement. I applied to join the Communist Party when I was ten. They sent me a brochure about something called the Woodcutting Folk, a socialist camping project in the wild. Lots of fresh air and cold showers and healthy exercise. I wrote back, comrades, you are having me on. I want dank air, cigarette smoke in cellars, spiked marching boots to tear down Buckingham Palace. I never forgot this first disappointment with Social-Capitalist Revisionism. Hey, are you believing any of this? Boy, are human beings gullible.

A Broadway mental case, on the editing table screen, is telling Ben Tishman his wife is a creature from outer space. This is not a new theme by any means, and bears an uncanny similarity to my own hillbilly tale-cum-script. He claims she was sent down by the Grand Council of Venus to diddle him out of his social security. She left him to live with a telephone engineer, and now both of them were sending secret messages to home base, on Venus, through his skull. The man drools and dribbles, he is in bad shape, but only Ben Tishman will listen to him. Personally, I disagree with this thesis on women, though I would not go so far as Vince Epiglotis. My problem has always been a romantic view of women as the repository of worldly wisdom and compassion, the old earth-mother shtik syndrome. But whenever I had close dealings with the other sex, the truth turned out to be quite different. Women were just as fucked up as I was. My episteme could not deal with this let down. One has only to think of Martha, the raving Trotskyite of Kentish Town, whose permanent revolution extended to the burning of my Erle Stanley Gardner collection. It was this that traumatized me completely from the private-eye-cum-legal milieu. She wanted us both to take menial jobs in a factory or sweatshop, so that we should feel the oppression of the working class in the daily aching of our bones. Oh yeah?

There is a sound of someone in the corridor turning a key in the lock of the company's door. I turn off the editing table and extinguish the light. Something in the air makes me shaky. I peek round the edge of my door. It is Vince Epiglotis, looking unusually furtive. He goes into his office and emerges with a hammer and a large spanner, padding softly back into the corridor. I follow. He disappears into the men's room, a renowned danger spot where one might, upon squatting quietly, minding one's own business, be approached by the Puerto Rican messenger boy, Angel, leaning over the half-locked booth door, with offers of a less than appealing nature.

I wait outside. It seems bizarre, to say the least, of Vince Epiglotis to turn up at two in the morning in order to carry out a little repair work on the bog. Still, one has learned not to question strange acts in the city. Sleep does not come easy.

Bang! Bang! Bang! Bang! Vince Epiglotis is hammering on the main pipe. It is a strange rhythm, resolving itself into what sounds suspiciously like the morse code. I never learned it, but one does get the general drift. Long, heavy strokes alternating with quick blows, echoing up the pipes, around the walls and ceiling. Then he ceases. Unmistakably, from somewhere behind or above the walls, there comes the dull hammering of an answer. It stops. Vince hammers again, ceases. The dialogue of the pipes, clanging on. Overtaken by a feeling of numb panic, I rush back into the cutting room, remove my viewing reel, replace the cans in their piles, and exit the building, gliding down alone, shaking baking, in the lift.

★

Time lapse: there is a curious further development. Two cans of Tishman's opus are missing. Having decided to dice with insanity again two days after my inadvertent glimpse of Vince Epiglotis' night life, I conducted an all-night random search through the film cans, which Tishman had stockpiled in his own order. He could not handle such a mass of disparate material without some form of logging control. In fact there were copious notebooks in the apartment, which I found on top of the kitchen cabinet, behind some cans of baked beans. It took some time to figure out the system. Tishman had his own view of what constituted clarity. Roll 23 was in Can 7, Roll 45 in Can 2, Roll 12 in Can 34, and so on and so forth. There was a rudimentary rough cut, consisting of 38 cans of 30 minutes' film each, with chapter headings such as: Night Pickets, Man With Pimple, The Sailor's Tale, Bag Man Blues, Cops and Schnorrers, The Vegetable Man, Feed The Birds, I Give Great French, Canarsie or Bust and Out of The Rising Steam. But the missing cans, 12 and 13, appeared to pertain to a single item, identified after exhaustive cross checking, featuring Rolls 25 through 27, and entitled The Mad Bomber.

Now we were really getting somewhere. The vestiges of a plot, Goddammit! Frank Zagdanovitch, the fowl detective, might well have raised a loud squawk, riffling his feathers and beating his beak against the wall. I summoned Ellie to a conference at Tom's Restaurant on 110th Street, another cheerful abode of the great New York breakfast, the jolly stodger, bathos banter, two eggs over easy, toast, no jelly, orange juice and fries.

'The Mad Bomber,' she said. 'Yes, Ben talked about him. But he never showed me any footage. He was an old man who'd served life for something he'd done back in the late Forties. I know, he had a grudge against the telephone company, and put bombs in their installations – offices, vans, telephone poles. I think two people were actually killed. He was a celebrity for a short while, when he came out, four or five years ago. I don't remember his name.'

'Could he have been part of a group?' I asked, sniffing conspiracy. 'The Semaphorological Liberation Front, Poste Restante Anonymous, Telecommunications Terror, the Popular Front of Outraged Subscribers? For Whom Ma Bell Tolls?'

'I don't know. Ben just said he was weird. But then so was most everybody Ben talked to. I remember he said they got along fine.'

'Sweet Nature of Arsonist. We Got Along Like a House On Fire. But somebody removed those cans, Ellie. It's all we have to go on so far.'

A dead issue. Headlines of thirty-two years back. The year of my birth, in fact, no kidding, 1947. My mother heaved, ho'd at Hammersmith Hospital. The Mad Bomber brought down telephone lines. And, today, I am abroad and destitute, and Vince Epiglotis talks to people in morse code over toilet pipes.

'Where does he live? Who would know?'

'Maybe at the cutting room.'

We're down to Vince Epiglotis again. Or Little Nel, who knows everything, or the little faigeleh Angel. 'Angel, do you know about the Mad Bomber?' 'Hey man, no way, but if you looking for a beeg bang . . .'

Ellie looks at me mournfully across the scuffed plastic table, wreathed in coffee fumes and potato grease. Maybe, after all, Tishman just met a blonde with big tits at Penn Station and went off to Tenafly, New Jersey. Maybe he took the Mad Bomber cans with him, to jazz up the hip moves. Ellie, in distress, is quite beautiful. I am in danger of human emotions.

'Tom,' I said, 'the Lon Chaney of modern American journalism. He probably knows the Mad Bomber's inside leg size. When is he due back in your flat?'

'You never know when Tom's going to turn up. We haven't seen him for three days. He's on to a scam involving poodle parlours. Dog pelts are being sold as muffs.'

The fuck. It is impossible to progress logically in this town. I return to 79th Street. The 'penthouse' flat, its peeling old plaster. Tishman's ashtray dregs. Files of his and his begging letters. Tishman's play: 'I conceive of this project as a grand attempt to portray the City in all its facets, to leave, as it were, no stone unturned . . .' And no turn unstoned. My own mounds of rejection slips, piss offs, mimeographed tips for aspirant hacks from Jake Akimbo's Magazine:

Why do we reject a story? There are a few general guidelines. We've mentioned Lecturing, Synopses and Vignettes. If your science or your logic or your characters aren't well done, then they Do Not Convince. A story that isn't about anything, that is Pointless, won't work either. While tragedy can be a powerful story basis, a tale that ends in Futility is not; put it aside until you are in a better mood. Sex, as a necessary part of life, is a necessary part of fiction. But sex-for-arousal and sex-&-sadism – no. (We're not all that interested in sexless sadism either . . .) When the reader (or editor) can't understand what's going on, not enough description to feel the setting, characters operating on unclear, inconsistent or unbelievable motives and the like, the story will be Murky or Opaque. Your story must Convince. You're allowed an outrageous assumption, but not violations of common sense. It's not easy to be entertaining and

convincing, and make sense, to have a point to it all –
but if you do, we'll send money!

Jake Akimbo, Proprietor

Convincing he wants? Believable motives? Logic? Sex without
Futility?? The rain has begun again outside, lashing the grimy
french windows, washing the terrace and obscuring the towers
marching solidly downtown. Vince Epiglotis, Little Nel, the
Mad Bomber and Tishman, even Ellie, will have to wait a
little. I can take reality, but should it defy Jake Akimbo's
demands to that extent? I am becoming bogged down with
too much social realism. This will not do at all. I must return
to the easier climes of Outer Space. The cut and thrust of alien
dolours. Vegetables from other galaxies. Quatermass and the
Pip. Stand still, Earth, sprachen Mister Fotheringay. The Hack
Who Could Work Miracles. Typewriter out, paper racked
through the roller. Fingers ready for action. Tippex poised.
A new ribbon, so one can actually see the consequences! Break
loose, Danny boy! Mush! Let's go!

SPACEPORT '99!

IN PANAFISSION AND SMELLOFEELOSCOPE

Starring:

SHARK BAGLE as HACKITT
GERTA GRABBO as PRINCESS BOPI
LAWRENCE PARVE as KOSHER
ELIZABETH FAILYOR as DEE DEE

and co-starring:
Mumblon Drabno as Pratt; Brute Miscaster as Zopi;
Roger Boor as Grun; Robert Dinero as Cash;
Bob Dope as Bing Frisbee;
John Drain as Aargh; Telisuk Fallus as Captain Gurk;
William Shitner as Captain Berk
and Groucho Marx as President Fard

A Sam Peckinapuss Production

1

The stewardess' voice came purring softly over the loud-speakers: 'Ladies, gentlemen and intermediates, you have been experiencing our in flight feelie *If It's Tuesday This Must Be Alpha Centauri*, with Dean Fartin and Geriatric Lewis. We

93

are now entering Solar orbit. Please secure your foamofoam coverings for imminent expansion. May we remind our Fnirgian passengers that Skwurltian Oscosis is not permitted during distension procedures. We hope you have enjoyed your trip with Pangalactic Thruways and will come back to Bounce with us again.'

Space Engineer Ssringh X. Zopi, known to his Terran friends as Matt due to his triple coat of thick fur, folded his copy of the *Jewish Martian Chronicle* and lay back in his couch, extracting an antenna to note the chronopod time. 09:55 12 12 2999 Solar Standard. The ship was slightly behind schedule. His incisors reddened in annoyance. Trust the Terrans to be sloppy, though the pilot of the ship was Princess Bopi, a fellow Aurigan. What was the galaxy coming to? Order, discipline, punctuality, all going by the board. In the old days a minopod might have been lopped off for every sec's delay. He sighed, slipping deeper into the enveloping foam cocoon.

Flight Manager Thnida Bopi, meanwhile, hummed the latest melody topping the Terran charts. It was a revival, a tango rescued from undeserved oblivion at the hands of the Bebop Police. She felt light craniumed and happy, imagining moments soon to come in the arms of her Terran lover, Bonzo Hackitt. The thought of him squirming in her, entering every one of her three hundred orifices, in turn, caused her to percolate with joy. But she had to return her attention to the controls. By her side, the two Flight Assistants, Gurk and Berk, floated in their ammonia baths. No joy for them on Terran shore leave. They would spend their liberty as always, locked in their hotel room, exchanging lewd limericks and getting sloshed on diluted nitrogen.

The Chief Stewardess was Dee Dee Grant, an ex-hooker from Macon, Georgia. She was returning incognito from a lucrative year on Omega, the pleasure planet, where perverts from all over the galactic lens came to indulge in inter-species sex. Her earnings for the year had been converted into a minute supply of Thrummadin, the universe's most potent drug, distilled from the Grompian flibberjib's spare vagina. One drop could turn a whole city mad with sex lust, guaranteeing five hundred orgasms per hour. Her entire stash was pasted to the inside of her golden nipple rings. She was extremely tense, anticipating the tough and thorough Terran Customs Check and Brain Scan. The penalty for dealing in Thrummadin was id-castration, a fate too grisly to contemplate.

The passengers were in various stages of alertness, apathy or stupor as the final lap of the journey approached. Travelling through hyperspace took different species many different ways. The craft was an Atomo-Jumbo, quaintly named after an antique vehicle and a defunct mode of propulsion. Like its medieval predecessor it seated over 300, 346 to be precise, though seated was hardly the right word. Many passengers had spent the journey reclining in hammocks, floating in glass tanks or openly in the lounge, swinging back and forth on threads and creepers provided along the walls. They were the usual assortment of trans-galactic travellers: a businessman, Bing Frisbee, returning from a Flub-dyer convention on Callisto. An emperor of a minor cluster in Orion exiled after a palace coup. A herbiform tourist from Jlunn, resembling a giant cabbage, who had spent the entire trip entreating the cabin staff to keep him away from the vegetarian passengers. A group of Christian pilgrims from Barsoom, tentacles waving, en route for the New Salt Lake Religiopolis. A little aloof from these, a Jewish convert from Tralfamadore, vainly attempting to adjust his prayer shawl and phylacteries over his jelly form. And so on. The ship catered for almost every taste, though Skwurlt was definitely discouraged. The kitchen observed the dietary taboos of 666 species. The bar stocked intoxicants from thirty systems. Two vug vugs had in fact spent the whole journey attached to it by their suckers, imbibing shasha-juice through straws and telepathically exchanging texts from newly rediscovered Philip K. Dick novels.

Such was Flight 117 from Cignus V to Terra. All in the day's work for Pangalactic Thruways and the New Washdelphia Spaceport down below.

The routine spiel continued on the loudspeakers:

'. . . as you aware the craft we travel in operates by the Jeeb–Wheegian Theorem. It was Professors Wheeg and Jeeb who established the maximum size of any object that could traverse and survive hyperspace as 200 by 250 microns, only slightly larger than one grain of salt. It was then left to Professor D'Pouf of Beta IV to develop the miniaturisation and expansion process used today in all galactic craft. On leaving Cignus V we underwent miniaturisation which has enabled us to cross hyperspace. Having now arrived within orbital distance of Terra we must now undergo expansion, or distension, back to our natural size and weight. Secure in your foamofoam, rest assured you will experience nothing but a mild jerk and momentary loss of consciousness . . .'

The usual lullaby, Zopi thought, to avert panic when first-time passengers experienced that inside-out feeling that took place during distension. Even he, a hardened traveller, had never become used to that horrid moment. He folded his antennae in their sacs and waited for the gut-twisting wrench.

It did not come.

Bartholomew (Bonzo) Hackitt could not believe his eyes when his deputy, Ms Thinga Mabob, handed him the printout. 'Get me Grun,' he commanded.

Grun was the monitor on duty at the New Washdelphia Spaceport's Incoming Console. He was a young caucasian bearing the large gold nose ring that was currently in fashion. 'Yes,' he confirmed over the viso, 'we have a problem, sir. Flight 117 has failed to expand on schedule.'

'Initiate malfunction procedure,' barked Hackitt. 'Throw

out maximal grid.' Ships in contraction were incommunicado apart from a placement blip until routine distension.

'We have the blip,' said Grun, 'but scanners report no distension. Even worse, there is a clear drift developing towards Terran gravity range.'

'Fnuth!' Hackitt swore. If the craft entered gravity range nothing might stop it drifting to the Terran surface in its present, miniaturized state. And expansion on land had not been attempted since the Great Jubilee Catastrophe of 2931. 'Pnokation!' he cussed again, 'Let's hope they have enough sense to switch back into Wheegian Drive and jump back into hyperspace.'

'They can't,' Grun reminded him. 'Crew and pilot will be in transicoma. Automatic landing synapses will over-ride.'

Hackitt's chin jutted firmly. He thought of Princess Bopi, trapped in earth-fall, presently smaller than a nit. The blissful hours he'd been anticipating, climbing in her thulma, the numerous sucking orifices and tactilia caressing his skin, the telepathic croon of union. He knew many would condemn his love as degenerate, but what was 'natural' in a galaxy with fifteen thousand intelligent life forms? Society sucks, he brooded, ruminating on the care he had to take to conceal his romance from the Decency Guild. They still had power where it counted, and Hackitt prized his job as Spaceport Co-ordinator, witnessing the hustle and bustle of galactic diversity, the multiform challenges of providing for races as far apart as say, the Frulvian Squid and the Utholian harmonoform, which was pure music encased for ambulatory purposes in a unicellular bubble . . .

The situation called for calm, proficiency and grit. Hackitt had all three. Putting his personal involvement aside, he leaned forward and flicked the Red Alert switch.

Aboard Flight 117, somnolence reigned. Captains Gurk and Berk, last to slip into transicoma, surreptitiously distilled with

their pseudopodia the last of the illegal jujo-sap they had
smuggled into their ammonia baths. Dee Dee Grant was
applying Slirgian Self-Discipline to her soon to be scanned
brain cells. Space Engineer 'Matt' Zopi, still waiting for disten-
sion-jerk, pondered again the maddening unpunctuality of
human-controlled affairs. Back home the whole lot would be
swiftly thrigged, he thought.

Only slightly larger that an average grain of salt, the ship
plunged down towards the Earth.

2

Bernardo Pratt was a small fish in a large ocean full of sharks.
He was a minor cut-throat, pimp and pusher of illicit feelies
in the most downtrodden, decayed quarter of Amazonia, the
megalopolis of fifty million that had once been the capital of
the Empire of Abrasil. Built in the Empire's heyday, in the
twenty-second century, as its showpiece and crown, it was
now, seven centuries later, the sort of urban monstrosity
legendary from the twentieth and twenty-first centuries. The
jungle having returned to the Upper Amazon after the decline
of the Empire, Amazonia was now a nation in itself, teeming,
vibrant and vile, a symbol of corruption for a mostly rural
world whose surplus population had long since spread to the
stars.

Pratt slouched down Castrato Avenue (no tree grew now
in that ferro-plastic jungle), glancing furtively this way and
that for any trace of Thirgo Aargh's assassins. He had to dance
sideways to avoid the spluttering sparks showering from the
ancient monorail thundering by above. The city was a mould-
ering museum of old modes of transport and housing. Abandoned hi-dwellos jutted on every side. The twisted ruins of
broken movewalks made any surface travel except walking
nigh impossible.

Feeling the need to get away from the open, Pratt ducked into the nearest public store – 'Pete Pepperoni's Pasticheria' – finding it satisfyingly full of its normal complement of down and outs, Inglish guest-trabajadores with their mean and evil looks, tourists in fashionable and safe rags slumming in Terra's last great urban nightmare. There were even two aliens, blue blobs encased in sheet armour to protect them from the xenophobia of the natives.

Pratt sat down at a corner table. A roboserve clanked up on squeaky treads to take his order. 'Spaghetti Bolognese,' he said, 'and custard tart to follow. And put some castrol on your own tracks, señor, I am allergic to such noises – fingernails on alligator wallets, you know what I mean. OK?' The waiter trundled grumpily away, calling out 'Una Spaga-boga! coostar pood!' towards the foul-smelling kitchen.

Pratt brooded, watching the door. It may have been an error to steal the cap of Thrummadin from Aargh's own courier, but who was Aargh to force a monopoly? He fingered the stunner in his pocket. Was not Bernardo Pratt entitled to a piece of the action, a place in that meagre greyness that stood in for the sun in Amazonia? His hand moved to the gold ring in his left ear which concealed the potent drug . . .

In the kitchen the roboserve waiter was in mid-slanging match with the rusty old mechano-cook. 'Whatsa witha Numero Quatro? Is Scaloppini alla Uranus, notta Pizza Tralfamadore!' 'Sforzato!' the cook waved his ladelpods, spraying the kitchen with cannelloni. 'You thinka my memory banks apazzo? Ecco, Numero Quatro – Risotto Saturnale . . .' 'Cretino! figli di merda! junka heap reject!' squawked the roboserve, grabbing the cook's pods with his tweezers.

Small wonder, then, that neither of them noticed a miniaturized spaceship, not much larger than a grain of salt, coasting in through the open service hatch and landing in one of the steaming pots.

Emergency sirens sounded in the ship as she entered Terran atmosphere in her undistended form. Gurk and Berk hiccuped into awareness. Princess Bopi broke out of transicoma with a start. The mainframe computer was highly agitated, squawking: 'MAN OVERBOARD! HOMME A LA MER! TENDER A ENGEBEN! WOMEN AND CHILDREN FIRST! PADDLE LIKE HELL FOR THE SHORE!'

The ship rattled about like a pea in a falling tin can. Passengers were spilled from their foamofoams and hurled this way and that. Ssringh Zopi had to extract all his grippers to keep some sort of even keel. Bing Frisbee became entangled with the Jewish Tralfamadore convert, who was slewing off epidermis on the floor, reciting the prayer of imminent death: 'Shma Yisrael, Adonai Eloheinu Adonai Ehad . . .' The two vug vugs underwent sexual congress under the stress. A Fnirgian attempted to Skwurlt, but was sat on and anaesthetized by two Ulrfilian symbiotes.

Ssringh thought: the morons have killed us! Disorder, indiscipline, laxity, this is where it all leads, to disaster, breakdown and death! We will crash in Terra's oceans and drown. The thought of water actually touching his flesh made him shudder. The ultimate blasphemy, reminiscent as it was of the actual reception of sexual fluid. Gogor preserve us! He curled up and began to pray . . .

Down, down the spacecraft rushed, Princess Bopi wrestling with thirty wheels and joysticks as Gurk and Berk, out of control, skidded and crashed into each other like dodgems, the flight assistants themselves vague shapes in ammonia bubbles thrown to and fro in their tanks. Shrieks, hoots, honks, bleats and yodels issued from the passenger lounge. A harmonoform burst into an old Pink Floyd number, 'Wish You Were Here'. The Barsoomian Christians clicked their worry beads in furious syncopation. It was all rather like the last trump rendered in a combination of Reggae and Stockhausen.

Frantically Bopi manipulated handles and steering pivots

and auxiliary thrusters, but the ship was not under control. Vast shapes danced outside the pilot's capsule windows, plastic turrets, steel buttresses and spires, flashing gargantually by as the ship's buffers hurled it between them, avoiding collision, manoeuvring her emergency course and movement and swerving her, down Lower Amazonia, through the open hatch of Pete Pepperoni's Pasticheria, to lurch to a confused and entrapped stop just above the open cooking pots. Then, assuming, as dumb machines are wont to, that enclosure meant arrival at an accredited port, the entire drive clicked off, causing the ship to drop, a negligible grain in the fetid air, straight down into the nearest froth of bubbles.

★

OK, OK, OK. This is a true mug's game. I clatter downtown from 79th Street in the IRT cattletruck, trying to reconnect the various parts of my brain with each other without experiencing rejection symptons. A sort of convention in the frontal lobes, an old boys' reunion of cerebral delinquents who had not met for ten years. What am I doing with my life, et cetera. Answers in ten words or less. Why am I pushing all this garbage in the direction of Jake Akimbo and his ilk? Ought I not to be resurrecting those painful pages of angst-ridden questing for the meaning of life scribbled during cold London nights of permanent non-revolution with 'Bronstein' Martha and the Cause . . . Painful experiments with content and form. Ultra-bourgeois navel-gazing. Torn pieces of paper in long lost wastepaper baskets. Fin-de-sickle garbage loads. The poets one used to see under the bridge from Charing Cross to Waterloo, at the Embankment, selling single sheets for 5p. 'Are you interested in poetry, sir?' The free damp of total destitution. Not that many laughs there.

Coughs, sneezes, farts, retching erupt up and down the subway cars. People who have sat here all the way from Lenox Terminal or, God help us, 241st Street, looking like condemned travellers along the lower routes of Hell. We Have Seen Everything and Nothing. And only another thirty stops to Flatbush. I suppose what attracts me to this is precisely – it is a macrocosm of my own head. The subway map as the channels of my own nervous system. The bile ducts of the consumer society. Don't flush! Don't flush!

And my situation is rapidly becoming more absurd by the minute. I have lost the only true friend I have in the city. I think I am falling in love with his girl friend, the ballet dancer. To make things really peachy, I am in transit to seek out the Mad Bomber, an old maniac who has, apparently, not given up his lifelong feud with the most powerful Corporation on Earth, the American Telephone and Telegraph Company.

Whither, wither, Danny boy. I remember the first time I met Tishman. It was, oddly enough, on the airport bus coming in from J.F. Kennedy. I had just crossed the ocean for the first time, from Albion, the Perfidious, and he, rather than returning from Outer Mongolia, had just been seeing off a girl friend who had gone to join the Peace Corps in Ethiopia, then still an American fief. She had decided, she said, that New York was too savage. She set off in search of civilization, which Tishman spurned, returning to his own native hut-ments. We found ourselves in adjoining seats and chatted. I took his phone number, as one does in the wild. I had the address of an acquaintance who turned out, for my sins, to have regressed from Revisionist to an old-fashioned fellow traveller of the American Communist Party. You don't believe it till you see it. He took me to an old battered cinema on Bleecker Street, which was running a retrospective of agit-prop documentaries by a veteran Soviet cineaste. Shots or portraits of J. Stalin appeared frequently on screen, to be greeted every time by the audience with an immense burst of applause. I felt as if I had dropped in from Uranus and had taken the wrong galactic turn. Then the Trotskyites were denounced for betraying Spain. The audience bayed with approval and began eating the seats. I escaped, and soon after gave my host the slip. This was the first of my many SOS calls to Tishman, saying: 'Help! The Reds are on my tail.'

At that time Tishman was living in Avenue A, a part of town which deserves an epic of its own, in the apartment of one of the film editors from Expedition Films. There was a fair deal of room for us and the roaches, who saw no cranny as taboo. They especially liked one's underpants, slung over a chair. The lowest sleaze was their stock in trade. They, too, deserve an opus of their own, a musical. But Realism must still wait its turn . . .

I exit into the Times Square labyrinth, uncoiling my reel of mental thread. The smell of freezing, congealing piss and the dank cold are all pervading, iron gratings swing on lost platforms. The number of tokens one has lost here mounting to one's chosen line, only to find oneself back out in the main concourse. Or descending into the bowels, to a disconnected service. The slosh of vomit on the floors. The furthest west one can penetrate on the Metropolitan Transport is the AA or CC down 8th Avenue. The portal too to the Port Authority Terminal, the magic Greyhounds to the outer worlds . . . Feeling not much larger than a grain of salt myself, I stagger up the furthest outpost of the system, the peeling exit of 44th Street. Down then, beyond 9th Avenue, towards the No Man's Land of 10th, 11th, even 12th. The true arsehole of the city, by the Hudson, along the old decayed docks. Rumour has it this entire area is due for development, like Greenwich Village and SoHo, so that middle-class persons and 'artists' might live in it with a life expectancy of more than twelve hours. But, as yet, there is no sign of this. It is the Mad Bomber's perfect venue. Decaying tenements, residential and warehouses, strange clubs and cafés at the end of the line. One of these, picturesquely dingy with an on-off sign saying Paula's Café, is exactly opposite the corner tenement in which, according to Ellie's flatmate Tom, the bloodhound, is chez

Bomber, ground floor, Flat Two. Tom just pulled it like a rabbit out of his memory, having turned up at 112th Street at two in the morning, with two black eyes, clutching the torn skinned pelt of a once beloved Bazenjee. 'The Mad Bomber? Sure, everyone knows the old man. His name is Rudolph Fihser. He lives at . . .'

Zonksville. Castrato Avenue. And not even the hidden balm of Thrummadin. I look at my watch. Twenty-two thirty. What would Frank Zagdanovitch have done? Marched in and pecked the bastard half to death. Vomit up Ben Tishman, varmint! An odd image enters into my head, of the crocodile in Disney's *Peter Pan*, following Captain Hook with an alarm clock ticking in his insides. Tick tock. What new outrages is red-nosed Rudolph planning in that thieves' kitchen?

What I really need is a bagful of oats, Zagdanovitch says, twitching a feather. Let us hie to this greasy spoon establishment which has manifested at our wing tip. Eh, Danny boy? I enter Pete Pepperoni's Pasticheria, alias Paula's Café, through squeaking double doors, taking my choice of the empty tables by the plate glass window, with a clear view of the entrance to the tenement dingily lit across the street. I order a coffee from a waitress who might have been Paula, a frowsy, rather vacant presence, taking out my usual scattered sheaf of papers and my pencils and pens. The ambience seems congenial. What the hell. The Mad Bomber ain't goin' nowhere, far's we know . . . With luck, only time would be killed –

*

. . . After the first flush of panic, some equilibrium was restored in the passenger lounge. A Hvulvian doctor was already at work telekinetically healing fractures, leaks and burst sacs, simultaneously performing primal scream therapy with his alter ego on those the shipwreck had traumatized. The harmonoform had now become Bach's Prelude in D Minor, enveloping all with soothing chords. The vug vugs had separ-

104

ated, and the fruit of their union was bouncing all over the lounge, blurting out entire sections of *Ubik*, a Philip K. Dick novel long thought forgotten. The only exception to the calm aftershock was Ssringh Zopi, who burst into the flight cockpit to give his compatriot, Princess Bopi, a piece of his mind, only to be brought up short by the stench of ammonia emanating from two evaporating lumps of flesh on the floor.

'The tanks collided and burst,' said Bopi. 'Gurk and Berk are dead. Help me vent the gas outside.'

'What on earth happened? Where are we?' Zopi asked, his indignation balloon sagging.

'Amazonia, Abrasil,' said Bopi. 'We have failed to expand. I have the computer working on an analysis of our environment.'

The said machine emitted a long series of beeps and trills. Paper unrolled all over the console. Bopi perused the printout and turned to her fellow Aurigan with that faint twitching of minopods that denotes a wry smile.

'We have an analysis of the composition of our environment,' she said.

'Well, what is it?'

'Spaghetti Bolognese.'

The ship suddenly lurched terribly, again. Passengers fell free in the lounge. The Jlunnian herbiform fell into the mouth of a Foubian Vegivore who had been eyeing him throughout the journey. The Foubian sped off on suckers to consume his lot in the toilet. No one noticed in the confusion.

Stem over stern the ship tumbled and turned, twisted and dropped on its way.

Bernardo Pratt savoured the mouthful of spaghetti as it slid down his gullet. He felt lucky to have received what he ordered, he thought, as the roboserves argued on in the kitchen. The whole principle of robot-humanization was a double-edged sword. Other customers, who had ordered risotto, were angrily eyeing the spam fritters or saveloys that had been plonked before them. He ate rapidly, one eye on the doorway, alert for Thirgo Aargh's assassins.

'Fnuth and Fnard!' Hackitt swore at his post at the Spaceport Emergency Bubble. 'What sort of idiots are on the scan here? While we've been debating whether touchdown occurred in the lasagne or the cannelloni, some bastard has gone and swallowed the spacecraft! Who the gnuki is this person? Where's my hot line to the Amazonian lawforcemen? Don't they know that expansion in a closed environment will inevitably set off a nuke explosion? Where are my Amerindian tweezers?' He slumped in his chair, burying his head in his hands. His deputy, Grun, bent towards him, murmuring soothing words in his ear. The nuzzling of Grun's nose ring was calming, but no substitute for Princess Bopi's three hundred odd orifices. A tear trickled down Bonzo Hackitt's superficially tough face.

Pratt saw the uniformed men appear at the doorway in time for decisive action. His stunner arced round. One, two, three, four, the assailants fell. But others rushed in, with multibeamers. A yell came from outside: 'Set to stun! Don't kill him!' Not likely, Thirgo Aargh, he thought grimly, you won't get me alive to shrink in your dungeons. He dropped three more, but others entered, firing. He was saved by the crowd in the restaurant. The bums, the Inglish guest-trabajadores and the slumming tourists fell in the crossfire, blocking the space in a welter of threshing limbs and smashed tables. The robo-waiter speeding out from the kitchen, spraying pasta and sauce from its armtrays, croaking: 'Stronzos! Assassini! I break-a your bons! Vai, vai funculu, cazzi . . .' But he was mown down by a laser burst from one of the incoming lawforcemen and expired in a jumble of screwbolts and busted relays.

There are too many of the bastards, Pratt thought. His hand went up to the ring on his left ear. Lucky I had this installed, he reflected. A flick of his finger released a spring which shot a very minute dose of the superdrug Thrummadin into the rancid café air. And instantly, before waiting for any effect, he was off, sprinting like hell for the door. It hit him before he reached it, but his momentum was enough to carry him out to the street. Lawforcemen moved to intercept him, but then the drug hit them too.

All around him, men tore off their clothes, grabbing each other with reckless abandon. Moans and bellows of frustrated passion rent the air. Within three seconds everyone within three hundred yards radius was copulating with everyone else, in twos, threes, fours and larger groups if at all possible. A dog that was peacefully passing was seized and abused with great savagery. Squeals and shrieks of pain and delight echoed from within the restaurant. Pratt tore himself free by a super-human effort from the grasp of two burly lawforcers and streaked down the road, his heart pounding, his clothes in shreds, till he stopped by a monorail underpass, threw himself to the ground and jacked off until his yearnings subsided.

'All right,' said Hackitt, 'let's keep calm and review the situation. We now have a printout on the man in whose stomach Flight 117 now reposes. His name is Bernardo Pratt. He is a small-time hoodlum in Amazonia's main slum. Fedinfo reports he is currently being sought by one of the major capos of the area, the extremely seedy though powerful Thirgo Aargh. Our man is on the run from said Aargh, bearing a stolen supply of Thrummadin. He cannot therefore be safely approached by any sexually aware person at this stage. We are tracking Mr Pratt by our ship's placement bleeper. The ship is safe as long as he remains out of reach of Aargh's assassins, but the local lawforcemen are unreliable. One option is to buy off this Aargh before he blasts our 350 passengers to kingdom come. Another is, concurrently, to send in an android unit, immune to the drug. But, ladies and gentlemen, there is a third, radical option, which we cannot now avoid. May I present Professor Sorn Plattvogel, the world's greatest expert on Wheegian Drive Theory . . .'

A small, dapper man, aged about sixty, with a craggy face and an aftershock of white hair, stood up briefly at Hackitt's side, said 'Plisst to meet *meine Herren*,' and sat down abruptly again.

'Professor Plattvogel,' said Hackitt, 'has a proposal which may help us out of our dilemma. He is convinced it is possible to modify the ship's drive on the spot, so as to carry out a gradual, rather than instantaneous expansion to life size, thus avoiding the danger of nuke explosion and causing damage only to the craft's immediate environment, i.e., Mr Bernardo Pratt, regrettably.'

'He vill go shplatt,' said Plattvogel.

'Professor Plattvogel,' Hackitt continued, 'has volunteered himself for his exceedingly hazardous mission. He has offered to be miniaturized here in our laboratories, together with a volunteer assistant and the necessary equipment. They will be conveyed to the scene by one of our scanners, and shot into Mr Pratt's bloodstream by means of a robodartgun. A homing device will lead him to the swallowed spacecraft. Once inside he will proceed to work on the drive. The estimate is two hours and fifteen minutes for that phase. We will in the meantime be proceeding with the other two options concurrently. Is everything clear? Right, let's get to work. We have customers in trouble out there!'

★

'You writin' a thesis?' the vacant presence, Paula, trailing blondish wisps, glided up as if on rubber treads and refilled my coffee cup. I looked across the table, where, in the haze, Frank Zagdanovitch waved a small Panatella in his claw. He flicked a roach from his beak, which landed in a tab of jelly, subsiding in mute ecstasy.

'I had a regular who used to sit right where you are and write for hours,' the waitress said. 'He was a stoodent at Columbia University. He was doin' his Ph.D. on Quantum Physics an' the Heisenberg Principle. Somethin' to do with Uncertainty, he said.'

'Yes, Uncertainty,' I concurred. 'That's about the ticket. But I'm not a stoodent. I'm a failed professional writer. I am writing a story about a spaceship on an intergalactic flight which fails to expand on its return to the Earth and ends up in a plate of spaghetti.'

'You never know what'll end up in a plate of spaghetti,' Paula agreed. 'In this joint, nothin' at all would surprise me. I once read a story in which a vegetable from outer space comes down in some farmer's backyard, an' then it makes love to his wife, transformin' itself into all sorts of famous film stars . . .'

'What?' I said.

'Clark Gable, Cary Grant, Humphrey Bogart . . .'

A Black Hole opened in front of my eyes. I grabbed her arm. Frank Zagdanovitch chortled.

'Where did you read that story?' I hissed.

'Or maybe it was a movie.' She shook me off like a flea. 'But then where would they have got them dead actors? It makes ya think, don't it?'

'Please,' I said, taking hold of my aura. There are a few times, in this town, when I have found my English accent standing me in good stead, setting me apart from the normal run of local barbarians. 'It's important to me! Can't you remember where you read or saw that?'

'Naw,' she said. 'My memory's like a sieve. I can catch drips, but that's about the size of it.'

'A magazine?' I said. 'Jake Akimbo's Science Fiction Magazine? *Archaeos*? *The Parmesan Review*? Would you have a copy of that issue somewhere?'

'I never keep anythin',' she said. 'What's the use? The boy

friend uses up every snip of paper snortin' his stash. I have little cones all over the place. Still, I do like a weird story now and then. Tell me when they're goin' to publish yours.'

When Hell freezes over! Thieves! Pirates! Footpads! Men have died the thousand cuts for less! I'll get you, Jake Akimbo! There'll be nowhere to hide! This galaxy is too small for the two of us!!

– Bernardo Pratt lurched down the pitted road . . . His feet were leaden heavy, he felt worn out by fatigue. The lawforcers had not pursued him, but he could still see three roboscanners circling and swooping above. One of them had dived low and he'd felt a sharp prick in the side of his neck. For a moment he thought they'd got him, but no incapacitating or lethal drug appeared to course through his veins, so he scrambled on. Perhaps it is a delayed-action capsule, designed to hit me when I'm least expecting it . . . I must find a doctor, a stomach pump . . . but there was no one he could safely approach . . . Thirgo Aargh, in league with the lawforces . . . his heart sank. I am on my own, he thought. He was entering that area of the city which seemed in the aftermath of a nuclear war, though it was just the legacy of six centuries of neglect. The ripped-up movewalks were hills and mountains in his way. Cracked empty shells of vast hiveapartments loomed on either side, but it was not possible to tell whether in their heyday they had been twenty or two hundred storeys high. Piles of rubber and plastofoam reared like giant termite castles. He had to cover his nostrils as he ran past a tower, thrusting up towards the steel grey sky, of garbage and debris left from habitable days. Not even the lowest of the low could live here now. Everything scavengeable had been scavenged. But still, here and there, he spied movement. Another ambush, perhaps, but more likely the man-hating Untouchable robots, escaped malcontents fused and rusted to madness, their brain pans busily breeding plague darts to fire at any human

110

encroacher. He hurried on, past this excrescent nightmare, towards the plastibox 'Riverside City' . . .

I climbed up the cracked steps towards the block entrance and took a look at the door bells. Sure enough, there was one marked Fihser, R. I pressed it. There was no trace of a sound. Everyone in the building seemed either not there or dead. Frank Zagdanovitch stood below, clawing the centre of the road, cawing jeeringly, pecking at a bag of corn. 'Go to it, Danny Boy, snoop that stoop!' I pressed the useless bell again. The intercom by it rasped suddenly, as if a cobra inside it had sneezed.

'Who dat? What you want? Go 'way.'

'Is that Mister Rudolph Fihser?'

'Who wants to know?'

'I'm a friend of Ben Tishman . . .'

'Who?'

'Ben Tishman? The film-maker . . . remember, he did an interview with you . . .'

'You from Doubleday?'

'No.'

'Then get lost.'

'You must remember Ben Tishman . . .'

'Never hoid of him.'

'He filmed you, with his camera . . . listen, can I come in and talk for a moment?'

'You a joinalist?'

'No. I'm a writer.'

'You got money?'

'No.'

'Get lost.'

This was not very fruitful. And Frank Zagdanovitch had vanished from the road. Probably taken back to the battery farm. Steam oozed from a subway vent. I staggered back towards the café. Paula the waitress, from behind the grimy window, was beckoning oddly to me. I re-entered the sanctuary.

'Hey,' she said, 'I remembered where I heard that story. The one about the vegetable from outer space. A friend of mine told it to me. He said he had a writer friend.'

'What was your friend's name? Or his friend's friend's name, friend?'

'Ben. Ben Tishman. Right, I see you know him. So you're the friend. Well, ain't that somethin'.'

It certainly is.

'When did you last see Tishman?'

The memory drips plopped through the sieve.

'Couple of nights ago. Three nights. Tuesday. He was in Tuesday, not for long. But that ain't when he told me the story. That was quite a while ago.'

Tuesday. While we were all still out checking the garbage cans and alleyways for bodies. And all the while the man is still in the city. The plot thickens. Into bouillabaisse.

I spilled the beans. 'Tishman has been missing since the weekend. His girl friend thinks he's in some sort of trouble. He had some business with a man who lives across the road from here. A man he interviewed for a film.'

'You mean our Rudie?' she knew it all. 'He's our local celebrity. He's been on NBC and Channel Five. And Nine. I don't like him. I think he's one big pain in the ass. But Ben got along with him just fine.'

'Ben got along with everyone just fine,' I said. 'So where is he now? Do you know?'

'Search me,' she said. 'He just comes in and goes out. Say,' she said, suddenly looking all thoughtful. 'Can I trust you?'

This is the sort of question I dread. 'Can you trust anybody?' I asked.

'Probably not,' she said, 'but you don't look mean to me. Is that why you came here, lookin' for Ben?'

'Yes.'

112

'Well, you know, he left me somethin'. It's a bit weird. He said he didn't want to . . . Listen, would you come up to my apartment? It's a bit messy, but the coffee is an improvement on this dump. This is my clockin' off time. An' believe me, not a moment too soon. Harry!' She untied her apron and vanished behind the counter for a tick, returning with a battered fur which covered the top part of her waitress gear. It made her look like a werelemming. 'Let's go,' she said, leading me out, across the street into the same apartment block from which the cobra rasp of Rudolph Fihser had evicted me a few moments before.

'If you were tryin' to get to see Rudie,' she said, 'you're wastin' your time. He's gone professional. There's a guy writing his life story for Doubleday. Rudie's buyin' his way outa here. He's after a summer house upstate where he wants to spend his last years shootin' bears. You ever shot bears, Mister?'

'Danny, Danny H—.' I said. 'No, I never shot bears. The closest I got to a bear was Baloo, in the *Jungle Book*. I would have loved to shoot him.'

'Yeah, wasn't that some show. You English?'

'I am afraid so.' She had finally input my hints.

'I had a boy friend once who was English. But he was a pusher, I got rid of him. Now my boy friend just consooms the stuff. He's too timid to push. I ought to get ridda him too. Don't worry, he's in jail right now. Some people have all the bad luck. That's Rudie's door right there.'

It had a large poster tacked to it:

DOUBLEDAY PRESENTS: THE COMING NO. 1
BESTSELLER: A REIGN OF TERROR IN THE CITY!
THE MAN WHO PARALYSED NEW YORK STATE!
SETH OVERSTOAT: THE MAD BOMBER.
A TRUE NIGHTMARE OF OUR TIMES!!!

A shadowy profile leered over the background of the city skyline, with explosions.

'He killed two people,' said Paula, 'an' he'll die a rich man. How many d'you think we'd have to kill?' She led me stomping up the dank and broken stone steps, storey after storey, dragging, to the fifth floor, unlocking a nightmare of four locks and bolts, pushing open a door heavy enough to guard the Federal Treasury of Munchkinland. The rooms within a tangle of used cartons, discarded tinsel, cardboard boxes, a double bed with piled sheets and a bilious riot of coloured beads and gew-gaws hung all over the walls.

'I used to go with a painter,' she said. 'He did the crucifixion, over and over, from every angle. I had blood oozing everywhere. I couldn't sleep a wink for months. He used to have crowns of thorns, to model from. They got all over the place, the bed, the toilet. I told him, it's either Him or me. He got the message, all right. Tried to nail himself up at the Rockefeller Center. What's with it with these kooks an' me?' She hung her fur on a peg and climbed on a rickety chair to reach the dust on an old wardrobe. 'This is what Ben Tishman left me. He said he didn't want to carry it around. You have any idea what it is? I don't.'

An exercise machine, for blind mice? It was a little gadget like a wire cat's cradle, with what seemed like an antenna poking out from one end. There was a sort of metal grating, with small holes, at the bottom. No sign of anything to plug it into anywhere. It seemed to have come from an assorted box, somewhere on 14th Street, marked 'Useless Gadgets. Annoy Your Friends'.

'What did he say about it?' I asked her.

'He said to believe him, it was important. Just that. If you know Ben you know he likes to tease. I took it in to yoomor him. Hey, maybe it's somethin' to talk to outer space, you know, like another galaxy, in your stories.'

'Mayday. Mayday,' I said into it. 'Centaurian marooned on

114

alien planet. Send platoon of sabre-toothed armopods. Or three cans of frorlma soup.'

Nothing at all happened. We put the doo-dah on the shelf.

'Shall I make some real Colombian coffee?' Paula asked.

'Yes, for God's sake.' I appealed. I lay back on the bed, exhausted, fingering my sheaf of first drafts. Poor Bernardo Pratt, hunted down in the lowest dregs of Amazonia, with an intergalactic spaceship and a plateful of Pete Pepperoni's worst spaghetti lodged in his intestines. What on earth could he do next? Particularly with Professor Sorn Plattvogel and his assistant Moishe trundling down his thorax, through his lungs, in their miniaturized probe. 'As zis man ve are inside off iss running, his breazing vill be heavy unt irregular. Be prepared for gusts of force zibben to acht. Pliss be careful off zat naughty antibody vich iss comink tovards us. Ve vill repel him mitt antibody repellent, like zo.' A grey-coloured spray whooshes out of a tube in the bubble-sled's outer hull and the menacing blob scampers off, muttering. The sled continues on its downward path, as walls of cellular tissue streak by . . .

– Nevertheless, Zopi reflected, our own value system cannot rationally be claimed as the only true condition of being. Twenty-four per cent of known galactic societies are as puritanical as we, or even more so. But forty-five per cent are permissive in varying degrees (while the rest look upon sex as an amusing invention of foreigners). Do we Aurigan Brulbers genuinely hold the key to the Universe? Was suppression of our desires the true path of Gogor? If so, why did Gogor create us with so many sexual facilities, more than any other known species? Was it truly to test our steadfastness and discipline? Have all our sages been wrong, as dissidents like Princess Bopi and the Affirmatists allege? He watched her pseudopodia curling round the flight console with a new rising excitement. But this was neither the time nor the place.

To have come so far, only in order to betray his race, his faith, his philosophy, for the prick of illicit desire?

'Do you want cream in your coffee, Danny?'
  'No thanks, love. Black as sin.'

The passengers were attempting to come to terms with their dire predicament. The Foubian, who had devoured the defenceless herbiform, was lying on a couch in the economy lounge recounting his early podhood to the Hvulvian analyst and the Tralfamadorian righteous convert: 'Don't worry,' the Tralfamadorian jelly was saying, 'it's nothing that a bowl of frorlma soup can't cure. The number of times I've regressed myself, eating pork, or, God forbid, even pipiklech–mit-milch . . .'

'My main problem in podhood . . .' began the wretched Foubian, but the Tralfamadorian continued unchecked: 'My own cubhood, what a cataclysm! If I had a galactocredit for every trouble in my life, I'd be a Snofthild today. In my nest nobody kept kosher. There was no shul within three parsecs, Yiddischkeit was unknown. All they wanted to do was crooble, crooble, crooble, all day long . . .'

Dee Dee Grant was necking with the exiled Emperor from Orion, who tore off her flimsy bouse. 'Hnn, hnn, hnn . . .' he grottled, as he grabbled hold of her ample boobs. Dee Dee Grant let his fingers stray where they wished. She did not notice as they inadvertently shook loose the tiny caps of Thrummadin attached to her nipple rings. Her mind was very much elsewhere as the tiny but terrifyingly potent pellets rolled down on the floor. A robocleaner sweeping by with its brushes gathered them up with the rest of the litter and happily buzzed on its way . . .

Paula did not have a bad body at all, quoth the male chauvinist. It was her somewhat blurred face that was the problem. But

116

one could not blame her for it. In New York City, the face is moulded by force majeure. It is the field of life's blitzkrieg. Firing squads file along its ravaged defiles, finishing off the wounded. She squealed a lot, keeping time with the bed. I had mislaid my caps of Thrummadin. Then, the skirmish over, she sat up and smoked. I gruffly declined the cliché.

'What are you doin' in New York, Danny?' she said. 'I mean, don't think I'm nosey. Me, I'm used to the place. I can survive it. What's your excuse?'

'I can pretend to be someone else,' I said.

'But you're a writer. That's your profession. Even if they don't pay you now. When you got talent, you gonna make it. That's what I believe anyhow.'

'I don't know if I have talent,' I said. 'I'm just pissed off, and that's not enough. There ought to be something affirmative to say.'

'My boy friend used to affirm Jesus. But that got him straight into Bellevue. I think you have to take the rough with the smooth. Mostly it's the rough, I guess. But you're sweet, Danny. I like you.'

'Thank you. And Ben Tishman, too?'

'He's a charmer. He gets what he wants. But I don't think he wants that much. You, I can feel you burning with want. Do you know what I mean?'

'I want to save the world for democracy. I want a chicken in every poor man's pot. A long, long life to Chairman Mao. I want justice in every corner of the land. I want to see my name in lights.'

I want to find Ben Tishman, to make his girl friend Ellie, the beautiful little ballet dancer, happy. I want to perform a selfless mitzvah, for once in my lousy life. And even that, fat chance. Perhaps I should beam my wants into Tishman's wire gadget, and bring down the flying saucer over the Natural History Museum, complete with magic tail light, to whisk me too, into the Ne'erworld . . .

'Tell me that story you're writing, Danny,' Paula said, 'the one about the spaceship in the spaghetti. It sounds a real hoot.'

'It is a machine for the destruction of Jake Akimbo,' I said, 'the man who almost stole my plots. I am hoping to give that man a real heart attack one day, and shuffle off his mortal coil. Have you ever read Jake Akimbo? the "Substratum" series, I thru IV?'

'Is he the guy who writes about the pacifist robots?'

'Yeah.'

'I read a few. But I like 'em with a bit more action. You know what I mean?'

Indeed. There might be problems in that department. Perhaps I should have smoked too.

'My stories are all full of action,' I said desperately. 'A race against time. Professor Sorn Plattvogel and his assistant Moishe have just reached the site of the trapped spacecraft, in an intestinal fold, when another crisis strikes: the cap of Thrummadin, the universe's most potent sex drug, has been vented out through the vessel's waste disposal chute into the outside environment, which happens to be Bernardo Pratt's stomach. Despite being diluted by miniaturisation, it drives Pratt totally sex mad. He staggers about, grabbing hold of the first living being that comes across his path. It happens to be a goat.'

'Hey, that's disgusting!' says Paula.

'It becomes even more so,' I relish. 'Professor Plattvogel, who has just exited his miniaturised bubble-sled, is sucked along by the trauma towards his host's genitals. Mein Gott! he cries, it's ze gonads! I am makink medical history here . . . ! *Hilfe! Hilfe!* Zey are all around me! Halt! *Achtung!* I am der married man! Ach, ze acceleration . . . at least tzvantsig g's . . . *Hilfe!* Moishe! *Hilfe!* aaaahhhhhh . . . Pratt lets the goat gallop away, with Professor Plattvogel trapped in its vagina. Then Pratt continues, into the bowels of the city . . . Meanwhile, at mission control, panic ensues . . .'

118

'I ain't surprised at all. Danny, you've been in the city too long.'

'I know.'

'Tell me about where you were born. Was it an English country village?'

'No way, José. I was born in a London suburb called Wembley. It is now the abode of upwardly mobile Swedish salesmen. There are three synagogues and a kosher butcher. It has the ugliest town hall in Europe. It is also the main sports stadium of the capital. Football hooligans invade regularly. There are also pop concerts and conventions. The Pope might visit next year.'

'Well, it sounds better than Brooklyn.'

'Is that your native turf, Paula?'

'Lafayette Avenue. It's the pits. Not that this is Paris.'

'I have been to Paris, Paula. It is truly beautiful. I hit a policeman with a brick.'

'I've often wanted to do that. But they're only doin' their job.'

'It was a long time ago. Eleven years now. They thought they were having a Revolution.'

'Yeah. The French are always having those, ain't they?'

'It comes with the package tour. A friend of mine burned down the Stock Exchange.'

'That would be un-American, here.'

'But blowing up AT & T pylons?'

'That's American as apple pie.'

'Listen,' I sit up. 'Can we get into your neighbour Rudie's apartment? I'm sure there's some clue there to Ben Tishman. Maybe those missing cans of film. Does that bastard ever go out, or does he stay in the centre of his web all the time, waiting for the man from Doubleday?'

'He has breakfast at my café.'

'Ah.'

'He has ten locks on his door.'

'Fire escapes? Back entrances?'

'He has burglar alarms, and cut glass. He thinks agents of the phone company want to kill him in revenge even after all this time.'

'There must be some way . . .'

'Let's get some sleep, huh? I'm bushed.'

She begins to snore, loudly.

Sirens rattle outside.

I curl metaphorical smoke from my nostrils.

Ven zere's a vill, zere's a vay . . .

*

'. . . I don't know how he meant to achieve it,' the young assistant, Moishe, said, 'but he was very certain, though, that it could be done.'

'Yes.' Princess Bopi's antennae curled in sudden excitement. 'It should be possible. I suppose it wasn't considered before as an acceptable process as it would entail a longer period of discomfort for the passengers during a slow expansion. Matt, you're a Space Engineer, Fifth Class. What do you think?'

'Hmm.' Zopi mused, curling his own antennae. 'Why not? We don't have much to lose. It might take some time, but the sooner we start the better.'

'Right,' said Bopi. 'Then let's don the spacesuits and open up the drive.'

'Do you think,' the sad Emperor-in-Exile asked the Tralfama-dorian convert, 'that Judaism could hold the answer for me too?'

'I'm convinced of it,' said the quivering jelly. 'When we get out of this, why don't you come with me. There's a tiny yeshiva in Kansas, thirty-six souls, all new converts. The Rabbi's a mollusc from Rigel . . .'

'With us,' the senior vug vug was explaining to the Bar-

120

soomian pilgrims, 'Philip K. Dick is not just a great literary figure of antiquity. Not that he is a deity, but we do find, hidden in his writings, the various codes and phrases that are the very root of Vrin. For example . . .'

Dee Dee and Bing Frisbee were fucking.

Professor Plattvogel was still wandering in the goat's vagina. He had broken away from the doomed young sperms and was approaching the creature's ovaries. 'Very interesstink,' he mused aloud, 'a most yoonusual eggsberience. Ziss younk lady zeems to haff ze most eggzdra-ordinary internal structure . . . it calls vor furzer eggsplorink . . .'

Pratt woke with a start. It was night, but a glow lit the interior of the tiny plastobox in which he had come to rest. An old hag, who appeared to have materialized out of the night, laid a wrinkled hand on his brow. 'It's all right,' she said, 'you have reached sanctuary. Neither the lawforcers nor Thirgo Aargh can reach you here . . .' He sat up, a terrible pressure in his bowels. He pleaded at her with his eyes. She motioned to a curtained-off partition, bearing an ancient porcelain privy, leading down to a primitive open drain which led straight down into the mighty adjacent river. He took down the rags of his trousers, squatted on the bowl and heaved.

'Here we go again!' cried Princess Bopi. 'Hold on to your hats, mateys! Our host is at it again!' Groans and honks of ennui breaking out in the passenger lounge as the tossing and tumbling recurred . . .

'What's that?' cried Hackitt, shaking sleep from his eyes, as Ms Thinga Mabob pulled his ankle.
'Sorry to disturb you,' she said dryly, 'but this came in just two minutes ago. The spacecraft bleep has moved again. The

mainframe has analysed the drift as out of Mr Pratt's bowels, down the drainage system of Amazonia's plastobox city, and now floating down the river, along the Amazonian coast.'

'Call all units!' yelled Hackitt. 'We're in business again, Snuth and Fnood! Where are my bicentennial underpants??'

'Saltwater,' said Bopi, 'slightly diluted. The man has shat or puked us out into the river.'

'The perfect venue for expansion,' cried Zopi, 'no population, no dangerous material obstacles! At last we can get this thing licked!'

'We seem to have steadied again,' said the Barsoomian pilgrim-chief, hopefully.

'Never trust appearances,' said the vug vug. 'The world is a vortex of fact and illusion. Take any chapter of *Eye In The Sky*. This is probably all happening in the diseased imagination of some Bowery drunk, or tertiary syphilitic . . .'

'Ecclesiastes . . .' said the jelly.

'Marry me!' said Bing Frisbee.

'Oh, Bing!' Dee Dee said. 'This is so sudden . . .'

The craft lurched again. 'What was that?' shouted Zopi, popping his head out of the engine.

'Running printout . . .' said Bopi. Her calm was like steel. Nothing could surprise or faze them now. They had found contentment together in crisis that nothing could match or destroy. 'Amino acids . . . salt water . . . this is not unexpected . . .'

'We've been swallowed by a fish,' Zopi guessed.

'Well, we shouldn't let that stop us,' said Bopi. 'If we're ready for distension, let's prepare to go ahead and activate . . .'

'They've located Plattvogel, sir,' Ms Mabob informed Hackitt. 'He's inside a goat, it would seem. But he seems to be acting rather strangely . . . he thinks he is inside Ms Feelie of

2998, and adamantly refuses to leave. Our psycher, Admiral Cornelius Noodle, fears the Professor has flipped his lid . . .'

'Forget him,' said Hackitt. 'I have 350 passengers to get out of dire jeopardy. We are on the point of slowed-down expansion. E-hour is only three minutes away!'

'Ten . . .

Nine . . .

Eight . . .' counted Bopi.

'*Yitgadal ve'yitkadash* . . .' intoned the Tralfamadorian.

'Our Sporefather that art in Thulma . . .' chanted the Barsoomians.

'My name is Mrs Tilly M. Benton and I wanted to get out . . .' quoted the vug vugs in unison.

'. . . five . . . four . . . three . . .'

'This is exciting!' said Dee Dee.

'Yes, isn't it?' said Frisbee.

'. . . two . . . one . . . activate . . . !'

'I,' said Zopi, 'looove yooooooooooooooooooooo . . .'

Implosion . . . the Big Bang . . . nebulae like slow-motion farts . . . a billion multi-coloured stars shivering shimmering shimmying bobbing tossing oooooooooooooooo . . . a trillion frying pans sizzling . . . muffled gongs ong bong donggggg-gggggggg . . . swelling surging spreading smergling . . . bursting . . . crescendoing . . . bong bong big bang implosion and so on and so forth, an endless catherine wheel swirling whirling rippling out out out . . .

And then, with sledgehammer suddenness, stopped.

Eyes, opening slowly. Antennae unfurling on stalks . . .

'We've done it! We've done it!' cried Princess Bopi. 'Look at the dials! We're back to our normal size! We've done it! We're free!!!'

'Not quite,' Zopi said, in an ominously quiet tone. 'Look out of the window, please . . .'

Outside – instead of the rippling water, shimmering trees, brown landfall and dim grey skies of an early Amazonian morning, that should have been – it was still as black as pitch.

'Don't tell me,' said Bonzo Hackitt. 'I don't want to know.'

'Sir,' Ms Mabob was firm, having taken command. 'This is Professor Pescus, of Marine Biology. He will explain the new problem.'

The marine biologist was a little dapper, swarthy man, with an immense sword-shaped proboscis and two lovely emerald earrings. 'A most unique phenomenon,' he said. 'History made before our eyes.'

'Urk. Urk. Urk,' said Hackitt. 'Nobody takes away this egg.'

'The distension field activated,' said Professor Pescus, 'covered an area much larger than the spacecraft itself. The fish which swallowed them, normally no more than five centimetres long, thus grew to an incredibile length of five miles, retaining, unfortunately, the spacecraft within its now gigantic abdomen. It is amazing that the creature in question still lives, but live it does, with its normal attributes magnified a million fold. Now, perhaps it wouldn't have mattered much unless. . . This is no ordinary fish, signor.'

'Oh?' Hackitt, despite having draped a towel over his head, peeped out for a brief moment.

'Si, certo, not a common fish at all. You must understand, the marine history of the Amazon in modern times is a fascinating subject. A teeming freshwater environment turned by engineering into an oceanic ecology. And this is an area where flora and fauna were always extremely adaptable. So, for example, the doras, a genus of Siluridae, which had the remarkable ability to walk overland when drought dried up its habitat. Many other Amazonian species developed this latency in the wake of so many man-made changes since the twenty-first century. A scant eight centuries, an instant in the evolutionary scale, but these species were always in a hurry . . . They can and do mutate readily, this has been observed all along . . . particularly this genus which has swallowed your ship and holds it still within its belly as the Biblical whale held Jonah. Pygocentrus of the Characinidae! What a marvel! What a miracle of nature! Maintaining down the centuries its peculiar strengths and talents, adding to them the abilities of Doras Siluridae, that is – the facility to walk on land. A freshwater fish now adapted to the ocean, able to traverse and survive any marine environment. Able to live, in short, on land or sea, with, in its present size of five miles' length, with commensurate breadth and size of its, ah, attributes, its appetite increased a million times! What an ecological marvel! A tragedy, unfortunately, for us, its poor human rivals. We shall regret very soon, I fear, our banishing of nuclear and other power weapons from this earth . . . very, very soon, I am afraid to say . . .'

'What are you saying?' Hackitt grabbed the man by his emerald earrings and shook his head from side to side. 'What are you telling me? What's the name of this paragon, this Pygo Charlie or whatever?'

'Pygocentrus Characinidae,' Professor Pescus said morosely, 'or in common, vulgar and colloquial use, for you, signor – a piranha.'

FIRST IT SNOWED AGAIN, then a thaw came, turning the thick fall to slush. Then the temperature dropped below zero, then rose, it rained, the ice froze. This created the New York climatic condition known as the Soft Shoe Death Walk. It was impossible to keep one's footing on the pavements, even with rubber boots. Vast puddles of icy slush separated each pavement from the centre of the road. One had to waddle great distances up and down blocks to find a survivable crossing point. The cold air reverberated to the cries and curses of those who failed in this course. Flailing arms and gumboots flying. Old ladies, infants, and grown veterans carried shrieking downstream. How are the mighty fallen. And the sky, steel grey.

What are the grounds for optimism in *l'affaire* Tishman? Well, at least I could convey to Ellie the hearsay good news of the living Ben, wandering out there on the West Side. A Tishman sighting, from the horse's mouth, as it were. And definitely some connection to the Mad Bomber. Not that I could make any move on breaking and entering the said ex-con's powdered glass abode.

'I'm a bad shamus,' I said to Ellie. 'Castigate me.'

'Don't be silly,' she said. 'What could you do?'

But the issue had at least taken on some attributes of a narrative, plot, scenario, chronicle, despite its unsettling loose ends blowing all over the place like scattered spider webs. The strange doo-dah from outer space or from the five and dime, the lurking shadow of Jake Akimbo, the bizarre behaviour of

Vince Epiglotis, talking to God knows who or what by toilet pipes. Reality, gone more than a mite askew. I once wrote a short short story along these lines, which I sent nowhere, but dedicated, now that I remember it, to Tishman, and his search for the extraordinary in the contours of the everyday . . . In fact, I just happen to have it right here. All right, all right, it's a very short one. I called it:

ANOTHER FINE MESS

'Another hard day at the shops, dear,' Mildred said, floating in at the porthole, 'The butcher was completely out of missionary, the cornflakes were rioting again and the green-grocer was off sick with the mildew. The canoes came as usual in clumps of four or five. The councilmen had all the machines in the laundrette – it made you sick seeing their smug, grinning faces going round and round inside the front-loaders. And the workmen still haven't repaired the assholes in the driveway. And, to cap it all, the postman nearly got me right on the corner and I had to fight him off with my panga.'

'Never mind, dear,' I said, 'Just relax and put your feet up by the fire.' She did so, hanging them up on the peg and in no time they were done to a turn. Nothing like domestic bliss, thought I, as we each gnawed an anklebone. Franz the cat lay on the settee with his Proust, annotating the margins with his eyestalks. Bongo, the performing alligator, swam in his jar. In the telebowl the kojaks slaughtered each other as usual with lasers and machetes. I got bored and zapped them from my chair. I really didn't feel like a trip to the bodybank tonight, but if I put it off we'd both be putrid by morning. It was an evening, more rightly, for some quiet self-mutilation followed by suicide by panga or flamethrower. Tomorrow a hard day's squawk at the office.

Oh, the dreariness of it all.

*

But how can I save the damsel in distress? Especially as she is just due to begin rehearsals for a shmuntz performance in the city, a show due to open in the spring. Presidential primary time. The whole hoo-hah. Re-elect Jimmy Carter. Oyf kapoyres. The wags say this is going to be the Year of Ronald Reagan. I tell them: I make the jokes around here. The doctors who host Ellie at 112th Street are nevertheless convinced this is the Shape of Things To Come. When will the winter lift from the city? The barking man slushes up Broadway. 'Arf! Arf! Arf!' he cries. No one follows him with a brush and pan. I lock myself in the 'penthouse' with Entenmann's Donuts. Kill or cure, that's my motto.

Re-engaging the brain, there may be some points to touch here. If Tishman is out there, he needs a base to work from. It is wintertime. Bong, bong, bong, the boy wins the cigar. He can't be sleeping on the streets, like a bagman. He can't be domiciled with lemming Paula, or I wouldn't have been sleeping there. Nor could he be staying with the Mad Bomber. (No? No. Well, that had some bizarre attraction.) There is, of course, an obvious alternative staring me in the face like a mackerel.

The Arab-loving cousin's pad on the East 50s. A chicken feather playfully tickled my nose. In fact this had occurred to me, but I had found the spare keys hanging in the kitchen. I had not followed from there to the high probability of a second spare set, on Tishman's person. We had always juggled about that one set of keys as if it were the Antigua Penny Brown.

Four o'clock in the afternoon. A reasonable time for action. I take the keys and don my booties. Under normal circum-

128

stances I would enjoy the walk down and across town along the south end of the park. Charabancs and drunken bums and the elegant hotels, flitting by the glass towers of Sixth to Madison Avenues. The wide swathe of 59th Street, Grand Army Plaza, the traffic jams up and down Park Avenue. The view down to the PanAm building, with the great glass towers on either side. You feel the centre of the world, firmly anchored. Cash money, in concrete and steel. But also delicatessens, cinemas, ritzy fashion stores, pâtisseries, frozen yoghourt shops. The whole area of affluence which is creeping up to engulf my sleazepit of the upper 70s Broadway. The times they are a-changing, but Danny H— is not. Loath to try and navigate these delights by the Soft Shoe Death Walk, he takes the Independent subway. Down on the rattling AA train from 81st Street, change to the Eastbound E train at 42nd. Exit at 53rd and Lexington. This used to be a male whore pick-up. Strange characters lunged towards you in the dark, offering their somewhat warped bodies. Absent now. Yesterday's sleaze is today's haute couture. And I, with my unreconstructed hopes and prejudices . . .

Tishman used to suggest to me that I ought to hitch my waggon to the new rising fashion of minorities. Black up my prose, feminize my output, emphathize with the oppressed. I empathize with the oppressed, but on a purely personal front, as a self-enrolled member. Auto-Suppression In the World of Plenty, that should perhaps be my opus. I saw two paths in a forest glade, and I, I took the path more strewn with rubbish, leftovers and Pepsi-Cola cans, spurning the freeway of Prosperity, where I might be run over anyway. Sheer cowardice, masquerading as class treachery. A Moral Tale of Our Time. But I cannot think in terms of What's Good For Women? What's Good For Blacks? What's Good For the Jews? The Gays? The Midgets? The Tralfamadorian converts? Though I tried, for Tishman's sake, as I was staying in his flat, eating his slops, fouling his air, disrupting his sex life. I sent a story off to *The Gay Post Bag*, mouthpiece of the City's ever-burgeoning homosexual community. It came to me out of the depths of my childhood. It returned, of course, by US Mail:

WINNIE THE POOF (*and his chum Faglet*), Part I:

When all the cuddly lady bears waved and displayed their honeypots at Winnie as he walked by them on his morning constitutional, he shook his head politely and strode on.

'I am a Poof Bear,' he said, 'I enjoy my roll in the hay, but only in my own way.' He was a very Independent Bear, and apart from a talent for poetry he had, as we can see, his own strong likes and dislikes.

He walked down the path, humming proudly to himself, until he came to a little hut on a small knoll, surrounded by rhubarb and jerusalem artichokes. On the door was a bright green sign saying: 'Faglet's Hous. Positively no Grils.'

Winnie knocked on the door three times and Faglet poked his little head out warily. 'Oh, it's you,' he said. 'Come in. I'm glad you're not a gril. They've been bothering me all day, despite my sign.'

'Are you sure you don't mean "girls"?' said Winnie, settling down on the settee.

'Dear, oh dear,' said Faglet, mournfully, 'So that's the explanation. No wonder no one paid any attention.'

'Never mind,' said Winnie, 'Tell me how the plans for the Kinema are getting on.'

Poof and Faglet had applied to the Bearville County Council Arts and Recreation Committee for a permit to open a Gay Kinema on Poplar Avenue, so they and their friends could enjoy screening all their favourite films and serials, such as *Poofbeats* and *Fiddler on the Poof*.

130

'The lady bears are objecting,' said Faglet. 'They say no one will want their honeypots any more.'

'I'll tell you what,'said Poof. 'Let's go and have a word with the fairies. They usually have an answer for everything.'

'All right,' said Faglet.

As they walked off together down the hickory path towards the woods, they could see someone trying to hide behind a willow tree.

'Come out of there, Eyesore,' said Poof. 'We know you're there. You don't have to hide from us.'

Eyesore stepped out slowly from behind the tree. He was a very melancholy fellow and his tail was dragging on the ground. 'Nobody wants to see me,' he said, 'My ears are too long, my teeth are crooked and I have pimples all over my face.'

'Come with us, Eyesore,'said Winnie, 'I'm sure the fairies can fix you up too.'

'Do you really think so?' said Eyesore, and he joined them happily, dancing and jaunting down the road, crying out, 'The fairies are going to get rid of my pimples! My teeth will be put straight and my ears folded up and held with safety pins!' None of this had been promised Eyesore, but that was what he was like – if you offered him a finger he took the whole hand.

Phallus In Blunderland

The Chief of all the fairies was called Grumpy Blintsies. He was a little old man with no clothes on and a very long grey beard which covered his naughty bits. He said: 'I don't think I can help you till spring, because I've had to pawn my magic-making things to buy enough Kentucky Fried Chicken to last me the winter. However, if you go down the valley, through the Mould Forest, over the Marrow Downs and past Filth-wood, you might come across the Fag-norns. Among them lives a very old and extremely stupid man called the Ombuds-

131

man and he might just have his magic Anti-Committee Spell Kit. On the other hand, he might not; it was all a very long time ago and my memory isn't what it used to be.'

'That's enough for us,' said Poof, 'Thank you very much. Come on, friends, let's be on our way.'

'Will the Odd-bod-man have safety pins for my ears?' Eyesore called back as Poof led them back up the path.

'Yes, yes, yes,' said the surly old fool, curling himself into his beard to continue his afternoon nap.

So Poof, Eyesore and Faglet started off towards the Mould Forest. At first they were light-hearted and gay, whistling so cheerfully the butterflies joined in, but as they approached the Forest the sky darkened with clouds and it began to get quite chilly. 'I don't like the look of those trees at all,' moaned Faglet, 'What about all those stories of Poof-bashers hiding in the branches with knobkerries and bicycle chains?'

'Stuff and nonsense!' said Poof, and, chin up, he strode determinedly into the wood. Faglet peered right and left but followed, his little heart thumping, while Eyesore sauntered after them, secretly glad they were going somewhere his long ears and pimples would be hidden from the banter of respectable folk.

'This *is* very dark,' murmured Poof, not as brave as he had made himself out to be.

'And gloomy,' said Eyesore.

'And cold,' wailed Faglet, 'I should have brought a jumper, or my old Grandmother's Paisley shawl.'

'Oh, shut up,' said Poof, 'You're making us all very nervous.'

Just then there was a skittering noise in the shadows and something black and medium-sized skimmed past them and knocked into a tree, squawking and beating with its wings.

'Belay there, shipmates!' it cried, 'All hands below decks! Avast, landlubbers! Splice the mainbrace! Pieces of Eight! Pieces of Eight!'

'What is it? What is it?' screeched Faglet. Eyesore had already hidden behind a tree.

The creature staggered to its two taloned feet, spread its leathery wings and flew up again, though it didn't get very far, banging its head on a branch just above Winnie's head. Its feet caught on the branch and it hung there upside down, panting heavily.

'Why, it's a bat!' said Winnie, 'but not a very efficient one, it seems. I thought bats had a special sense which made them avoid bonking into things like you do.'

'This is generally true,' said the Bat, 'but I am, alas, a very special kind of a bat. I am a Cheshire Bat, and my radar has been dulled by my exclusive diet of Cheshire Cheese and Fish Fingers.'

'Why don't you eat something else then?' asked Winnie.

'Nothing else agrees with me,' said the Bat. 'I've had a very mixed up life. I was brought up by an old and very near-sighted seaman who trained me as a parrot. In fact my education has fitted me out to be a Grade A parrot, but as a bat I am totally useless.' And little tears fell like dewdrops from his head on to Poof Bear's small snout.

'Why don't you come with us, then?' said Poof, 'We are going to find the Ombudsman who lives with the Fag-norns past Filthwood, to ask him if he can make the Bearsville Arts and Recreation Committee give us a permit for a Gay Kinema in Poplar Avenue.'

'And so he can give me safety pins for my ears and clear up my pimples!' said Eyesore, coming out from behind his tree.

'And perhaps he can make you a true Bat again,' Poof wound up.

'That's very kind of you,' said the Bat, 'and I may be able to help you find the way, if you describe the things you see as you go along. I've been in the Forest for a long time, and, although I can't see where I'm going, I've picked up some bits and pieces of knowledge about the Forest's secret paths.'

'What does a piece of knowledge look like?' asked Faglet.

'It's usually round and crumbly round the edges,' said the Bat, 'but I've also found ones that are oblong and squishy. You'll probably trip over one sooner or later. They fly about mostly in the evenings, after teatime, looking for places to sleep.'

They went on together deep into the Forest, the Cheshire Bat perched on Poof's shoulder, saying, every now and then, as Poof described a special sort of tree, or a small grassy clearing: 'On course' or 'turn to starboard' or 'alter course twelve degrees larboard' and so on. Once they were surprised by the sight of two odd figures sitting on a rock. They were identical fat twins, with striped jerseys and schoolboy caps, and one of them was mouthing silently and desperately at the other, who just sat there looking very glum.

'It's only Tweedledumb and Tweedledeaf,' the Bat explained. 'Tweedledumb is as dumb as a dodo but doesn't know it, so he keeps shouting at Tweedledeaf, who can't hear him, and he thinks he's totally batty to pretend to make sounds. But Tweedledumb thinks Tweedledeaf is just making fun of him. So they'll both go on for ever, unless they can stop to think things out, since they're both right about each other, and wrong, as well, contrariwise.'

'It's all much too complicated for me,' said Poof Bear, and Faglet just moaned in confusion.

Soon it became very dark, and the Forest no longer seemed as empty as before. Legs of mutton flew through the air, black puddings leaped from tree to tree and shepherds' pies crawled warily across the ground. Another odd figure, dressed in white, stood with what appeared an old book in hand, leaning against a tree and quoting poetry. It had a long white beard and matching whiskers and a snow white cap on its head.

'That must be the White Rabbi,' said the Bat, when Poof

had described the figure to him. They caught a couple of verses before going out of range (and you should try catching verses sometime, nasty squirmy things that they are!). The verses were rather sad and languid, like putty passing through a sieve:

> Twas yontiff, and the shabbes loaves
> Reposed on Myron Gimble's table,
> The payments on the borrowed stove
> Were rather more than he was able.
>
> Beware the chapper's knock, my son,
> The law's quick bite, the formal snatch,
> Beware of sub-jus-gentium,
> The frum old banker's touch . . .

'We should hurry on a little,' advised the Bat, 'If we're not out of the Forest by midnight we might come up against the Wicked Bitch.'

'What would happen then?' asked Winnie nervously.

'Well, if we meet her close to midnight,' said the Bat, 'she could turn us all into bumpkins.'

'I don't like the sound of that!' said Eyesore.

'It won't make any difference to you,' said Winnie, 'but I'm an intellectual Poof Bear and I'd rather stay that way if you don't mind.'

They began to walk faster and faster, almost running as the Forest grew even darker than before, and then darker, and then darker still.

(Don't Miss Part 2 – incorporating SNOW BLIGHT AND THE SEVEN POLYMORPHS, POOFEYE THE SAILOR MAN, THE BIONIC WOMBAT and LARD ON MY WINGS.)

★

But there was not much trick or treat on East 52nd Street. I breezed past the liveried doorman, whose photographic memory passed me as an occasional sub-tenant, climbed in the swift, noiseless lift in which well-dressed couples contemplated their good looks and breeding, to Floor 9, exiting in a brown panelled corridor reeking of good maintenance. More tasteful persons padded past in rubber soles on their way to the incinerator. Standing with the keys poised before the double lock, I put them away and rang the doorjamb bell. Footsteps, a voice calling for identification. A small pudgy Middle Eastern looking gentleman then unbolted the door, looking me over, with a bag of frozen bagels dangling in his right hand.

'My name is Akram,' he said. 'You are a friend of Adam? Please come in. I was just going to hit a beagle.'

Would that not cause trouble with the SPCA? I thought, but my brain re-engaged, as he headed for a small microwave in the kitchenette, unwrapping his bag.

Tishman's uncle, it seemed, called his two offspring Adam and Eve. Ben's own father was, luckily, more conventional. There is something in the Jews that tends to overstatement. It's probably in the DNA. But I sat by a coffee table which was piled with pamphlets in English and Arabic, advertising the pleas of the Association of the American Friends of Palestine. Once that used to mean geriatric Jewish ladies from Flushing attending raucous Hadassah meetings. No more. But all Akram was toasting now was another bagel. The pad itself was much as always, the bachelor's dream: one dinky room with folding kitchen and bathroom, double bed concertinaing neatly into a sofa.

'I was actually looking for Adam's cousin, Ben Tishman. He told me he would be staying here this week,' I said, enunciating slowly, as we racially patronizing persons do when confronting the wily Pathan, especially when they are

136

engaged on assaulting our native tongue, 'You know how the keys of this place circulate . . .'

'Adam is very generous,' said Akram. 'But I have been staying here all the wick. Nobody else has been. Adam is in Hartford. You know Hartford?'

Thank God, no. But this was not doing us any good. I could not see Tishman in these surroundings. The sufferings of the Palestinian Arabs, let alone the Jews, were not the sort of cross he would bear. I think he told me he had made one trip to Israel, in his youth, to the communal farm. New Yorkers sometimes undergo this atavism. I am told all of Brooklyn was once fertile topsoil. Cows grazed where now only the D Train cuts deep into the fallow dirt. Pilgrim fathers or sweaty Hebrew pioneers. I don't think Tishman thought much of it. 'It was good while it lasted,' he said. 'But not the life for me. My lungs are addicted to the smog.'

And Akram, burning his fingers on heated bagels in Jew York, deep behind enemy lines. 'You are a poet?' he asked me.

'What makes you think that?' I asked.

'It is the gays,' he stated. I was about to deny all, indignantly, when he added, 'the gaze, the way you are looking at things.'

'That's the New York skewer,' I explained to him. 'It's a defence, you know, like poisonous snakes. We try to terrify and entice our victims at the same time.'

He nodded vigorously, as if he knew what I was talking about. Which made one of us, anyway.

'Urban angst,' he said. 'I am writing my doctorate about it for Adam. This is why I am in the city. I walk around, looking at the people. I return their gaze. I talk to them in subways and parks. When you break the eyes they are very friendly. They like to tell you all their problems.'

'Not me, mate,' I said, 'I'm all right, Jack.'

Everyone I meet is into social observation. Tishman, Tom

137

the Joinalist, Angst Hunter Akram. Another wild goose chase. Or is it? Is it an elaborate ploy? Is Tishman actually curled up in the sofa while I consume the ethnic leaven? Or his body in the dinky kitchenette freezer, cut up in frozen bagel bags, to be removed in a suitcase by Raymond Burr as in *Rear Window*? The fruits of his discovery of a terrorist plot to blow up the Bnai Brith Anti-Defamation League and all its works? No, that would not be Tishman's bag of beans. Squabbles over distant lands and foreign battlezones. Not a very likely cause. Invaders from outer space, yes. Jews and Arabs, absolutely not.

'Have a good day,' says Adam's latest rib, as he tips me politely into the corridor.

Out in the street, the observed subjects amble on, ogling the antiques and greeting card shops. An eminently observable eight-foot-tall black man in an overcoat hands me the following message:

MADAME CLARA!
Clairvoyant, Spiritualist, Advisor, Palm, Card & Crystal Ball Readings, Phrenologist & Astrologist.

To all she has the Power to help and Heal you of All your Ailments and Troubles. LOVE – MARRIAGE – BUSINESS – HEALTH. She removes Evil Influences and Guards you through Life. If you're ill or unhappy or bad luck seems to follow you everywhere she can Succeed where others fail. She has God-given Powers to help and solve all Problems. Praise the Lord, HALLELUJAH. One visit will put your mind at ease.

The address is a mere stone's throw from my billet at Tishman's abode. Another option to conjure if all else fails. As it seems. Tuesday, and Tishman has been missing for eleven days. What price Urban Angst now? There is either more or less than meets the eye. So what next, eh, chicken shamus?

No answers in the East. Re-try the West. Another crack at the Mad Bomber? I press phone numbers. Ellie is deep in rehearsals. I do manage to raise the 112th Street bloodhound. He cannot offer much more dirt than I already have sopped up on Rudolph Fihser.

'Yeah, I heard something about a book. After Watergate, the publishing business is a crook's charter. But that's the name of the game, Danny. Money talks. Don't you hear it? It says Fuck Off. You should have seen the Medicare frauds. Doctors hand out placebos to patients and keep the real pills to sell private while they claim the cost of the drugs. People piss blood and die because instead of antibiotics they're taking in wee tabs of sugar. It's the survival of the unfittest, the morally debased and deranged.'

Don't I know it, returning to my other life, slouching by the doorman, Jesus, his eyes fixed on the game shows, edging up in the slowest lift in Christendom looking through the porthole at the numbered floors floating by in incredibly slow motion, perusing for the hundredth time the notice:

Please Do Not Leave Your Laundry Unattended In the Boiler Room – There Is a THIEF In This Building!

Another possible case for Frank Zagdanovitch. 'The Longjohns' Goodbye'. Unlocking the 'penthouse' door to repossess my file of put downs and return of mail envelopes:

Thank you for your manuscript BEYOND THE PLANET OF FUCK, which you sent to Mrs Blighton who is no longer with this company. Although there is certainly a place for space age satire, we have a very limited science-fiction list and have to cater for the mass market in our editions. Your novel, I'm afraid, while full of colour and zaniness is a bit way out. I think that you should bear in mind that its many references to a special

'Sixties' cynicism will result in it being nearly twenty years out of date by the time it could get published, in the '80s.

Yours sincerely,
C. Highton, Editorial Manager

Bye-bye Danny boy, last dinosaur of a long forgotten age. Perhaps they'd go for the real thing, the little homilies of hard core porn from my little stash of wolf hour magazines, true up-to-date Seventies prose this, the absolute ungilded lily:

'Judging from the reports of anthropologists, oral sexual techniques are fairly commonplace throughout most primitive societies. For example, the men of the Ponape tribe, located on an island in the Pacific, who stimulate the labia with their tongues and teeth.' (What else is there to do on a Pacific Island, *Gott sei dank*?) 'One of the ceremonies finds a man placing a fish in the vulva of his partner and gradually licking it out prior to performing coitus.' And this over a picture of a girl in a dentist's chair being penetrated by her orthodontist. Why don't they just stick to the illustrations? No, they just want to pretend vice is good for you. 'Thus while we know from the *Satyricon* that a guest at a party gives a girl a bellyful of wine, from his mouth into, not her mouth but another orifice of her body, we have no way of knowing how common these practices were among the other classes of that society, much less which orifice.' Siegfried von Schmeck, Penisologist. What do they want from our life? Rub-a-dub-dub, rub-a-dub-dub . . . (What fish do the Ponape use? One hopes it is not a carp . . .)

Despair, as I collapse, post-pump, on to the spare camp bed, trying to banish the Ponapes, Madame Clara and Frozen Bagel Akram and Adam and Eve from my reveries, adopting the theory that the next move must come from the random forces of kismet and entropy. Always potent forces around here as the lingering winter night takes hold . . . The house

140

steam, bubbling through the old heating ducts, wheezing like an old man's guts being mangled. The muffled boom-te-boom of partygoers in another part of the building, kidding themselves that life has some purpose. To contrapunkt, the late-night, small-hour sounds of 79th Street, as the whackos, crooks and insomniacs claim their kingdom, with wild arguments that call for more cotton wool tightly balled into the ears: 'I'll slit your throat, your mangy motherfuckin' bitch!' 'Oooohhh! Oooohhh! Oooohhh! Oooohhh!' 'You think I'm a ratbag?! Eh? you bitch? You think I'm a motherfuckin' ratbag?' 'Eeeeee! Eeeeee! Eeeeeee! Eeeeee!' 'I'll put your pieces in the ashcan. I'll cut you, woman!' 'Aaaahhh! Aaaahhh! Aaaahhh!' and so on and so forth.

Or, there is always the possibility of that night-time phantom telephone call. The heavy breathers, the strangled larynx, the depth croaker, the demented tooth grinder, or just the whisper of the lines. Answering machines, wooing each other, over the humming wires of Ma Bell: 'Hi. This is Expedition Films. There's nobody about raht now, so ah can have you all to ma-self . . .' Mmmmm. Dig them electronic jolts, robie! What does it feel like to be the model that wasn't Asimoved? Is this the origin of the species?

Or Tishman, calling from a phone booth in Texas, using the old credit card scam. 'Listen, Danny, I don't have much time. I'm using the Chase Manhattan Bank number. You won't believe what happened to me the other day. Tell Ellie I . . . aarrg . . . uuugghhh . . . rrrr . . . zzzt . . .

'Put your dollar eighty-five in please, caller!'

'Rrrr . . . brrr . . . zrrr . . . grrrr . . .'

Boom-pa-te-boom-pa-te-boomp. I wrote a story once, in one of these night downturns, when Tishman was away with Ellie elsewhere, and the swingers were on the go somewhere on Floor 8, and the screaming neighbour across the street, or down on the pavement, being beaten to death again, and sent it off the next morning, in a fit of rage and frustration, to

The Parmesan Review. Is this avant-garde and nouvelle prose enough for you?! I called it –

THE STORY OF E

'Eeee, eee, eee ee eeeee eeee!' eeee Eeee.

'Eeeeee? Eee eee ee eeeee . . .'

'Eeeee.'

Eeee eeee eeee eeeeeeeeeee e eeee eeeee Eeee, eeee eeeee eee eee eeeee. Eee eeeee eeee ee; eeeeee, eeee eee e eeeeee eeee, eeee eeeee.

'Eeeeee. Eee e eeeee, eee eeeee eeeee eeeee eeeee eee.' Eee eeee eeee ee eeeeeee e eeeee. Eeee eeeeeee eeee. Eeeee eeee ee eeeeee ee, eeeeee: 'Eeee! Eee! Eee ee eeee!' Eeee eeeeeee eeee eeee eeeee ee. Eee eeee.

'Eeee eeeee eeee eeee.'

'Eee eee eeee eeee,' eeee Eeee, eeee eeeee eeee, eee eeeeeee eee. Eeee ee eeee eee. 'Eeee eeeeeeeee eeee.' Eeee eeee eeee ee eeeeeee eeee eeeeeee eeee eeeeeee ee eeee. Eeee eeeee eeeeeeeee eee. Eeee e eee eeeee eeeeeee eeeee; eeeee eeeee eeeeeee e eee ee eeeeee eeeeee eee, ee eeee eeeee eeeee eeeee ee eeeee ee.

'Ee eee eee eeeeee, eee eeee eeee eeee eeee.'

'Ee eeee?'

'Eee.'

Eeeee eeeee eee eeeee eeeee eeeeee. Eee eeee eeeeee eeeee, eeeeee eeeeeeee eeee e eeee eeeee eeeeee ee eeee e eeee. Eeee eeee eeee eee ee eeee, eeeeee eeee eeeee eeeee Eeee eeeeeee eeeeeee eeeee ee eeee eeeeee eee.

'Ee eeee eeeee eeee eeeeee e eeeeee eeee.' Eeee Eeee. Ee eeeee eeee eeeeee eeee eeeeeeee eeeee ee, eeeee eeeeeee eeee eeeeee ee. Eeee eee eeeeee, eeeee, eeeee ee eeeeeeee e eeeeeeee.

Eeee! Eeeee! Eeeee!

142

Eeee eee eeeeeee eeeee eeee eeee eeeee, e eeeee eeee eeee e
eeeeeeeee eeeee.

Eeee eeee: 'Eeeeeeeeeeeeeeeeeeeeeeeeeeeeeeeeeeeeeeeeeeeee!'

'Eee eeeee eeeee. Eeee eeeeeeeee.' Eeee Eeee.

'E eee eeeeee ee!' Eeee Eeee, 'Eeee eeeeee eeeee eeeee eeee
ee ee eeeee! Eee eeee ee eeee eeee eeee, eeeee eeeee eeeeee ee e
eeeee e eeeeee eeee, eeeeeee e eeeeee eee eeeeeee, eeeee eeeeee
eeeeeeeee eeeeee eeeee, eeeeee ee eeeeeeeeeee, eeeeeeee, Eeeee?
Eeee ee eeee eeeee eeeeee eee e eeeeee eeeeeee? Eeee eeeeee
eeeee eeeee eeeee ee eeee eeeeeeee ee e eee eeeeeeeeeeeeeeee?
Eee? Eeeeeee eeeeee eeee!'

Eeee eeeee eeeee eeee eee.

'Eeeeee eee eeeeeee eee, eeeee eeeeee eee eeeeee eee e eeeee.
Eee eeeee eeee eee eeeeee?'

'Eeeeeeee.'

'Eee! Eee!'

'Eeeeeee!!!!!'

Eeee eeeeee eeeeee eeeee. Eee eeeee eeee ee eeeeee eeeee,
eeeeeee eeeeeeeee ee eee eeeee, eeeee eeeee eeeee.

Ee eeee eeeee eeee eeeee eeeee E.

E eeeee eeeee, eeeeee ee eee E'eeee.

E eeee eeeee eeeeee eeeee.

E? E?

eeee eeeee eee ee eeeeeeee . . .

I pricked my ears for the shrieks of sub-editors leaping to their
death from fifteenth floors. But they maintained their sang
froid, returning the text without comment, but with another
subscription demand.

However, the forces of entropy never fail one. When in
doubt, Raymond Chandler said once, always have a man come
through the door with a gun in his hand. I switched on the
early television news in the morning. I sometimes do that,
when prey to real masochism. The subliminal messages, in
particular. 'Mouse racing at Four. News at Eleven.' And lo,

a local item leads the pack: fire at an apartment block in Midtown West Manhattan. An unflappable lady woos the mike:

'. . . An old, only partly tenanted building looking out on to the Express Highway. The fire apparently started on the fifth or sixth floor, and spread downwards along old rotting brickwork. All the inhabitants of the building were swiftly evacuated but it is as yet too soon to tell whether anyone was actually trapped in the blaze. Firemen were on the scene within minutes but it has taken them until the early hours to get the fire under control . . .'

Oh God. Poor Paula, smoking in bed again. Or was it Tishman's doo-dah, suddenly emitting a powerful beam from Tralfamadore? I threw my togs on and rushed to the subway, grabbing a couple of garlic bagels on the way.

It is a strange image of cliché writ there on the street as I arrive. Firemen, still training two hoses upon the smoking front of the building, the long twisting pipes leading to the whining engines of three great red firetrucks. Ambulances, police cars, uniformed cops holding back the sidewalk crowd of gapers, onlookers, hopefuls of a closer sight of human pain. No sign of waitress Paula amid the slack jaws, gleaming eyes. Smoke still billowing from the front of the building out of soot-blackened gutted windows. I push my way here, there. The tingle of excitement in the air. Something's happened. Praise de Lawd. The humdrum trance of life is broken. I zig-zag among the ghouls, adding my own vacant stare, unable to see through the blackened front and blind eyes of the burnt building. The crowd has almost obscured Paula's café. I push my way in. No Paula. A small sweaty man with an apron I deduce is the chef/partner Harry is looking out from inside.

'I'm looking for Paula,' I tell him. 'I was talking to her the other day. I know she lives across there. Is she OK?'

'I ain't seen her yet,' Harry said. 'But the firemen have been up there. Nobody's been trapped, thank God. But she weren't at work last night either. I just hope she's OK.'

A harassed policeman edges his way in, removing his cap and mopping his brow.

'Gimme a coffee Harry,' he breathes. 'All these people. What do they expect to see?'

'Death,' says Harry. 'They wanna see death. And they wanna make sure they're still here.'

'I guess so,' says the policeman. 'It still gives me the creeps every time.'

'I know two people who live in that building.' I sit by him at the counter, on a low plastic stool. 'A woman on the fifth floor and someone on the ground. Is it sure everyone is clear?'

'Well, we ain't sure how many people live in the building,' he says, grabbing his proffered coffee. 'Lots of the apartments are empty.'

'Paula, who works here,' I say, 'and Rudolph Fihser. The Mad Bomber. He lives on the ground floor.'

'You from Doubleday?' says the cop. What's with the world? I am constantly identified with my predators.

'No. I have a friend who filmed an interview with Fihser,' I explain to him. 'And that friend has disappeared.'

'Lots o' people disappear in the city,' the cop says. 'Sometimes I wish I could. Have to get back,' he has gulped his coffee. 'Thanks, Harry. Jack's a busy man, friend. Try the casualty ward at Roosevelt. 58th and 9th. We took a few people there.'

Half of New York is still standing outside. I breaststroke through, looking for a familiar face. I see it. But it is not one expected. 'Hey!' I swim through the human gridlock. The man walks on, towards the De Witt Clinton Park. I push on, getting closer. There is no doubt now. It is Vince Epiglotis, the toilet-pipe basher of Expedition Films.

'Vince! Vincent Epiglotis!'

He doesn't hear, but walks on, hurrying towards a car

parked by the north-eastern corner of the park, a battered old Dodge. I run up to it. Vince is in the driver's seat. Little Nel is smoking a cigar beside him. In the back a haggard-looking old man is hunched up, almost totally covered by a blanket.

'Vince!'

'What the fuck you doin' here, Danny?'

'That man is Rudolph Fihser. Aren't you, sir?'

'What the fuck you doin' here, Danny?'

'You know where Ben Tishman is, don't you, Vince? It's something to do with this asshole.'

'The only asshole around here is you, Danny.' Vince gunned the engine. 'Go away. Quit sticking your nose into other people's business.'

'Where's Ben Tishman, Mister Epiglotis?' He reversed the car a piece, to clear a van parked ahead of him, running the window up to clear my hand. 'Who do you talk to over the toilet pipes, Vincent? Why do you bang with spanners on loo walls?'

He gave me a look that should have dropped me on the spot and accelerated forward, clearing the van by inches. The battered Dodge bucked over the pitted swathe of Eleventh Avenue, off towards the bowels of Downtown, the Mad Bomber still wrapped in the back seat, Little Nel calmly chomping her stogie.

God Damn!

I sat down on a bench and Frank Zagdanovitch skittered up and sat by me, holding out a bagful of greasy french fries.

'That's a real turn up for the books, eh Danny boy?' he chortles. There are dirty feathers on the french fries. 'Sounds like you got a real pretzel there, my son.'

'I refuse to talk to a chicken,' I said morosely. 'Especially a figment of my imagination.'

'Will anyone else speak to you, Danny boy? Will anyone else endorse your own morbid existence? Anyone else give you the time of day?'

'Get lost.' But he waddles after me, as I hurry down Eleventh, in the wake of Vincent's exhaust. A thousand other cars hooting, burping, retching, wrenching down the avenue. The backside of the city, glimpsed as the street blocks flash by: 49th, 47th, 45th, 44th Street. I turn down 42nd, towards the bare back of the New York Times, the crumbling towers of Times Square. To my right the needle of the Empire State, and further Downtown, lost in fog, the twin chopped-off peaks of the World Trade Center. No sign of King Kong, with or without giant penis. Or of Frog-In-My-Throat, meditating on Skinnerism, or Godzilla, on the loose. Just the usual down and outs, hawkers, spitters, and this mad fucking chicken.

'You need my help here, Danny boy. Years of experience, in the shamus shmeerkez. Philip Marlowe of the Bay Area. Who put the Zipper Murderer behind bars? Who tied up the Potrero Hill Strangler? Who nabbed the Nob Hill Rapist? Face it, kiddo, it's an art. You either got it or you ain't.'

'Free chicken soup!' I called out. 'Bring your own cleavers! Pulkes and white meat on the house!' Nobody even turned a hair.

I walked up, across 10th and 9th, towards the Central Core, the gaping neon incisors on either side, advertising motorcycle movies, soft core, the worst turkeys in town, Z features by Irving Klotskashes. THE HILLS HAVE EYES. THE RATS ARE COMING. THE VAMPIRE HOOKERS. DRIVE IN MASSACRE. THE SILENT SCREAM. Touts try to entice me, even at this pre-noon hour, into the Live Acts and Peep Shows. Check it out. Triple X, quadruple Z, quintuple Yecch. Even the ubiquitous leaflets for Madame Clara –

ARE YOU LONELY? ARE YOU FRUSTRATED? LET MADAME X SEE, SOOTHE ALL.

147

Ach. At the corner of Eighth, lightning sheers the sky. A clap of thunder precedes a sudden downpour. New touts emerge from their holes, offering umbrellas for a dollar, as if they had been frozen in bottles, ready for this very moment. The sky is sort of deep purplish red. The thundercracks burst right above. Cars swerve upon the flooded road and vanish, as if swallowed by the ventilation shafts. Pedestrians disappear, each with his newly-bought umbrella. I stand at the deserted junction of Times Square, Number One, looking up Seventh and Broadway. Discount shops, topless bars, the hard core movie houses, triple bills of XXX delights. The man eternally blowing the Winston smoke ring is now gone, replaced by Japanese slush. Messages, news flickering round the Times building, barely visible in the flood. The neon ripple forming odd mirages on my eyeballs.

BEN TISHMAN SAYS: DON'T FRET DANNY, EVERYTHING IS UNDER CONTROL – FRESH UFO SIGHTINGS IN NEW JERSEY – VINCE EPIGLOTIS SAYS: GET LOST . . .

At least the giant chicken, with its crushed fedora, has stopped following me. I duck into a souvlaki stall. There are rows of stools along an L-shaped counter. I sit down by a small dumpy man. A swarthy youth with Yasser Arafat chin growth approaches me and says 'Yes, sir.' 'One medium souvlaki,' I say, 'without hot sauce.' The dumpy man turns towards me and exclaims.

'Hey! You are Mister Adam's cousin's friend. Remember me . . .?'

It is the angst hunter, Bagel Akram. The odds on such a coincidental meeting in a city of ten million souls at a random time and place are probably thirty-five quantillion to one. In other words, a sure thing.

'Oh yes . . . how're things on the East Side?'

'When I left it was all sunny. And now look at it. Is this not a compounding city?'

'Ah . . . it sure is.'

'This is my friend Nabih, who works here. Nabih comes from a small village in the hills not far from Haifa. Now look at him, like me, in this massive city. It is a very strange exile.'

'Onions? Pickles?' said Nabih. I waved assent. He piled them on.

'You know,' said Akram, unfurling a notebook with pages thickened by his tight scrawl, 'there are both Arab and Israeli kebab and falafel stores in the city in almost equal numbers. But the Israelis, wishing to differentiate, invented a new format, the falafel and pizza store. There are two hundred fifty thousand of them, in the five boroughs.'

'Pizza stores?' I marvelled.

'No. Israelis. Many of these places are fronts for the Jewish Defence League and the Israeli Secret Service. It is a known fact. You would not believe what happens behind the scenes.' He moved closer to me, conspiratorily. 'Do you know, I have been doing research. I have a friend in a Downtown police precedent. He tells me there are statistics for the large number of people who disappear every month in these Israeli falafel and pizza stores. It is quite a compounding figure. None of them is ever seen or heard of again. But I know what is happening.'

'They kidnap them, put them in crates and take them to Israel,' I said, 'to beef up their flagging population, which is so depleted by emigrés who open falafel stores.'

They both looked at me with worried eyes. 'You are in serious danger,' Akram said, solicitously. 'You are a man who knows too much.'

The rain has stopped by the time I leave the souvlaki store, the four exiled eyes boring into my back. I walked across the Avenue of the Americas towards Bryant Park, where I sat gingerly on a soaking wooden bench. The loose joint vendors were out of their rain bunkers like rabbits who know carrots are in season. It was a nice warped thought to add to the options: Ben Tishman abducted by the desperate Renascent Hebrews, currently ekeing out his life pulling cabbages out of the ground of a collective farm, scourged with whips made out of holy phylacteries. Take that, reluctant Zionist swine! Down, among the sacred dung beetles of the land of milk and honey!

Beam me up, Scottie. My brain is congealing. My Time on this Earth draws to a close. All the avenues of investigation appear to be fading out one by one, as the harshness of real-life absurdity and mangled language intervenes. A pretty girl in an old mackintosh hands me a leaflet. 'I already gave,' I say, but she disappears. It says:

> Festival of Small Presses. Bryant Park. Saturday–Sunday, 14–15th March. More Than Fifty Independent Publishers & Small Presses Will Be Represented. Sponsored by ARCHAEOS MAGAZINE, THE PARMESAN REVIEW and the Association of Independent Publications. Small Is Beautiful. Come One Come All! Special Booths for Genre Magazines – Crime, Westerns, Science-Fiction, Sponsored by THE LARAMIE PRESS and JAKE AKIMBO'S MAGAZINE.

A convention, no less, of mine sworn enemies! Rudolph Fihser, Mad Bomber, Where Art Thou Now?? Drops of rain fall from the tree above me on to the leaflet. I carefully wipe it, fold it and proceed. A gathering of the clans that cannot be gainsaid. A voice, somewhere, perhaps, is calling . . . Is that Akram, darting behind the trunk of a tree there, following me from the souvlaki store? Or was there perhaps a trace of feathers? . . .

Return 'home'. The 'penthouse' time warp, always waiting. A whole afternoon to pass before I can phone Ellie. Not that

I can lift her spirits any. There's a real problem out there. Some genuine monkey business. Compounding falafel. Vince Epiglotis and the Mad Bomber. And Little Nel, chomping on her stogie. That shuts me out of Expedition Films.

When in doubt, escape, inwards. Always have a man come through the swing doors of your brain with an idea in his hand . . . the *Laramie Press*? I did try one story for them. Tishman encouraged a spate of 'genre' efforts. I sent them this rather offbeat western, somewhat in the style of the earlier hillbilly feature, 'I Divorced a Monster,' etc. I know I have it somewhere, at the bottom of my suitcase. It was called –

BUFFALO BALLS FROM WICHITA FALLS

Shore, you young whippersnappers kin scoff 'n' sneer but that won't change the goshdarned truth, an' that's a fact, so thar!

In them days I was a young buck, bushy tailed an' rarin' fer trouble. They called me the Toyota Kid, an' ain't nobody west o' the Mississippi nor south o' the Rockies but were sure to know ma name. Ma handsome young puss were displayed in every Sheriff an' Marshal's office from Yuba City t' Okee-chobee. But -

Oh God. I could hear that text dying in the office of the *Laramie Press* like Tweety Pie in a convention of Sylvesters . . . My deathless prose, falling like tin tacks . . . their cast steel noses tethered to the daily grindstone of the mun-dane . . .

– Yessirree, Dead Dick Gulch was one hell of an ornery town . . .

No, this will not do at all. It was good while it lasted, but the milk sours when it's left out on the stoop too long. Where is that jwah–de–vivray now? The joy discovered, alone in Tishman's 'penthouse', when it still held its romance, on my first stay within it, summer of '77 . . . He absent on long hauls to the Bronx, to sojourn with a group of ex-nuns who still worshipped the Pope but were not averse to delights of the flesh. It was another of his gorgeous blondes, Elena, I now recall, he had a thing for girls whose names began with E. He was the only sane man I knew who had seen all the Emmanuelle films, from white to black, from A to Z. In fact, Tishman came close to being the only sane person I had ever come across since 1968, period. The living proof of possible survival. And he was madder'n'a coot anyday . . .

– 'Respect fer the law . . . the very maidenhead o'liberty! Why I'd no more countenance wrong doin' an' chicanery than I'd beat ma own mother to death with an iron bar . . . Poor mother . . . she could lick the twenty best men in the territory, drunk or sober . . . I remember her rhubarb tarts pertikerlarly well . . .'

Yea. Bash, bash, bash on the battered keys of Tishman's old Remington typewriter. Churning out the entire oeuvre. 'Drekula.' 'The Thing in the Bog.' 'The Globble Village.' 'The Screaming Biscuit Tin Strikes Again.' 'The Yoke of the Egg.' 'Winnie the Poof.' 'I Divorced a Monster from Outer Space.' 'Buffalo Balls.' 'The Oi Vei Machine.' 'Computer Whx/5 Goes Apeshit.' 'Battle Shriek.' 'Haywire-Five-O.' 'Frog-in-my-Throat.' 'Your Monkey's Shmuck is in my Beard.' 'I Was Godzilla's Mother-in-Law.' 'The Story of E.' And of course, that doomed opus, 'Beyond the Planet of Fuck.' I intended it as straight porn. But, as usual, it turned into something else. The original spinoffs like the late 'Spaceport '99'. Requiescat in pace, old friends. If each man kills the thing he loves, I ought to exterminate the lot of them. Instead, they are preserved, like pickled gherkins. PROTO-

COLS, FOUND IN A PICKLE JAR. Now there's another title to ponder . . .

Love. It's an old wives' tale. I don't think I have had the pleasure. The agony, yes, but where's that ecstasy everyone seems to be talking about? Ellie . . . Now that's just another romance, a fantasy of Danny's escape lines . . . I am simply presenting myself as a proxy for Tishman. I am sorry for her. I envy them both. Fucking, yes, a fair amount of that. Or unfair, if one recalls the slings and arrows of politically zealous Martha . . . always hot to Trot, but not quite in the way one hoped for . . . Perhaps I should put an end to it all. Tie all my manuscripts round me, soak the lot in petrol, and leap off the 'penthouse' terrace, merrily ablaze. *Morituri te salutant!* Get lost, sucker, comes the mob's response. The rain alone would put me out by the seventh floor, leaving my prose and ballads fluttering –

I knew a man, a certain man,
Who came from Wichita Falls,
He was a gunplay artisan
An' his name was Buffalo Balls.

> Ohhhh Buffalo Balls from Wichita Falls,
> He'd run from no one an' he'd shun no brawls,
> But he'd shoot nobody if he had no call
> Ohh, he stood so steady an' he walked so tall . . .

When he came in an' threw me a glance,
Ah missed all ma curtain calls.
Ah could see quite clearly ba the cut of his pants
That this was Buffalo Balls . . .

Au secours! Au secours! Au secours!

The phone rings. I am saved by the bell. It is Jack Pritchard, the Honest Capitalist from the eleventh floor, below.

'Anything from Tishman?'

'No.'

'Let's go eat.'

We steamed in the Manhattan Restaurant, on Broadway, just down from the H & H Bagel Shop. The bustle of the early evening crowds. Car honks. Buses, cabs, transport trucks, thrusting up and downtown.

'Well, we can scrub one theory,' he informs me, ordering just a coffee and english. 'Remember the "flying saucer" Ben said he saw over the Natural History Museum?'

'Who can forget such a visitation?'

'Well, anybody with half a brain. I checked it out. There were several sightings. But it turns out some advertising company was flying a small Cessna kitted out with circling lights. They were supposed to be dragging a sign for some new nightclub, but it dropped off over the park. The Galaxy Club. Get it? Several people were taken in. One man went beserk in the Zoo and attacked an owl.'

'Wha'd'you say.'

'I say that's life. No mystery. Just a mundane cock-up.'

I ordered a cheeseburger. Anything more unusual might destroy me. Cause me to disappear in a puff of green smoke. The waitress asked: 'How's your friend, Ben?'

'He has gone AWOL,' says Pritchard, 'absent without leave. But we've established he has not been kidnapped by spacemen.'

'Well, that's something at least,' she says, moving on a table.

'OK. Give me a mundane explanation for this one.' I told him the tale of the Mad Bomber, the 50th Street fire, Vince Epiglotis, toilet pipes and all. Not omitting the strange gadget Tishman left with much hoo-hah on Waitress Paula's shelf, but keeping stum on the San Francisco chicken.

'You know Ben would do anything to impress a girl,' says Pritchard. 'Gadgets from outer space are small beer. You get

154

offered things like that on every street corner. The city's full of them. It's in vogue. I've never met Vince Epiglotis. His name sounds like throat gargle. With such a heritage anything could happen. Of course, it does sound like there is a remote possibility organised crime could be in on this. That would not be good news.'

'The toilet pipes? What about the toilet pipes?' I press him.

'Everyone has their own kinks.'

One cannot argue with an aspiring Capitalist, a man who tries to sell Nigerian biros to Ceylon and Dutch bottlecaps to Costa Rica, all over a telex machine installed in his broom cupboard.

'Things are looking up, nevertheless,' he says, over an english muffin (one seldom sees one of these strange objects in England, they are generally Yankee). 'There is apparently a strong call for coat hangers in Madagascar. They've had a rash of bad winters.'

'And it so happens you are neck deep in the critters.'

'That's right. It's a marriage made in heaven.'

It's a good thing I haven't mentioned a chicken with a bag of greasy french fries is after me. Not to speak of the latest Palestinian theory concerning Israeli falafel and pizza stores. There remains nothing but an abject retreat back to the womb in the cold grey Manhattan sky, dropping Pritchard off on the eleventh floor and rising alone in the lift to the hum of another rejected stanza of the Ballad of Buffalo Balls (sung by the Grand Dame o' Bourbon Street, Flower Belle Lee, in the Last Chancre Saloon):

When ah grew up, an' started to dance,
Ah met with all sorts o' molls,
They all said, Flower, you won't know romance
Till you meet with Buffalo Balls.

Ohhhh Buffalo Balls from Wichita Falls,
He'd run from no one an' he'd shun no brawls,
But he'd shoot nobody if he had no call
Ohh, he stood so steady an' he walked so tall . . .

Ah. Them was the days. Innocence, Danny Boy, That's Entertainment. Back o' the bus, soul brother. Where is it all gone now? That sense of surreal freedom? Tishman filming plastic steakburgers in drug-sodden SoHo lofts? Chelsea Girls? Now we're left with Ellie, rehearsing *Swan Lake* or Rigatoni or Cannelloni or whatever they call those opii, those overblown sperm whales of kulture . . . Avast, the hwite hweal . . . ! I nail up this doubloon, me hearties! I stomp up and down, on my wooden leg all night, striking fear into incipient Ishmaels. Call Me Fishmeal . . . another title? MOBY'S DICK. OMO. TYPO. Grand masterpieces of the oeuvre. KNUCKLEBERRY THIN. TOM SCHNORRER. A CONNECTICUT HANKIE IN KING ARTHUR'S COAT. PASTRAMO. NSU. FOR WHOM THE BALLS TELL. THE OLD MAN AND HIS PEE. AN AMERICAN SCREAM. Ah, the Masters, fondled, feted, asslicked to the grave. *Te salutant!* Danny H— in the dumps, salutes you! Vengeance is mine, saith the Lord! Out of the grimy french windows of my Pequod, I poke my rusty harpoons. A mere scratch, and blood poisoning will do the rest. What else is left, but the ultimate absurdity of unobserved Creation? Will the phone ring again? Will the landlord call, waving his rentbook? Will the heating ducts ever get up steam? Will Ben Tishman, or Danny H— for that matter, ever be seen or heard of again? Watch this space for new developments!

I flex my fingers at the keys:

Hackula

1

It always struck at night.

Take for instance Paul Tallow, world renowned Nobel Prize Winner, who had only just published his latest pièce de résistance – *To Petah Tikva and Back* – to glowing and reverent reviews. Imagine the scene: there he sits, tapping away at his typewriter, never at peace, always groping for new literary frontiers, never resting upon his well-deserved laurels, when – Shazam! it hits him. His fingers jam on the keys, he stops short in mid-sentence, goes rigid, stiffens, rolls his head wildly, begins to dribble and drool on the unfinished page. Then, gasping and retching, he staggers into the bedroom, twitches the bedclothes off his half asleep wife and stutters out:

'Mildred! it's finished! no words . . . no words . . . it's all gone . . . gone . . . my brain . . . !' And he drops to his knees and sobs pitiably, rending the winter downy cover in his inconsolable grief.

Imagine Karl Burns, New York's foremost literary critic, the man who could make or break any aspiring young writer and many established reputations, twiddling his goatee uneasily and pulling at his earring as the dressing gowned trembling figure of the once great Tallow is trundled off on a trolley down a hospital corridor by anonymous young men in white.

'How long can this last?' he appeals to Fay Chaffee, Tallow's ex-agent, standing chalk faced at his side.

159

'Froth, Bashful-Stinger, Pippa Dong and now Tallow, snuffed out in the twinkle of an eye, every idea, every simile and metonym, every pattern of syntax and grammar, snatched out of their minds as if by some malignant force! Four unconnected writers, living in different parts of the city, each within a week of the other. It's impossible, strictly impossible!'

Take a look at the impossible city. Concentrate on its core, the island of Manhattan, that grimy modern enigma bought for $24 from the Indians in 1626, reined into the mainland by fifteen spiderweb bridges and four tunnels pushing underground, along which shellshocked guestworkers dash in vehicled hordes at day's end to the shelter of open parts, leaving behind the several millions who live, eat, fuck and bed in the cavernous towers. Fly above it, gaze down at the gleaming skyscraper centre, the rotten edges crumbling into the dank and putrescent waters on either flank, the poor besieged by the rot of the city, the rich besieged by the poor. In between them the 'artists' scurry about, playwrights, film-makers, musicians, writers, et al, repelled and attracted by both ends of the spectrum, dreaming with equal passion of prestigious success or a death of neo-tubercular grandeur. And spare a twinge for the vast army of secretaries, clerks, bus and cab drivers, shop workers and owners and so forth who, like everywhere else, are merely content to survive, ducking and bobbing to avoid the sparks struck by the warring social poles.

And then, the journalists. The recording hacks. The rats, scampering in the walls of the decayed mansion. Like, for example, yours truly.

Let me introduce myself. My name is Jake Mishkin. My father, perceiving the twin sons who squirmed out of my poor mother's loins, one smooth and saintly, the other hairy and gross, wished to call upon us the cosmic joke of naming us Jacob and Esau. But my mother kicked up an unholy fuss with the result that the whole idea was turned round, Esau dropped in favour of Benjamin, and I, the red-haired nomadic one, ended up as Jay, Jake or Jacob. Thus, I moved about, first in my playpen, then around the US, then a little trotting around the globe, while my brother Ben stayed to tend his flocks in the city, and became involved in arts and crafts. Me, I became a journalist of no mean repute. A Pulitzer Prize winner. No shit. This I earned by my series of articles exposing Medicare frauds in the City. You know the game – you step into the quack's clinic with a mild headache, you come out laden with pills prescribed for athlete's foot, diarrhoea, gonorrhoea, anaemia, high blood pressure, low blood pressure, angina, anthrax, you name it, then they bill the City accordingly. And to cap it, all the pills and lotions are bogus. Oh, it's a fair old scam. After that I surpassed myself, researching another series on the down and outs of Times Square. The bums, the muggers, pushers, pimps, whores, hustlers, junkies, priests and do-gooders. It netted me a broken arm and twenty-four stitches. But circulation showed a definite upcurve. So –

'You are the man,' said Don Krankman, sub-editor of the *Post*, his cracked shoes poked in my face from his desk, 'to track down and extract the tale of whoever, whatever it is draining the faculties of our finest prose writers. I do not fear for your own safety. Plagiarists seem exempt. The Thing goes for originals only.'

'Oh yeah,' says I, 'wait and see. You might find yourself suddenly gagging at the door of Boss Legree's office, struck down at the brink of a deadline.'

'Speed the day,' he replied, 'I shall take early retirement, vamoose to the mountains, and live off raw fish and wild berries.'

'And how about the Mad Bomber story?' This was an assignment I was just getting the measure of. A celebrity of the late Forties, having served his life sentence for sabotaging Ma Bell's installations in retaliation for an unfair telephone bill, the old coot appeared to have disappeared from his East Side fleahole, amid rumours that he had in fact taken the rap for crimes committed by someone else . . .

'Forget it,' said Krankman. 'I shall put Tom Knish on the job.'

'The hell,' I said. 'Tom Knish couldn't find a rabbit in the rutting season. He is practically Elmer Fudd.'

'Clear off, Doc,' he said. 'Find the Mind Stealer. And give him my mother-in-law's address.'

'What makes you suppose,' I asked, 'that there is a single person responsible, with some sort of psionic power, I presume, in this world of electrobionic scoopers, CIA and KGB dirty tricks, alien probes from outer space and all that jazz?'

'This is the post-Watergate age,' said he, 'Jimmy Carter. Détente. Peace and Apathy. Zzzzzzzz. The public's not into Soviet secret mind rays these days, or diabolical Chinese Fu Manchulah. Perhaps those joys will return, but for the moment it is not the tale of foreign invasion or even the perfidy of our own government that will frighten stiff the American people and boost our ailing circulation, but rather the fear of the lone chuckling fruitcake, imbued with terrifying unexplained powers, casting down the high and mighty of belles-lettres with his foul telepathic blows, reducing celebrities overnight to fellow shufflers in gloom-laden dole queues. Go forth, Mishkin, and find me this new American hero, this leveller, this bell ringer of the doom of our moribund "higher" culture. Is he a heroin fiend scraping in the grime of an ashcan? A petulant idiot savant schoolboy? A mad scientist, fooling with death rays in Brooklyn? Or a critic – there's a good lead – or even a writer him or herself, green with envy, nursing dreams of revenge, perhaps even one of the stricken, acting the victim as camouflage? I don't have to tell you to suspect everyone! Now between you and me, Mishkin, I think it's baloney, just a naturally infectious psychosis. Writers are all crazy anyhow. Do you get my drift? But that's not copy, that's old print shavings. I want my perpetrator – my lone, raving loonie! Get out thar, Mishkin, and don't dare come back without our man lassooed to your spurs!'

'To hear is but to throw up, oh Bwana,' I told him. '*Morituri te salutant*. Love and kisses.'

I have not told my sub-editor, but his assignment has for me a certain piquant personal angle. I have, for several years, secretly spent my spare time, holed out in my East 50s pied-à-terre, penning my own humble attemps at the lit shtik and sending them off under an assumed name. Most of the time I called myself Danny Hohenlohe, but occasionally I adopted a more vernacular handle, such as Zack Armitage, or Pedro Rojas. I even tried the feminist magazine, *Aphra*, once, under the label Maria Papadopoulos. But the Pulitzer Prize by another name smells as rotting cowdung. The forces of Kulture always spurned me. Was there now a sweet come-uppance? . . .

The slaughter continues. Jon Downhill, Lou Cleaver, French Postman and Kathleen Zeus succumbed in quick succession. Then the plague began to spread further. Imagine the scene: a sunny Sunday morning. Cornelius ('Cracker') O'Shea, the city's top television comedy scriptwright, wakes with a start, sweat covered and mumbling in helpless terror, every wisecrack, witticism, chochmeh and bon mot wrenched out in slumber, every vestige of wit whisked away. He shrieks, leaps out of his bed, batters his wife's brains in with his latest Emmy, and jumps out of the window to his doom twenty-five flights below.

Now this is getting a little close to home. They had set up a special ward, in Bellevue, for the victims, who could not be cared for domestically and couldn't afford to be shut away in upstate arboreums. Not everyone was affected totally, as the Effect spread to minor talents. Two poets, Chosen of *The Parmesan Review*, for example, though smit, simply continued their normal life – signing on at the Welfare office, spurning shaves or baths, boozing and shooting up at night in bars or in the stairways of fleapit hotels. They just ceased verbal output, which made little difference, as no one had ever heard of them anyway. Another writer of forty-five bestsellers simply took off and vanished on the prizefighting circuit, his secret ambition forced on him by circumstance. Still, fifteen miserable souls shuffled morosely in Bellevue, Ward 13B, in faded blue dressing gowns, settling only to play leaden games of gin rummy on a little plastic-topped table.

'There is some hope,' Doctor Houseman explained to me, 'while they are groping for the concept of trumps. A vestigial interest, a surviving spark perhaps, of some creative endeavour. But for most the creative part of the brain has been scooped out, effectively vacuum cleaned. What's left is like fluff obstinately stuck in a carpet, but not of much apparent use. They have reverted to their original, pre-creative pattern, be that goodnatured, petulant, or destructive. Some are like five-year-olds, two have regressed to three months and are on the bottle. Three are fed intravenously, two are in catatonia, and one, the poor soul, has returned to the womb, thrashing mildly about, now and again, in a peculiarly fish-like demeanour.'

2

I went to work with some trepidation, feeling an ominous force closing in. Determined to leave no stone unturned, I began with the real pits, the IRT underpass of Times Square subway station, where I found Conway Stebbins, my favourite undercover cop, exposing himself to the passers by. Total immersion was his forte. He had a trim beard and hair tied in rastafarian dreadlocks, blue *dashiqi* and sandals, brass bangles on both arms, and a long dutch pipe hanging sideways, its stem wet with his spittle. His penis, the *dashiqi* was flicked up to reveal, was rove with a ring through the foreskin.

'Where the cops?' he whispered to me as I drew up, pretending to look for a lost coin. 'Where the motherfuckin' cops today, man? I got to be busted. I ain't been busted all week. The Chapter brothers are gettin' fuckin' suspicious.'

'I can arrange your arrest,' I said, 'but I want some information. About these writers who are being knocked off like ninepins. What's on the grapevine, Stebbins?'

'Don't use that name!' he screeched softly, 'I am Haile Mengistu Sion Mariam down here . . . There ain't much around but rumours. A Pentagon plot. A nerve gas gone wrong. Biowarfare. The Jaguars say it's a fallin' out between the boojwah innligenzia an' the military-industrial combine. The Farajuli Moslems say it's God's final vengeance on the Jews. If you ask me they're all jackin' off. There are no hard facts, no leads to go on. They all crazy anyhow, ain't they, these Jew scribblers? Hey, move on, Jake, do me a favour – I see a nice fat policeman a-moseyin' this way . . . gwan, scram, do a buddy a good turn . . .'

I passed him a portrait of Lincoln and walked off down the tunnel, hearing the crack, as I rounded the corner, of the cop's nightstick connecting to Stebbins' head and the latter's happy cry of pain.

He was right. There were no true leads down there. I had to cut through, and turn my trump card. This was clearly a case for my deepest throat, Van Gardner, née Ivan Gargarin. He was one of that crop of Fifties defectors whose only hope to escape KGB retribution was to accept a menial life job with the opposition, and do the bidding of Langley, Virginia. He fed me tidbits, now and again, just to be on the good side of the Free Press, you never know which way the wind might blow. I always figured he was either telling me the truth, or selling me a pup to take me off a certain trail, which was also useful to know. He was a small nervous man who looked like a bankrupt Polish grocer. This was due to his job: he was in charge of signing out ordnance to agents going on field duty, you know the sort of stuff – collapsible bazookas, poison dart guns, triple-strength durex, prepared packs of contents-of-typical-Russian-wallet, cyanide pills, depilatories for bearded revolutionary leaders, reinforced plastic testicle-protectors, LSD sprays, artificial foreskin for use by Jewish agents in Arab countries, and the usual mini-cameras and electronic bugs and doo-dahs. This gave Ivan an insight into ongoing operations way beyond his own Stage Three rating.

We met in Bloomingdales' lingerie department, conversing while pretending to browse through brassières.

He said: 'It is not a Company Operation unless,' he hesitated, 'it is the Others . . .' he has made this hint in the past but never yields beyond that, 'the Gamesmen have been on to it, trying to plot a pattern. But the computers yield nothing but what you know. There is no evidence of electromagnetic or microwave action by either the Soviets, the Chinese, the French, the British or the Israelis. Paraphysics have seized on the issue but we cannot depend on them. Last year they proposed raising Jesus in Madison Square Garden to lead a new anticommunist Crusade. All those chaps are now under constant surveillance, armed guards, male nurses, drips, catheters. Not to speak of the UFO Division, please don't ask . . .'

'I won't ask, Ivan. But does no one have an inkling? A theory?'

'Writers!' Ivan shrugged. 'Who knows what goes on in there? You will note it's only New York hit so far. Perhaps it is the air, like the summer smog of a million automobiles, trapped by the tall buildings. Perhaps it's the same with people's thoughts, the vibrations of their souls, rising, trying to escape in the air, but they cannot, they sink back, all the fears, hates, frustrations, falling like flies looking for a carcase. Certain people, particularly attuned to sickness of mind and

166

depredation, the fly finds them, it dives, presto – like a vampire!'

'Why only writers? Why now?'

'Who knows? Accumulation past tolerance. It might spread on, to artists of all kinds. Students of the humanities, all those with a sensitivity to the general miasma, social workers, policemen. Who knows, in the end perhaps no one will remain untouched but a few politicians, publishers, semiologists and of course, some journalists.'

'Thank you, Ivan. You fill me with hope.'

'I do my best, Jacob. I wish to offend no one. It is, of course, just a theory.'

'All right, you two lovebirds.' A large, jowly store detective approached us. 'Time to make your purchases. Cash desk over there.'

'We have decided not to purchase,' said Ivan.

'Fuck off then,' the store cop said amiably. We obediently filed off towards the escalator. 'Damn faggots,' I heard him mutter behind us as he called a clerk over, 'Delaney, check this merchandise for jissum. You'd be amazed what them preverts get up to.'

3

But a strange feeling of eager anticipation grabbed me as I made my way on the first really bright weekend of the spring, the Ides of March, to the Festival of Small Presses in Bryant Park, on West 42nd and Sixth. I even avoided my favourite hard core shop, a block behind, which was surely surviving the mind-blitz.

'OK gennelmen, time to pick up them magazines!' What sweet music to the ears . . . ('The practice of fellatio among Egyptian and Phoenician women has been credited with the invention of lipstick. The women of the day used paints on their lips to advertise their speciality . . . when Julius Ceasar first pushed into Egypt his sexual tastes were primarily oral. He was said to perform either cunnilingus or fellatio with equal fervor. As a dictator he could undulge in all forms of lovemaking without fearing censure . . .' Yea! Give 'em hell, Julie!) The Small Presses are in a large tent erected at the back of the New York Public Library. An air of some trepidation about the small stalls, as if people are walking about with time bombs in their underpants, but can't defuse them in public. I know that one of my enemies, Al J– of *The Parmesan Review*, has already gone with the wind, stricken in Bellevue, amid the crowded wards, which now held a hundred and forty victims. Some luminaries had already taken the logical step of evacuating the city. Loading their trunks of china and old manuscripts, they filled the concourses of Penn and Grand Central, en route to the safety of the Catskills. But the fool-hardy still remained.

I caught sight of him, behind the wooden desks which bordered the booth of the Science Fiction titles. There was no mistaking that large, ebullient figure, stalwart of Breakfast TV and afternoon science shows. Author of *I Turbot, Naked Moons, The Starlike Crust, No Room On Earth, The End of Fraternity, Feeble in the Sky* and *The Bicentennial Ham*, not to speak of the *Substratum* trilogy. The man who had written me, when I had foolhardily sent him a story under my own name: 'I'm Jake, and you're Jake, but this story ain't jake.' The one and only Jacob Akimbo. It was said he could complete a novel in three days, and edit twelve anthologies on a weekend. So what was he doing here, swanning with the proletariat, going 'Ho,ho,ho!' and swilling a paper cup of red wine? I recognized a literary agent, fawning at his trouser leg, whom I had encountered some months before, at a terrace party I had attended incognito. I had been invited by a friend who wrote for a Yiddish newspaper which nobody under the age of ninety read, but who also, under

168

a closely guarded alias, which everyone knew, wrote crime novels and space adventures. 'Here, meet Glib Gormenghast,' he pushed me at this klutz, who had managed to spill beer down his neckbone. 'Danny,' he was using my normal nom-de-plume, 'writes good S-F, but with humour . . . you know humour – the stuff that makes you go ha, ha, ha . . .'

'The bottom has fallen out of humour,' said the rat. 'The market is a real bear for funnies. What tickles you pink stinks to the other guy.' Then he slipped on his beer can and had to be hauled off and placed inside, on a plastic bin liner.

Now the man ogles the great guru of the future, holding back a small army of devotees waving autograph books and manuscripts. Other dainty people mince and twitch about the modest desks of such grand successes as THE GREENWICH VILLAGE FIGLEAF and THE SOHO BACCHANAL. I'll give 'em back canal . . . I press forward, fumbling in my pocket woefully for any miraculous visitation of a cosh, or Gatling gun. But my great moment is pre-empted, as I place my hand on the buttocks of a lady with a maroon haircut, causing her to displace twelve steps backwards, and reach out to grab the scrawny gizzard of the gormless Gormenghast, for suddenly, without any trace of a warning, in mid wine gulp and guffaw, the Great Man arches up, stiffens, emitting a terrible choked-off squeal. His wine cup crushed in his muscular hand, spraying all with dark red goo. His eyes glaze, the pupils disappearing up, showing the whites flecked with veins. His forehead literally bulges, his grey hair literally stands on end. Foam gushes at his lips. His fingers reach out, clawlike. He falls, like a great, cracked pillar. The entire temple goes bananas.

'It's the Plague! He's got it!' cries of terror pierce the close air of the tent. Art lovers clutch their handbags, scatter, running screaming towards the open park. They crash through the cloth flanks of the tent, rending it with fingernails, scissors.

Like rats fleeing the sinking ship, they spill out of the enclosed place of doom, leaving me alone with Jake Akimbo, frothing and kicking on the ground. I did not win the Pulitzer Prize for nothing. I bend my lips towards his ear.

'Can you hear me, Jacob Akimbo? Do you hear these words? This is the other Jake, the Jake that ain't jake? Remember? Remember Danny Hohenlohe?'

'Aaarg . . . barg . . . garg . . .' was all the Great Man could emit, eyes thrashing.

'What does it feel like, having your mind plucked out?' I asked, enunciating firmly. 'The three million readers of the *Daily Post* demand an answer. The public has the right to know.'

'Grrg . . . mrrg . . . trrggg . . .' frothed the Guru of the Future.

The ambulance men had arrived.

'This man is in bad shape,' I told them, standing away from the pitiable human shell, wiped clean of prognostications. 'Take him away, chirurgeons.'

I walked away from the scene of destruction, sloshing about with mixed feelings.

4

What is New York without its starving writers, jacking off in their lofts and garrets, subsisting on bagels and Entenmann's Donuts while hammering away at the Great Manhattan Novel, dreaming of Guggenheim Fellowships, gazing with bilious envy at the portraits of Knut Fornicutt and Flipper Froth from the back jackets of coffee-stained paperbacks?

I confess I was stumped. It was time to consult the more sensitive part, as it were, of my ego. My runaway id, in other words, or to put it another way, my twin brother Ben.

The problem was, I had not seen Ben for three years.

Although we both live in the city, our paths had diverged, since I plied my twin conceits of exposé and short stories, while he bought himself a 16mm movie camera and joined a studio of avant-garde deadbeats in SoHo. I think they alternated between 'alternative' or 'underground' abstract films, and long Warhol-like epics of Bowery bums relating their life stories. In theory we should have interfaced somewhere along the line, but in fact we moved on separate planes. I slummed, but I always had my swank bachelor's pad to retreat to on East 50th and 3rd Avenue. My brother Ben lived among his people. To root him out, I would have to dig deep.

Fortunately there remained a link, through my girl friend, the one and only honeypie, Ellie. As a practitioner of modern and classical dance, she once helped out Benjamin as a 'living sculpture' for some crack-brained celluloid folly. It was by this encounter that we met, then parted, then intersected again. Ellie lives on the more raucous West side of town. We maintain our separate lives and apartments. It suits both of us, since a disastrous early marriage for Ellie, and my own misfortunes with Shady Gertie, an ex-courier and street activist of the Socialist Workers of the World, a small group born and terminated in the Bronx. I was a little worried about Ellie, re Ivan Gagarin's theory of the vulnerability of all sensitives. For one has to hand it to my beloved, she feels the slings and arrows of everyone's outrageous fortune. But she sounded sane, if subdued, on the phone.

'I don't know about Ben,' she said, hesitantly. 'He seems to have dropped out of sight. You don't think something can have happened to him?'

'He hasn't been writing prose?' I said, alarmed.

'Not that I know. It's still the art movies. But I'll make a few calls and ask around.'

'How about a movie tomorrow night?' I said.

'OK. Maybe I'll have something by then.'

Cast thy bread upon the waters, and thou shalt get soggy

171

bread. The news she brought me was not encouraging, from a fraternal point of view. We sat at a Bagel Nosh, nursing hot chocolates, waiting for the hour of glamour to dawn. An apt choice, *One Flew Over The Cuckoo's Nest*, at the 57th Street Playhouse.

'Ben's been doing some work at a Times Square cutting room,' she said, 'for a man called Vincent Epiglotis. They produce exploitation films, cheap thrillers, horror, and, it seems, a little hard core. My friend, who was an editor there till last year, said they were shooting some biographical picture about a guy they call the Mad Bomber. Ben did some camerawork on that picture. But she hasn't heard from him since.'

'These are not good vibrations,' I said. I am wont, now and again, to slip into long deceased argot. 'I have been researching the Mad Bomber, a man named Rudolph Fihser. He served a life sentence, it appears, for crimes he did not commit. Rumour has it a rival telephone company conducted the campaign against AT&T, framing Fihser for the bombs he did not in fact plant. But why has he kept silent for thirty years? Vincent Epiglotis? With a name like that no one can be up to any good. I shall look into it, and God damn Don Krankman.'

'For God's sake be careful, Jake honey,' she said.

'My life is charmed,' I reminded her. We saw the movie. The large mad Indian escaped at the end. The entire audience cheered. Several women wept uncontrollably. I made love to Ellie with reckless abandon that night, in her 79th Street penthouse. It seemed to me that the forces of entropy and perdition were closing in, relentlessly, one step at a time, and, when we were not looking, three steps.

5

I should not have allowed this to happen. Alienation from my own twin brother. It is not as if one can find another twin

172

brother in one's life. But have I lost him to the old or new plagues of the city? Can he have gone the way of Froth and Jake Akimbo? The blood very definitely curdles. I have invented a name for this unseen, unknown scourge, which has caught on, to the chagrin of Don Krankman, my sub-editor, who certainly hoped I would be reduced to gibberish, like all the other scribes of the city, babbling about mystic, satanic forces, harassing pregnant women who look anything like Mia Farrow, covering exorcisms performed in upper East 80s apartments, adopting their favourite witch-hunting tone while landlords inform on tenants seen working their typewriters, on the grounds that any writer remaining untouched must be an automatic suspect . . .

HACKULA! Hack the Rip-Off. Fear stalks the upper wards of the city. Every thought is suspect. Every concept a danger. An idea might have lethal consequences. Self-expression is no longer a harmless proposition, a way to pass the time or hoard shekels. We are reminded of the envied fate of the author or poet behind the iron curtain: imprisoned for a phrase, shot for a sentence. Entire oeuvres burnt for a paragraph. For the rulers quake and shake at each mark on paper issuing from an independent mind. Whereas here, at the font of freedom, who gives a monkey's fart, until now? . . . But will anyone notice, even now, when the whole schemoz is endangered, when intellectual life is suddenly ferkakt . . . Will any of us be missed? The acid test of our values is upon us . . . Now, in our gross, materialist society – and so on and so forth . . .

But is there an actual perpetrator? Is Hackula Man, or Miasma? Perhaps we must wait for some totally unknown little person to come forward with the manuscript of the century . . . an amalgam of all those styles and themes of the stricken big shots and high palookas . . . and Shazam! The lawforcers pounce! One can imagine the Trial of the Millennium: Bring in the accused! Hiram Nebisch, a pretzel bender in a bagel factory, dried snot caking his jacket sleeve, indicted

173

for turning New York's finest minds, and some less fine, into so many babbling baboons, for profit. Grand Thought Larceny One is the charge. The witnesses tumble into court, tripping over their falling soiled underpants. Demonstrators of the Socialist Workers of the World howl at the gates: Free Hiram Nebisch, Our Hero! Screw the writers! Ofay the Thought Police! My ex-wife, Martha, Shady Gertie, waving Trotsky's *Terrorism and Communism*, kicking a policeman in the onions. While ace scribe J. (Pulitzer Prize) Mishkin, exclusively interviews the defendant in the death cell at Sing Sing . . .

But I digress. I am nowhere near this consummation. I have my family affairs to sort out. Disguised as a City Sanitation Inspector, kitted out with a large moustache, browned features and matted black, greasy hair, I present myself at the cutting rooms of Expedition Films, at the office of Vincent Epiglotis. Time to resolve the affair of the talking toilet pipes and the ubiquitous french-fry trailing chicken. Not to speak of the Mad Bomber, whom Vincent had obviously spirited away to no respectable purpose . . .

'Your premises are infested,' I inform him. 'Roaches, dragging rolls of film, have been seen leaving the building.'

'Go ahead,' he says affably. 'Kill 'em all. Leave not one soul alive.'

'I shall begin with the toilets,' I state. 'I require to be left alone there for thirty minutes.'

'It's all yours,' says he. 'If anyone gets caught short, we shall hang our weenies out the windows.'

Thou shalt not suffer a witch to live. I push past the nymph Adelia at the reception desk, steadfastly ignoring her giant bazooms, which she points towards me like cruiser cannons, carrying my little bag of instruments down the corridor towards the men's convenience.

There is always a strange lack of silence in toilets, even

174

when one is not speaking to one's own turds. The maze of rusty, paint-peeling pipes, emerging mysteriously out of the floor, twisting this way and that, exiting either sideways and vanishing into compartment walls, or up into the higher spheres. Sludge and cleansing water grumbling and gurgling past one's efforts of evacuation. Not to speak of Puerto Rican messenger boys, making nasal offers offscreen. But everyone was kept away now. I was alone with the chugging and squelching of the pipes. Thumps, thuds and low pitched whines and droning circulating through the walls. It was almost like the creaking of a ship, reluctantly moored, and keen to set out to sea.

I looked around again to make sure no one was lurking, took my spanner out and banged on the pipes. Nothing happened. I banged again, trying to dredge up the dimmest memory of the ur-call of morse code: dot-dot-dot, dash-dash-dash, dot-dot-dot: S.O.S. Save Our Souls. From somewhere beyond the right-hand corner ceiling a faint but definite reply. I climbed on the toilet seat and examined the peeling plaster. There were the definite contours of a compartment or loft door. I tugged with my fingernails at the crack and it suddenly swung open, showering me with plaster and dust.

Luckily I had brought a torch. I shouldered my bag and swung its light around. Metal handles, fixed in the wall, led upward into a man-sized shaft. For the first time I regretted not having brought a weapon. But what is a weapon to the Pulitzer Prize?! I grabbed the handles and swung myself up into the ceiling. Rubble and plaster fell beneath me. All about me the guggling and chugging of hidden pipes echoed, laughing and chortling in the walls.

When I was a child I used to hide in cupboards. I used to imagine I had escaped from the world. I remember a large wardrobe filled with my father's musky jackets and suits and shirts. My mother, pathologically terrified of moths, filled the corners of the closet with mothballs. No moth would ever dare attack my father, in the broadest daylight or the darkest night. But I always used to imagine they clustered in the closet, forcing themselves to become immune. I was also, I have to shamefully confess, hiding from my brother, Ben. Like Greta Garbo, I vanted to be alone. But I had no suite in the Grand Hotel. A part of me, all my life, has looked for that cupboard. A psychoanalyst might have kittens with this. 'Your vomb image, it alvays hass mossballs. You haff ze problem mitt vomen, nein?' Jah. Vomen, Men, The Other terrifies me. So I have driven myself extra hard. To the extent of wooing polecats like Don Krankman. Now there's a sacrifice for a solipsist . . .

The shaft opened into a small storeroom, filled with cardboard boxes and wooden crates, some partly covered by tarpaulins. A thick maze of piping came from the floor by the shaft exit and, intertwined like the veins of some giant muscle, thrust up into the next floor. The strange thuds and clatters of the pipes were ten times louder here, as if some giant beast were in agony. The sound was amplified further by the smallness of the room. The cardboard boxes and crates were full of old and new cans of movie film. They were labelled in a crab-like writing I recognized. I looked closer. It was definitely that of my missing brother. I'd know that scrawl anywhere, though I could hardly decipher it, even after thirty odd years together. They were strange headings – 'Upper Seventh Level', 'Christopher St Blues', 'Triboro Bridge Song', 'Basement Bedford Park Boulevard', 'The Barber's Chair', 'Red Alert – Battery!', 'Rockaway Rocks Forever'. I could not make head nor tail of this. I opened a few cans. Neat rolls of film, on the usual bobbins. I cast my eye about for some means of enlightenment, and spied a metal base under a dark tarpaulin. Lifting it, I found an old, virtually extinct model of an editing Moviola, cabled to a plug conveniently lying by a socket in the wall. I conjured up some dim memories of days helping out at Ben's avant-garde SoHo studios, where something like this had been around. I threaded a small reel through the doo-dah, plugged in, remembered the strange pedal at the base of the thing, and something flickered on the screen. A grey, seamed metallic surface, a microphone poking into frame. Goddamn, I needed the magnetic soundtrack that matched to this. I turned to rise.

Looking into the small barrel of a .38 handgun, held in Vincent Epiglotis' paw.

'You never listen, Danny boy,' he said. 'Poking your nose where it really will get chopped clean off.'

'I was just following the roach trail, Senor Vincent,' I said, vainly resuming my disguise. 'They led me to this storeroom. I wished to check if they were carrying away any, ah, import-ant footage . . .'

'Isn't he a honey?' Vince said to the figure which followed him, hunched, into the room. The old coot I had last seen crouched in the back seat of Vince's car, or waiting for the man from Doubleday.

'What is he doing here?' whined Rudolph Fihser, the Mad Bomber. 'What does he know, Vince? What does he know?'

'We're going to find out, ain't we?' said Vince, offering his epiglottal smile. 'Let's go, sanitation man. It's much too cramped in here.' He motioned me out on to a larger ware-house floor, completely hemmed in by massive pipes covering all four walls. A great hum of quiet determination came from the arterial complex. A massive iron tube ran like a pillar floor to roof in the centre of the room. The old bastard tied me to this with a filthy length of rope.

'All right, Danny boy,' said Vincent. 'Sing us an aria of your choice.'

'Figaro!' I gave voice. 'Figaro! Figaro! Figaro! Fi-ga-ro!'

'He needs elocution lessons,' said Vincent. The old man rummaged in a corner of the room and staggered up, beginning to wire me with a cat's cradle of handgrenades and dynamite sticks. I remembered I had described just this sort of situation in my ill-fated (as were they all) literary contribution to the *Laramie Press* – 'Buffalo Balls from Wichita Falls'. The Toyota Kid, Mayor Twillie of Deaddick Gulch, Bar girl Flower Belle Lee, Sam Clemens and two ill-fitting brothers, Hugo Z. Hackenbush and the Eyetalian Emmanuel Ravelli, are all tied by a sputtering fuse to a barrel of dynamite by Buffalo Balls, alias Captain Pile O'Manure, the roughest toughest orneriest bandit west o' the Pecos. 'Well,' Hackenbush says, 'Here's another fine mess you've gotten me into.'

But Mayor Twillie muses, with his usual nasal sang froid: 'This reminds me of an old Chickamuck from Pensacola. I had saved his seven squaws from a rapacious alligator on the Chatahoochie River. In return he promised to teach me the old Indian rope trick. I was on my way to Cincinatta at the time, having just recovered from that dread Everglades disease, Mogo on the Gogogo . . .' But I suddenly recalled ma hoss, Rudie, whose teeth could munch through these old ropes in no time . . . I mentioned this fact to the mismatched company an' we all began whistlin' 'Home On the Range', a-hopin' to attract the critter to our side . . .

'A true humorist,' said Vince Epiglotis. 'Maybe you wanna whistle that pitch for ever.' The Mad Bomber tightened a Mills grenade right up against my groin.

. . . 'I hear him!' Flower Belle shouted, 'I hear that dadblasted varmint!' We all stopped and listened. There was no doubt. A hoss's hooves, clip-cloppin' on the rocks. We redoubled our efforts, tootin' for all we was worth. Clip-clop, clip-clop, he came nearer. Then there he was, whinnyin' at the door, with Hackenbush's dumb sidekick Pinky leapin' off his back towards us. The hoss began chompin' through our bonds, but the fuse had almost reached the dynamite barrel . . . 'Quick!' Ravelli cried to Pinky. 'Cap a-da fuse, put-a dat light out!' Pinky darted forward, dashin' Twillie's hat from his head, throwin' it uselessly on the fuse wire, then grabbin' the oil lamp hangin' above us an' tossin' it out the window. 'No, no, no!' Ravelli yelled. 'Da fuse! stamp on-a da fire!' Pinky produced a book o' ten cent postage stamps from his pocket an' threw them in the fireplace. The fuse was fizzlin' inches from the barrel . . .

'Don't move!!'

The cry came from two voices at a kicked-open door.

'Freeze! Drop that gun! Move away!'

There was a flurry of feathers. Vincent and the Mad Bomber turned, flabbergation on their faces. I never thought I would be glad to see that varmint again – Frank Zagdanovitch, with his thin Panatella clamped in his oh so beautiful beak, cradling an Uzzi submachine gun in his right wing. And beside him, my wonderful waitress, Paula, holdin' up a Colt 45.

'Up against the wall, motherfucker!' The two galoots backed away from Zagdanovitch.

'A friend in need, eh boyo?' he winked at me, a fold over his beady eye. (. . . as ma hoss Rudie sauntered up calmly, liftin' his hind leg, shootin' a stream o' yellow pee skerwisshh! right on the fizzin' snatch o' cord. It sizzled, spat and whizzled out, a-drowned in the cascade. Then he calmly gnawed us all free . . .)

'Let's go!' Paula unwired me from the pipe. Frank covering us, we rushed from the room, down litter-strewn corridors, towards the lift, heart thumping as it glided up.

'What about Frank?'

'Leave him! OK. Let's go! I'm taking you to Ben!'

The lift arrived. Its doors opened, swallowed us inside. Paula punched for Ground Floor. I slumped against her. Her heart thumped through her massive breasts to my forehead. We hit ground. She dragged me outside. A yellow cab came coasting up Eighth Avenue. She thrust an arm up, stopping it dead. 'Avenue A!' she shouted at the driver. 'And don't spare the gas!'

'It's your funeral lady,' the man said.

'What did you say up there?' I sat up suddenly. 'What was that about Ben?'

'He wants to tell you what this is all about,' said Paula. 'Relax. We're going straight there.'

7

Dear Gentlebeing,

Our readers enjoy stories in which problems are posed but are, at the end of the day, solved. Stories with downbeat endings, in which the characters have no hope of solving their problems, are strongly disliked by our readers. Stories in which characters behave unrealistically are bound to be rejected. But bear in mind – a rejection doesn't mean that we hate you. It shouldn't hurt, either. (We know it does, but it shouldn't!) It's a learning experience, far more valuable than any amount of flattery and unearned compliments. To write, you must *write*, then recognize and correct your mistakes, then write some more. Learning to write, like growing up, can be hard but the results are worth it. They certainly are for us when you do!

Yours faithfully,

Bust, Sagass & Gasket.

TAGALONG MAGAZINE

Kill 'em all! Leave not one soul alive!

The cab drops us at the gateway to the underworld. Avenue

180

A, the worst scar tissue on the nether regions apart from Avenues B, C, and D. Decomposing, decaying, debilitating, abode of the wretchedest of the earth: The black, the Puerto Rican, the remaining poor Jews, the only readers of my friend's Yiddish essays. Spiky Hispanic music, the wail of police cars, the muffled cries of junky outrage. Apartments in the last stage of dilapidation and disrepair, rot, mildew, erosion, mould. Windows desperately strengthened by triple iron grilles, powdered glass strewn out on the fire escape. Poverty gapes in the very brickwork. This, in short, is it, rock bottom. The apartment Paula led me to was on the third floor of one of these blighted ruins. Waste, negligence, decrepitude, decline, opened cans of spaghetti and clam chowder every-where, buried in inches of dust and grime. Here and there signs of movement as some unknown vermin scurries deter-minedly through the muck. The abyssal ooze, from whence we came, and unto which we are all destined, Selah. Yellowed newspapers, canvases, old tubes of paint, sculptures of crushed Pepsi and Seven Up cans and ripped cereal cartons, Shredded Wheat, All Bran, Breakfast of Champions. A mountain of mould which may once have been bread and cheese, and, in a far corner, on something which may once have been an armchair, an outstretched figure, gaunt and dishevelled, with a five-month growth of beard. I could not believe that this raggedy-ann of a man, dressed in what appeared to be an old army blanket, could be Ben Tishman, my soul brother, my erstwhile twin, ever an untidy mother but never soft on dirt and filth. Cleanliness and good appearance were his watchwords. But the man facing me was far below his zenith. The nadir would be more appropriate. And yet, neverthe-less, that broad grin, lighting up even that shrivelled desolation.

'My God, Ben!' I could find no further words.

'We gotta clean up this mess,' Paula said.

'Ben, Ben . . .'

'Hallo, Danny.'
Antennae waved gamely through the dustbowl.

8

So there we are, Ben, Danny boy, alias Jake, and Paula,
treading the sidewalks of the wide frontier of 14th Street on
a crisp early spring evening. April 6, in fact, our common
birthday, though not that much to celebrate. We had got him
into the tub at least, washed and brushed up, his beard
trimmed, while roaches fought for the off-cuts. Paula clutching his arm, his own around her shoulder, myself meandering
by them in solitude.

'It's difficult to describe,' Ben saying softly, his voice almost
lost in the traffic and pedestrian rumble. 'I'm really sorry to
have caused my friends this anxiety, but . . .' We edged past
a prone body. A wiry black man approached us pushing a
pram full of knick-knacks, shaving brushes, baseball caps, odd
wire gadgets not dissimilar to the one I'd seen in Paula's
apartment. But Tishman waved him by.

'You have to trust me a little longer, Jake,' Ben said to
me. 'You have to digest this explanation. The thing is . . .
complicated, and on the other hand – simple . . . but it's the
simplicity that's terrible. Let's go to the Waverley,' the old
Ben asserting himself. 'Kurosawa's *Macbeth* – *the Throne of
Blood*, is showing. Then we can sit down at the Szechuan
House and do a proper Chinese. Maybe at that stage I can
begin to talk.'

Climbing through loo shafts, Epiglottal shock waves, tied
to kegs of dynamite, rescued by a chicken. The vibes of
Hackula full upon the night breeze as the unfogged stars punch
down. A movie, yes, what else remains? Wind machines blow
smog through a Japanese forest. A pile of skulls stands out in
an open glade. 'Just like the Bronx,' some wag in the back

182

cries. 'Shut up, asshole,' another ripostes from the dark. The city lives. It can never die. Toshiro Mifune, however, is shot full of arrows, expiring like a sneering pincushion. We pass down Waverley Place, rushing across Seventh Avenue before a massed onrush of cabs and cars. Egg Roll, Shredded Pork and Pickled Cabbage Soup to start, followed by Hunan Pork and General Ching's Tingling Chicken. 'Ah, this is it,' says Ben. 'There's light at the end of the tunnel. I can smell it. Paula, Jake, how about you?'

'I am still in the dark.'

'I have to take you further on,' said my twin. 'You might want to do it on drugs, amphetamines or Colombian. Or choose to take it neat.'

'I'll take it neat,' I said. 'My brains are sufficiently scrambled. Give, Ben, I've held on long enough.'

'Tell him, Ben,' said Paula. 'Maybe he can help us. Two's company, but maybe three's a real family. You know what I mean, honey? We need all the help we can get.'

'Well, I suppose you're in it deep enough,' Ben said to me, 'but do me a favour, Danny, keep Ellie out of it. She's sweet, she has her sights on success, and her whole life ahead of her.'

'Not much of a life if the Thing keeps spreading its tentacles,' I reminded him. He swallowed a baby corn.

'Do you want Kumquats or Stuffed Honey Banana?' he asked.

Steam trickled slowly out of our ears.

9

It was two a.m., after midnight. Imagine us, staggering through New York's nocturne. The sirens, the hawking up of phlegm, vomit. Climbing up Broadway towards Times Square. All three of us dressed in cast-off down-and-out costume, ragged scarecrows, even Paula, as an ersatz baglady. In fact she is carrying Ben's camera in her soiled shopping bags, while Ben and I each swing a bottle encased in a torn brown paper bag.

Imagine the city, a thousand black empty sockets looking down on the scuttling vermin below. Paranoid night bus drivers hurl their juggernauts by with their cargo of late-night shift zombies. Wary yellow cabs swishing by. Steam from subway vents. A drunk kicks a small dog to pulp. 'You bitch! You fuckin' bitch!' The dog squeals pitiably. The evening clear sky has dulled all over.

'Your researches were right about Rudolph Fihser,' Ben says to me. 'The Mad Bomber never bombed anybody. Details he told me when I interviewed him didn't tally with the original reports and court transcripts. You see, Vince was taken with the idea of shooting a feature movie based on the Mad Bomber, so we looked it up. Something was not quite right. On the other hand, the old man had a book deal lined up, to be ghost-written by some professional writer. He got scared and tried to shut us out. I persisted. And on the way, in that café, I met Paula . . .'

'Light o' my life,' she responds. 'Hic . . .' swinging a shopping bag against his thigh. He with his arm around her shoulder.

'Vince has contacts,' Ben continues, 'Enough said about them . . . he made enquiries, and suddenly froze on me. He called me in.

' "Benjamin," he says, "you know you've been like a true brother to me. I'd do anything for you, from the depth of my heart. But you gotta let the Mad Bomber go."

' "Come on Vincent," I say, 'it can't be that bad, can it? This is all ancient history. The AT & T bombings were in the late 1940s. The man's served life. But if he's innocent . . ."

' "Nobody's innocent." You know that old credo. "The old man did what was necessary. He found out something he shouldn't have, none of us should know. He wanted to live.

184

He kept his mouth shut. This is big, Benjamin, bigger than you want to know. Let's make a movie about Jack the Ripper. Alive in New York City Today. I can get a script by Harlan Ellison . . ."

'We split on that. He got very uptight. I said nobody owned my soul. I took the two cans of Mad Bomber footage and stashed them away in Avenue A, in that apartment, owned by an old friend, who is often up north in Maine. I went on staking out Fihser, with Paula's help. Then something else happened.'

'The UFO incident!'

'Right first time, Danny.'

I told him Jack Pritchard's rational explanation.

'Yes,' he says, sounding very paranoid now, 'but there are ways of covering up . . . Sure, there was an advertising plane up there. But it was something else as well . . . I didn't tell you the full story of that sighting. In fact I shouldn't have talked at all. But I was scared, and I needed to let it out. You see, I got a clear warning . . .'

We had reached our goal – the Times Square subway. Not for a long time had I been foolhardy enough to venture down that pit at such an hour. But we were armoured, to some extent, by our veneer of destitution. We staggered down the spew-flecked steps of the south side corner entrance of 42nd Street and Seventh Avenue. A man stands retching in one corner. Another seems to be attempting to sweep the floor by the ticket office with a coat hanger. Perhaps it is a left-over from the Madagascar deal. We stick our tokens in and push through.

Slip-slop, slip-slop, our cracked sparse footsteps, in the shabby bare passageways. I hope against hope Conway Stebbins, my IRT deepest-throat, is not around to pierce my disguise. But perhaps the policeman's nightstick, that grey day, laid him out longer than he'd bargained for. We are all helpless victims of our own delusions. *O tempora, O mores!*

This is the spookiest hour. No one who is up to any good at all can be around. We gingerly step on to the Uptown Local platform of the Independent Line. There are some figures on the benches. A man in a green *dashiqi*, with a painted face, massive earrings, a gold pince-nez and a fedora sits quietly perusing tomorrow's *New York Times*. A black bum, on another bench, is beating himself, piledriving bunched fists into his face, falling off the bench, dragging himself on again, punching himself off, and so on, muttering under his breath and sighing. A bagwoman lies stretched on another.

'I don't like it here,' Paula says, clutching Ben's tattered sleeve.

'Give, Ben,' I add, 'What's the big secret?'

'Just keep cool,' he says, 'Keep your receptors wide open. We're quite close. Just let it happen.'

New York City, 2.55 a.m. Paranoia hour. So what's new? The sound of a train approaching, rattling the tunnel. A disembodied voice cranks forth: 'Last train on the DD Line, Bedford Park Boulevard. Last train to Bronx. Last train.'

The train, an ancient monster of shaking cattle truck mien, festooned with aerosol graffiti to the last inch, clatters up, clanks to a halt. 'Last train. Last train from this platform,' the disembodied voice croaks. The painted man, the black self-hater, even the bagwoman, scramble on. The doors close. The train gathers speed, shudders, clatters down the north tunnel. We are alone. Marooned.

'What now?' I ask Ben.

'Now we wait,' says my twin brother. 'And the Lord have mercy on our souls.'

Silence, apart from the indeterminate subway hum of generators God knows where. The bluey glow of dim neon. An empty and meaningless purgatory. We sit on the only non-vomit-flecked bench, disembodied as that voice, in time and space. The harsh breathing of my friends beside me, the only kindred souls left me in the world. One feels as if The End

186

titles are about to roll in front of one's eyes, followed by the inevitable fade-out. The final flickering out of all we know.

But there is a sound, a rumble, in the distance. An unmistakably familiar thrum. The rattle of another oncoming train. I glance at Ben. He winks at me. So what's the big deal? Service carriages must rumble through here all night.

'This had better be good, Ben,' I tell him.

'It's a real howler,' he replies.

The train's bright eye trembles out of the tunnel. The train slows. 'Look at the cabin,' Ben shouts. I look. I get up and run forward. I poke my head in as the train stops.

The driver's cabin is empty.

'He must be at the back!' I say. I look down. There are only five cars. I run down the length of the train. There are strange figures here and there, inside, in ordinary passenger cars. But the doors have not opened. I stick my face against the grime-covered, unwashed windows. The figures inside do not move. Their eyes seem fixed open, with a metallic sheen. They are all wearing identical shabby overcoats. There is a metallic sheen to their hands. I run the length of the train. There is no one at the back. No driver or guard at either end.

The train starts up again and draws into the northern tunnel, vanishing down the hole. I watch its tail light fade into the black distance. I turn back. Ben bobs in my glazed gaze.

'This what you brought me down here for? They're running automatic trains. With dummies inside. So what?'

'There are no automatics,' says Ben, quietly, 'in the whole of the New York transit system. I've checked it out. It's not on. Freight and maintenance trains do run later. But these "others" are not on the board. They do not exist. No one sees them. And they are just one example . . .'

'Come on, Ben!' I look both at him and Paula, who is nodding sadly with him. 'What are you trying to pull? This is your twin brother here! Jake Mishkin! Danny Hohenlohe!

187

The king of the unpublished pulps! The scourge of Hackulas great and small! Don't pull some rotten con on me!'

'There is no con involved,' he protests, 'scout's honour! Listen, that day when I went to Penn Station. Do you want to know what happened to me? Why I dropped out of sight? Let's just get out of here, before they lock all the gates . . .' And he continued the running extravaganza as we tottered out into 42nd Street.

'Remember that day?' he said, 'A Friday in February – I was bent on keeping my appointment with Ellie's sugar daddy on Long Island. I was totally set on that. What I noticed here on the CC Local platform some weeks back was just ticking over in the back of my mind. What had happened then, I'd missed the last train, after a late-night session at the cutting rooms, still mulling over Vince's turnaround, and I hung about, God knows why, when the train you just saw here pulled in like a ghost and pulled out again. I stayed. Another, exactly the same, came and left. Then the maintenance train turned up. I asked the crew about the ghost trains. They thought I was strung out on hard stuff. They took me with them to their depot. Everyone swore blind I had been hallucinating. But when I came back two nights later it happened again. I got the wind up, but put the whole thing on the back burner. But in the following days strange things continued to happen to me – odd feelings of being watched, and monitored . . . Friday evening, I got my ticket at Penn Station and looked up at the big Departure board. Just as I looked the departure of the train I wanted flicked to a different platform. Level C, Gate 79, it said. I never knew a Level C at Penn Station but sure enough, by the toilets, I saw a sign to an elevator. I took it and descended, though I should have known better. Friday evening, you know how it is, you get fuzzy. I got down to this non-existent C and walked out, the door closing immediately behind me.

'I was at one end of a long, very dimly lit platform, over

188

tracks which stretched out into a strange, thick curling mist. Crisply painted signs said "Platform 79". But there was no one about but me. A train, looking brand new and gleaming, pulled slowly in to the buffer. I walked up, looking for a guard. There was no one. The train doors opened. There were no passengers. I walked up to the front. There was no driver. Just a ghostly, humming silence.

'I ran. I ran like hell for the liftshaft. The doors were closed. There was no button. I looked for stairs, and found emergency handles climbing up into the dark. At the foot of that ladder there was a strange little object that seemed to glow in the gloom. I took it with me, and pulled myself up the ladder. I don't know how long I climbed in the dark. I finally cracked my head against a manhole cover and pushed it up. I was on the pavement on 35th Street. Men were unloading vast vans of schmutters, pushing them into shops on long trolleys. I ran. Impelled away from the centre, east, to Broadway, then down, past Union Square, along 14th, to Avenue A. I had felt those emergency spare keys in my pocket. I holed out there. And that's about the tale. After a couple of days I crawled out, to make contact with Paula. I gave her the gadget, which I thought might be keeping tabs on me. But it seemed to call down trouble on her. She went to her own hiding place, at a friend's flat. I took the gadget back. Here it is.'

He took out that strange wire shape I had seen on Paula's shelf. It looked more like a piece of junk than ever.

'So what's the point?!' I shout at him suddenly, in the middle of a deserted corner of 5th and Madison, the tall blocks of midtown rearing all about us, the PanAm building majestically standing guard. 'What's the point of it all? What has this got to do with the price of bread, the leering zeitgeist, and Hackula??'

'Danny, Jake,' he said, 'haven't you ever noticed all sorts of bizarre incongruities in the city? Underground rumblings at night where there is no subway? Gusts of wind from nowhere in closed tunnels? Vapour rising from vents when the climate doesn't warrant it? The sound of trains on routes that have been discontinued? Have you ever felt the way buildings seem to watch you, not only at night, but in broad daylight? The way steam seems to stop and start in central heating ducts despite anything the super does or doesn't do? The sudden cataclysmic power failures which black us all out, trap us in lift-shafts?

'Jake – the city's alive. It's a living organism, a gargantuan Frankenstein monster. We built it but it is out of control. It has begun serious attempts to get rid of us. It needs more than our bureaucracies can provide to keep it going. Who knows what its values, its desires are? Why it needs to keep its own trains running like a bloodstream through the arteries of its subways? Sending out phantom trains to entrap someone who seems to have come too close to its secret? It began flexing its muscles in the late Forties, when the new total communications of the AT & T network posed a threat, or perhaps simply wakened it. Rudolph Fihser took the rap. He must have been contacted the way I was by the supposed fake UFO. Major politicians, crime syndicate bosses must have known of this Urban Assault Syndrome (UAS) from early on. Vince's contacts warned him off. Fihser panicked and ran. My own days in hiding might be numbered. Listen: it's learning, increasing its strength every year, setting itself bolder and bolder goals. Already it's pushed most of the middle classes out, but it must have felt threatened by the writers, the standard bearers, as they should be, of imagination. Perhaps it wishes to keep the poor, the blacks, Hispanics, down and outs, as a reserve army of its bile. What is its ultimate goal? Who knows, Jake, who knows? What is this steady build-up for? Maybe when it's ready the whole island of Manhattan will suddenly break loose from its moorings. Shuck off the bridges, Hudson, Washington, Brooklyn, the Queensboro

190

and Triboro, flood the Lincoln Tunnel – smash its way through the narrows like a giant Leviathan and take to the wide open ocean! Maraud up and down the coastline, or creep over New Jersey, trampling the helpless hinterland! I can see the headlines:

' "NEW YORK GOES APESHIT! MANHATTAN MANGLES MASSES! END OF WORLD IMMINENT!" And there I am, stuck in Apartment 3b, hanging desperately on to the lightbulb while Avenue A bumps and slithers all over Michigan and Wisconsin. Or maybe it's just the harbinger of a wider urban psychosis – with other great world cities going on the rampage: Great battles in mid-ocean, surpassing Godzilla – New York versus Rio de Janeiro! London versus Calcutta! Tokyo versus Los Angeles! Shanghai ravages Australia! And the few survivors drink corn beer in blitzed villages, or watch it on TV in Inner Mongolia. The Apocalypse Show, Walter Cronkite orbiting the Earth in the NBC escape capsule! Wouldn't you want to see the Nielsen Ratings on that, Danny?'

I grab him by the throat and shake him like a sack of straw, right there, at the gate of Grand Central Station. A JFK Airport Bus shuttle has just disgorged a slew of dismayed tourists into nowheresville. Paula tries to break me loose in vain.

'This is it?!' I cry. 'This is the great Truth for which I've addled my brains all this time?! This is Hackula?! This is the bottom line?!'

Paula and he tear me back. Bottles shatter on the walk. 'I told you it was hard to take, Danny!' Ben cried. 'I tried to shield you all, but you just came after me. If you can't stand the shit, keep out of the crapper!'

'Shit! Shit! Shit!' I cry, tearing off my false moustache, ripping off my filthy disguise, leaving myself in a torn shirt, thin jacket and underpants below the clock and nude bust pediment, one of the city's best examples, the guide book says, of Beaux-arts architecture.

'Danny, please!' says Paula. Ben stands with hands out-stretched.

'No way!' I cry. 'I still have standards!'

I run, pushing past flabbergasted trippers and returnees to the New World, Nieuw Amsterdam, the Rotten Apple, kicking a fat, mink-furred lady as she lies helpless on the ground, smashing a violin case against a lamp-post, scattering suitcases-ful of bilge, waving my arms, foaming at the mouth, leaving my last two friends behind, veering up Lexington, all the way to 59th, west past Grand Army Plaza and right through the park, ignoring the night death of muggerland, through to the Museum of Natural History and to the 79th Street penthouse. Throwing the double, triple, quadruple lock, tossing my entire stash of hard core on the floor, selecting the craziest, furthest out of them all, taking my meat in hand, and Presto!!!

Bring back the Ponape Islanders! Pull that deboncd fish from the vulva!

Ah! the misery! the misery!

10

Several months have passed. The city is completely transfor-med. For all I know I am the last 'creating' individual left unblitzed in town. Spring and early summer saw the Plague spread like wildfire among all questing minds. Playwrights, scriptwriters, composers, performing artists were taken in quick succession. Even rock musicians were engulfed. Bellevue and all other mental wards were full to the brim. Entire trains were chartered to transport the stricken to booby hatches upstate and elswhere. Survivors scattered in panic to the untouched hinterland, places like Tenafly, or Springfield. A colony, under medical supervision, has been set up in

Canaan, Maine. Others ran as far as the subcontinent could take them, to Salt Lake City, or Orange County, or skipped the country, to Mexico, Guatemala, England, France, Israel or Afghanistan. The day my own sweet Ellie was taken was the blackest in my calendar. She slumped, half way through a baconburger at the 100 Percent Charbroiled Burger Joint, and began asking for onion rings. Then she lapsed into a coma. I wept as the men in white coats materialised, roaming the city in their twenty-four-hour mobile vigil.

I am alone. I have not seen Ben or Paula since that fated moment at Grand Central. The city swallowed them up, or they found their own salvation in its mousecracks, or away in safety. Jack Pritchard packed his telex machine and loaded his battered Oldsmobile and rode off. 'Capitalists have been exempt so far,' he said, 'but I won't press my luck. If a vanload of coathanger returns turns up, hold 'em for me.' He was wise to vamoose, with or without coathangers. But I have determined to stay behind. I shall not be moved. This is my city. Born into, adopted, what's the difference. You make your stand somewhere. There is no option, unless you volunteer for defeat.

It's a sweltering hot summer in the city. Outwardly, many things appear normal. The traffic honks by irritably, only a little thinned out. The waitress Doris at the Manhattan Restaurant is as friendly, mourning about vanished clients, but then she always did. Come and go, that's the way it's always been. Some customers bewail the poverty of the newspapers. Yes, even the true hacks have been hit. Not all – enough remain to churn out the sports pages, local news, reprint the funnies. The powers that be have promised to lay the infection. The Mayor, the FBI, State, the White House. So what else is new? There are buses to run, shops to manage, welfare to dole out, business to keep running, Wall Street. A city to be kept ticking over, while it decides on its next move.

Even letter writing has become a danger. Ordinary, non-

'creative' citizens have been found slumped over their inoffensive scribbles to relatives, friends, business associates. But I am still here, poised at Ben's old typewriter, my fingers hooked upon the keys. I shall not be intimidated. I fight on. La Lotta Continua. Venceremos. Even though Jake Akimbo, the *Archaeos*, and *The Parmesan Review* and all the rest have gone bankrupt, their offices become empty shells, I bash them out, the ultimate short stories, the ones that would make their rotting hair fall out, their teeth rattle upon the ground. Again, I stuff them, uselessly, into an envelope. Traipse down to the oddly sparse Post Office . . . Now, at least, no longer the long, terrible wait in the shvitzbath, as the line stands in perpetuum, forced to listen to those endless harangues smart-asses bludgeon each other with in such a pass: 'So don't tell me about Religion. God, the Universe. We're all just bits and pieces of nothin'. Wha'd'ya expect? It's all just made for ya? God fixed the whole place just so it's pleasant for ya? You believe dat? Than you'd believe anything. I tell ya, this is just mind fucking. You know what I mean? You just jack off, in your head, all the time, ya get me? You tell me what's the use of sumpin' like dat? It's da same wid politics. You know sumpin' 'bout dat? So don't tell me 'bout Politics. The Superpowers, da President of de United States, Russia, de nookleer bomb, chemical warfare. Why, we could wipe us all out in a split second. Dat's politics. So what in hell's the use of it? You tell me. If you believe in what they tell you up there, you'd believe in anything. Ya know what I'm sayin' here . . . ?'

Gaa. Gaa. Gaa. But not now, in the blissful silence, a little plopping of rubber stamps, not much more. Handing in the envelope. The kindly black clerk: 'Are you sure, sir? I don't think this address is functioning.' 'Never mind, friend. I have included a stamped self-addressed envelope, for return of mail.' 'OK. It's your business.' Aye, it might well have been . . . It goes off, another pride and joy. This one I entitled –

THE NINE THOUSAND AND FORTY-FIFTH ATTEMPT BY THREE CHIMPANZEES TO TYPE SHAKESPEARE'S *MACBETH*

eifnkj fghr tr6ybc d hygsv chs 108 64'ds/*c gdh acxvzl hf
gdb vbbbbb sgsfa s hshhh dhd gg dggd j j jjjf fgg ggg sffa
sge65g bch dash dk
              ty dhga sl ldjkds dgfsr3hdjdfncmd;s
sgfsgbg hbghbgh bghbghb ghgbg hgbfdgd trs555 555 55555
rfedj fjfnv xcae2ds fggg gfhdgg sggd fhh VCGAS GSJHT
2434K.VNVB HFBC HD*/.B"][JDH D DS HA DHHJ
GHFJ FHFHDFKD $$$$ HDDJD KSLLL;D ;;D'LFJ& N
VBCV hgf da sssss cvx ca d skd;l fff ffjhf hkkj; gg df ahs
dga dsdll fj dhgds fdnc bv csd dfskfg;
fads lmvnmm mmmmmm mmm mmmmmnn nnnnnbb
bbbbbbbnn nnnnbvvcc ccvvvvvv vvcxdadd ddddd snnnnn
ndjj dffg svvvv x g g h j k ldhhh dggsff gdhyyy yyyyyyy
yyyyyyy yyyy fg ggdfs ab456j %%%% %% dfj alsl;d; gh
hvxcsd a fgkg hjfhd gada'lf jjh ZXCX DSFD JLHH HHH
JJ JJGA SFF DFD VC854 64; "DS. VNSF WRE D FGG LL
FHF LGKG KFJ&X 7 FGGGGG D FKJK mmv /b,b
mhgs. . . . . ///////* *** **** **" "" ';ljhf df
sdajd hfkfk gkgut jfj ghfgf bdf sdakd bvg dfsda vbgf fs vlk
fhfsda hgd fsd cvdf sds u tygfhg bfddskfkgh cbvsdaf dflfl f
gdfdas hfgd fsdak dsl afda ss fjhf gf abs dgsfda mdb dfat rj
fjfgd daeorf a gdfda s nhgkgk fhsf d dhgfd lspg oiyqeab x
mmsld dldl cbx. v;ghkgh jgs fh fg f f f yttrh fg gk fjf dasdl
lkfjhf dtnap dnhd fkjf lgl;gofj dgs ad d kdo fhgd fs dfkfnvakdp
===sh dg==== === ===== ===== ====
=======−−−00 000000 0009999 999999 8fgsan bsidunfhf
jhh gk sra2dl.f;g' "" ""s'dfl fjfkl f[[[[[]]]]]]]]as dfds hga
dghdgdegskd lkdlf f hjglg;g gd sdssae wteuro nvb dgsfads
reuyrlk hfgdfada s dgd h djf kflf;fjf lg;lg jhjhhhh flkl ghhfd

kf;g"h gffs dhfjf f ff hgfak djhdhf f hdh fhf fkglg dfs daew
XCXCXC XCXCXCX CXCXCXCXCX CXCXC
VBVBV BVB VBVBVBVB GJGJG JGJ GJGJ GJG J GJGJ
HHGHGHGHGH LKKLLK GDH GGD DDGDGDG
DGDG FHGFYTYHF FH$$$ $$$$ 11 11++——+++
++++——++—+—+ & &&&& &&**** *((((( ))))
)))————*&%$ £DCKG HG FFD SKD;F;;FLK GV FJFF
G;G GFGDF DDSFHF GHJGK cxdgaks fjfyr tgfd fl fh
fgffdlf wetr er t t t t tuty fgff das[gkg fhfgd ka;dkfm
nngkglfd agdk f;g' gafs d fkkgk

rotusi nefkf gogog ogogogo dhddaj sdnb
mf mfmfm fmgkg ifid
idididididi did didi
msa hdsld fjjj g gj j jjjgkl mmmmmm mmm
h dga ca c cc a cac a cacac dkdl fll;lg kjh
rhdg fggajdlf;;f fhg fgdsn bagsd
hgsjhs jdkjkjd fjjgk;g ggdfs dads dllfjk dace fos e s e sma am
ma aaa thgema lkdjher;;fjj ahgm, MAKSUHH ahhsmkk
AHAHS MA ASHSHS SDGAF anah fyiroo rhsfosmm

A
C
D
U
F
fffffff ffff fff fffffffgh gjhgkh kljljl&&&&&&&

So go stick that in your antipasto, Jake Akimbos of the world!
I, at least, am united! I shall not run from unknown horrors
when I've survived so many known ones! If I've held on till
now I can hold on longer. I shall hang on, to see what's going
down! And what in God or the devil's name will happen next?

You hear, that, Hackula? Here I am, boyo. Come and get
me.

Whoever, whatever you are – I'm waiting . . .

Is that a knock on the door?

196

* * *

AND THAT TEXT WAS ALL WE FOUND of our poor Danny when we finally made it to the 'penthouse' flat, Ellie and I, on a balmy, clear-skied spring morning. It had taken me all night to make my peace with Ellie, calming her down after my 'disappearance'. A long night of confessions and mea culpas and vows of future good behaviour. But what can I do? I am a creature of my passions. A light strikes in me and I am off, on all cylinders. What could I say? A billion to one chance meeting of an old flame who had kept embers going inside me for over ten years: radiant as ever, Scandinavian Monica, at the donut stop at the Penn Station concourse. Some things happen only once in a lifetime. When they happen twice, you have to obey the gods. Fate and an interrupted journey, and a two-week detour, through mountainous West Virginia. The Appalachians. Pocahontas County. A log cabin. The call of the wild. Who can resist? Mea culpa, etcetera etcetera. But there had been no need to panic, I would have thought . . . forgetting urban angst, and city blues . . . A storm in a teacup, no?

But there we were, in my ruffled apartment. Kept clean hygiene-wise by Danny, but the usual mess: opened cornflake packets, mugs of half-drunk coffee, balls of half-typed paper strewn all over the floor. The files of returned manuscripts in the suitcase. And the paperclipped pile by the typewriter.

But Danny H—, where art thou? Not a collar, not a button

or thread . . . Except – some strange, inexplicable omens of a fate beyond imagining: a strange combination of smells – cigars, which he never smoked, and the odd odour of a chicken coop, wafting about the writing table . . . compounded by two unusually large chicken feathers, appearing freshly plucked, lying by the completed manuscript. And the nondescript gadget I had picked up in a fleamarket, downtown, which no one could ever identify. Jack Pritchard claimed it was a Cheddar cheese-parer, but it had no effect at all on cheese . . .

Oddly enough, all Danny's clothes were in the closet, hung up with unusually neat precision. And it is true, my cans of filmed interview with Rudolph Fihser, the Mad Bomber, which I had brought home for safekeeping, have been spirited away. Like Rudolph Fihser himself, who vanished from his apartment after the 50th Street fire, never to be seen or heard of again. And yes, Vince Epiglotis has been acting strange lately, with none of his usual bonhomie towards me . . . you never know . . . Doubleday, at any rate, lost their shirt on the Mad Bomber. They had paid Fihser and his eponymous ghost, Seth Overstoat, a two-hundred-grand advance. They never saw a page of their story. Perhaps I should send them Danny's oeuvre instead. Take up the torch of his titanic struggles –

– Send the words out! Yes, that's really all I can do. A monument to my vanished friend, constructed of papier-mâché rejection slips . . . Poor Danny, disappeared, without trace, despite vigorous searches, into the labyrinth of his own story. *Morituri te salutant* with a vengeance . . . Or just another file at Missing Persons . . .

I send them out then. The longer tales, the short, the 'Planet of Fuck' novel. Even the defiant final text, with its inconsistencies, its co-option of my life for his, its twisted view of me and Ellie . . . The whole shtik, never mind the doubts, ever revolving. The rejection letters, continuing to pile up, filling the unused suitcases, the drawers, the cupboards, the shelves. Some I've papered the bathroom with, just to remind me that true existence is a thing hard fought for. But I have Faith in my friend, whom I have to mourn. His day will dawn, as ours, too, surely! We are with you in your just fight to Be, Danny boy, in that twilit roseland where Drekula hunts, where the globbles flail at each other, Sherlock Holmes and Moriarty track slithering mailboxes, Frog-In-My Throat runs the groove of the Subway, Flight 117 from Cygnus V to Terra still seeks its elusive port of call, the Yoke of the Egg racks its brains for its true identity, and poor Winnie the Poof Bear's ugly chum still seeks the Odd-bod-man, way past the Marrow Downs . . .

For at the end of the day, who really knows In Whose Beard the Monkey's Shmuck Lies?

Not me, but if you hum it I'll play it.

Dear Contributor — — — — —